SWANTON MORLEY

A DCI Tanner Mystery
- Book Eleven -

DAVID BLAKE

www.david-blake.com

Proofread by Jay G Arscott

Special thanks to Kath Middleton, Ann Studd, John Harrison, Anna Burke, Emma Stubbs, and Jan Edge

First edition published by Black Oak Publishing Ltd
in Great Britain, 2024

Disclaimer:
These are works of fiction. Names, characters, businesses, places, events and incidents are either the products of the author's imagination or used in a fictitious manner. Any resemblance to actual persons, living or dead, or actual events is purely coincidental.

Copyright © David Blake 2024

The right of David Blake to be identified as the Author of the Work has been asserted by him in accordance with the Copyright, Designs and Patents Act 1998. All rights reserved. This book is for your enjoyment only. No part of this publication may be reproduced, distributed, or transmitted in any form or by any means, including photocopying, recording, or other electronic or mechanical methods, without the prior written permission of the copyright owner except in the case of brief quotations embodied in critical reviews and certain other non-commercial uses permitted by copyright law.

All rights reserved.

Cover Photograph ID 202562873 © Richard Bowden | Dreamstime.com

ISBN: 9798879998016

DEDICATION

For Akiko, Akira and Kai.

DAVID BLAKE

THE DI TANNER SERIES

Broadland
St. Benet's
Moorings
Three Rivers
Horsey Mere
The Wherryman
Storm Force
Long Gore Hall
Weavers' Way
Bluebell Wood
Swanton Morley

"Do not seek revenge or bear a grudge against anyone among your people, but love your neighbour as yourself."
Leviticus 19:18

- PROLOGUE -

Monday, 23rd June

STEERING HIS DECREPIT old Fiat Uno left onto Dereham Road, Albert Sparks brought his eyes off the unlit road ahead to glance down at the fuel gauge, to find the needle resting firmly in the red.

'Shit,' he cursed, lifting his foot off the accelerator to further reduce his speed. He still had over fifteen miles to go before reaching Swaffham, and the post office where he was supposed to be working the early shift. That was also where the next petrol station was, if it was even open. 'Why the hell didn't I fill it up yesterday?' he asked himself, shaking his head in furious dismay as he returned his attention to the virtually pitch-black road ahead.

He knew why he hadn't. Until his next paycheque, which wasn't due for another nine days, he didn't have enough money to make his monthly mortgage payment, let alone all the bills that kept constantly piling up. His philosophy to just stick everything onto his various credit cards wasn't going to work either. All three had maxed out two months before, leaving him barely able to pay the interest on each. Subsequently, it was hardly surprising that he'd been putting off filling his car to the very last minute. The problem was, the very last minute had been the previous day, when he'd driven straight past his local petrol station on his way home.

When the car juddered suddenly underneath him, he was left gripping the steering wheel with ever-whitening knuckles. 'Not now,' he muttered, creeping slowly past the last of the road's few sporadic houses to enter what he knew to be a mile-long stretch of deserted woodland.

Thinking if he could just make it to Swanton Morley, the next village along, that he might then be able to find someone who was both willing and able to give him some petrol, he reduced his speed even more, only to remember the time. It wasn't even half-past four in the morning. There wouldn't be a single soul about, and he was damned if he was going to start knocking on people's doors at that time, using his jerry can as some sort of plastic begging bowl.

As the idea came to him that there was a slim chance that the village's newsagent would be open, the car juddered alarmingly again. 'C'mon on,' he muttered, urging it on with nothing more than the power of his panic-stricken mind. 'Just another half-a-mile and I'll be there.'

The moment he said it, it happened again, but this time, instead of spluttering back into life, the engine fell into a motionless, unwelcome silence.

'SHIT!' he shouted, in furious dismay, banging the steering wheel with his fists before steering reluctantly to the side of the road.

As it rolled to an eventual standstill, he tried turning the key in the ignition, but it was no use. It wasn't going to start. Trying to make it would only drain the battery, which was already on its last legs.

Turning the lights off, he wrestled the key out to think what to do. He couldn't call for breakdown assistance. He wasn't a member of any organisation, nor could he afford to be. He briefly entertained the idea of waiting for a car to flag down, only to remember the time again, and that he hadn't seen a single other vehicle on the road since leaving his house. His only realistic option was to grab the empty plastic jerry can from out of the boot to traipse the half-mile or so to the next village, in the hope that the corner shop would be open; not that they sold petrol, of course, but someone working there may be willing to lend him some, enough for him to at least finish his journey.

Having made up his mind, he shoved open the car's squeaking rusting door to be met by a cold, sterile silence. Without the lights from his car, the road was as black as pitch. He could barely see the trees he knew lined the road on either side, let alone where he'd been intending to start walking to.

Trying to ignore his growing sense of unease, as if a thousand eyes were watching him from the surrounding trees, he skirted his way cautiously around to the boot. Once there, he lifted it open, when a far off scream came tumbling through the air, like a sharpened axe being dragged along some distant concrete floor.

When it eventually trailed slowly away, he drew in an anxious breath. 'What the hell was that?' he eventually asked himself, his eyes staring down the dark, shadow-filled road towards where he thought the sound had come from.

With his heart pounding inside his chest, he held his breath to listen. But there wasn't a single sound to follow, just the hollow silence of the still pitch-black night.

'It must've been a fox,' he told himself, even though he knew it wasn't. It sounded far too human.

Doing his best to put it out of his mind, he pulled out the jerry can to close the boot, only to see a large, luminous full moon, sliding gracefully out from behind a silver-edged cloud.

Instantly being taken back to the very first VHS video he'd ever watched, when he was barely fourteen years old, he found himself frozen to the spot. He'd never been a fan of horror films. He'd always found them to be just far too believable, especially *that* one. *An American Werewolf in London* was the scariest film he'd ever seen in his entire life, and by a long way! Since the moment the final scene had leapt to its bloody conclusion, he'd had an all-consuming fear of being ripped apart by such an unholy creature. He'd never admitted as much, but that was the reason why he'd always refused to go camping, whether it was with his family, or when he was older, with his college friends. The flimsy walls of a tent were nowhere near enough to keep at bay whatever creature may have been lurking beyond. He could only ever sleep soundly when he was surrounded by at least four inches of bricks and mortar. He didn't even like to sleep on a building's ground floor, just in case some godless creature could sense his presence there to begin crawling inside.

Having to remind himself that he was now a grown man, and that werewolves didn't exist, nor could they have done, he pulled himself up straight to make his way around to the side of the car. Once locked, he glanced up and down the deserted road with the vague hope of seeing another vehicle. But of course, there wasn't one. There wouldn't be for at least another hour.

Grateful, at least, for the moon's ethereal white light, allowing him to see the road ahead, he steeled himself to begin marching forward, trying to keep his mind occupied by calculating how long it would take to reach the next village.

A minute later and he was already feeling better. What had his grandfather taught him? Action cures fear! The simple act of walking was enough for him to think about more positive things, like how he was going to spend the money he was due to inherit when his parents did the decent thing and died. Unfortunately, for him at least, despite the fact that they were both in their eighties, they were still very much alive and kicking. On the plus side, they were rich, at least they were by his standards. Their house alone was worth over a million. Then there was his dad's collection of cars, plus the fact that they'd also only bothered to have one child – him! And although he'd be left with a hefty inheritance tax bill, whatever was left was coming his way. 'A new car, for a start,' he mumbled to himself, a calculating smile playing over his thin grey lips, as he pictured himself climbing into the sumptuous leather seat of a Range Rover Velar.

Seeing the sign for Swanton Morley, he quickened his step, only to be brought to a gradual halt by the sight of something in the middle of the road.

Remaining still, he squinted his eyes, doing his best to work out what it was; a person standing there, or something less concerning?

Unable to decide what action to take, he was about to call out before changing his mind. If it was some sort of half-man, half-wolf-like creature, the last thing he wanted to do was to draw attention to himself.

Realising he couldn't just stand there all night like

a complete idiot, he took a steadying breath to begin inching his way forward, keeping his eyes peeled for the slightest movement.

After a few tentative steps, he was becoming increasingly convinced that it was nothing more threatening than a wheelie bin that some drunken idiot had parked there, perhaps with a bag of rubbish left on top of it, when the whole thing started to tremble.

Coming to a gradual halt, he tuned his ears for the smallest of sounds. That's when he heard the gentle, unmistakable murmur of a grown man crying.

Taking a much needed breath, he took another step forward, only for the crying to instantly stop. He couldn't see the person's face, but he somehow knew, with absolute certainty, that he was looking directly at him.

Unable to just continue standing there, gawping anxiously at whoever it was, he hesitantly opened his mouth. 'Hello?' he decided to call, to be left waiting awkwardly for some sort of response. But there was none. The man just seemed to keep staring at him.

Desperate to break the unnerving silence, he called out again. 'I've – er – broken down. My car's just behind me,' he added, gesturing back in a bid to explain his own presence there. 'I ran out of petrol. I should have filled it up yesterday, but I forgot,' he nervously rambled.

As Albert's words drifted pointlessly away, he heard the man start to cry again, this time mumbling something under his breath.

With his all-consuming fear becoming replaced by more curious concern, he began edging his way steadily forward. 'Are you OK?' he eventually asked. 'Can I help in some way?'

'I DIDN'T KILL HIM!' the man suddenly

screamed, the words left to echo through the surrounding trees, as if being whispered by the lips of a thousand lifeless souls.

'Jesus Christ,' Albert muttered under his breath, wondering what the hell he'd managed to get himself into.

As he heard the man begin to openly sob, he came grinding to a halt, wracking his brain as to what best to say next. His immediate thought was to ask *who* he hadn't killed, but he knew that was insanely stupid. Not only would it be highly unlikely that he'd know the supposed victim, but it could very easily be interpreted that he was questioning the truthfulness of his statement, as if the exact opposite was more likely to be true.

Next he thought to say something along the lines of, 'I'm sure you didn't!' but again, it could be considered to be framing the question as to whether he had or not. 'Can I call anyone for you?' he eventually asked. 'The police, perhaps?'

As the word "police" hung suspended in the air, like a corpse hanging from a tightening noose, he heard the man's sobbing come to a gradual halt. When he saw his head lift, as if to stare at him with a malicious, threatening gaze, Albert cursed himself for having said anything at all. 'I d-didn't mean I would,' he eventually continued, only to kick himself all over again.

'You're going to call the police?' the shadowy figure questioned, taking an ominous step closer.

'No, I – I mean – only if you want me to.'

The figure's shoulders hunched forward as his pace began to quicken. 'I don't understand. Why do you think I'd want you to do that?'

Albert began backing away. 'Because you said – you said you – you hadn't...'

'But you think I d-did, though, don't you?'

'No, I didn't. I – I mean – I don't!'

'Are you telling me the truth?'

'I am!' Albert stated, hoping to God he didn't trip over something as he continued reversing himself back down the road.

On the verge of turning to run screaming back to his car, he saw the man come grinding to a halt to hear him repeat, 'I didn't kill him.'

Again unsure as what to either say or do, this time Albert decided to keep his mouth firmly closed.

As the moonlit road returned to its previous state of uncomfortable silence, the glint of a cold steel blade, hanging by the man's side, had Albert's heart leaping into his throat. When he heard him start crying all over again, he took a very slow, and very deliberate backwards step.

With the person ahead seeming not to have noticed, he took another, then another, glancing over his shoulder to see how far he had to go before reaching the safety of his car. When he turned back, two things had happened. The first was that the man had once again become dangerously still. The second left Albert with a cold sweat breaking out over his face and neck. Unbeknownst to him, whilst they'd been talking, a bank of thick grey clouds had been inching its way over the face of the moon, leaving the road, his car and, more importantly, the man holding the knife ahead, to bleed slowly into the night, until there was nothing left between him and the increasingly shadowy figure but an impenetrable wall of all-consuming blackness.

- CHAPTER ONE -

'WHAT THE HELL'S going on?' muttered Tanner to himself, inching his way along the traffic-cluttered road leading to Wroxham Police Station in his slightly grubby, definitely dated, jet-black Jaguar XJS.

With nothing much else to do, he glanced impatiently down at the clock on the wood-veneered dashboard. It had already gone nine o'clock. Being the first day back since his emotionally charged honeymoon, he'd been planning on having his feet behind his desk by half-past eight. But with one thing and another, mainly their newborn baby, Samantha, throwing up all over him the moment he picked her up for a goodbye kiss, he had to change not only his shirt and tie, but his entire suit before eventually being able to leave.

Smiling at the memory of the smelly, milky-wet kiss, he glanced down at his tie, only to see a suspicious white mark about halfway down. Assuming it to be more baby vomit, probably from when he'd picked her up again for one last, even smellier kiss, he lifted it to his nose to sniff. 'Toothpaste!' he commented, annoyed at himself for not having spotted it before taking it out of the wardrobe.

Remembering he had another one, rolled up inside his glove box, he was about to lean forward to take it out when he heard some idiot beep rudely from behind.

Glancing up to realise that the car ahead was trundling down the road without him, leaving a gap that at least four other cars could fit into, he waved an apologetic hand at the driver behind to pull slowly away. It was as he was catching back up when he finally discovered the reason for the long tail back. Immediately outside the police station was an enormous news van, with a satellite dish the size of a nuclear power station stuck on top of its roof, endeavouring to navigate itself either in, or out of a space on the pavement between two more vans, both equally as large.

Wondering if it was really possible that they'd yet to move from when they'd been there to cover what had become known as the Bluebell Wood Scandal some two weeks before, he was eventually able to turn into the police station's carpark, only to find it was as packed as the road outside.

Unable to see a single free space, he was becoming increasingly curious to know what was going on, especially as he hadn't seen anything on the local news whilst he'd been away. Even the fabled Norfolk Herald had been unusually quiet. Their last big story, about a so-called rabid ghost dog, which they'd imaginatively entitled The Hound of Bluebell Wood, had died a death when the owner came forward to pick it up.

Forced to park around the back, he headed inside to find the reception no busier than normal for your average Monday morning. Seeing the duty sergeant sitting behind the plastic security screen, busily chatting to an elderly couple, he lifted a hand to wave hello, only to see him shift his gaze down to his keyboard.

Forced to assume he simply hadn't seen him, Tanner gave his shoulders an apathetic shrug to push through the double doors leading into the main office. There, he found the place buzzing with activity, with everyone either talking on the phone, studying a file in front of them, or staring with unusual interest at their monitors.

Remaining where he was for a moment, expecting someone to look up to see him, he eventually gave up. Everyone was apparently just too busy to notice his return.

Beginning to feel a bit like a spare wheel, he was about to slink his way to his office for a much needed coffee, when he finally heard someone say his name, or at least what everyone had been calling him since his promotion to DCI.

'Morning, boss!'

'Oh, good morning, Sally,' he replied, turning to see the attractive detective constable come hurrying out of the kitchen, two large mugs of steaming coffee at the end of each arm.

'How was your honeymoon?' she asked, 'and the baby, of course!'

'All good, thank you.'

'Unfortunately, I can't stop,' she grimaced, 'but – promise to tell me later?'

'Er...yes, of course,' Tanner replied, watching her scurry away towards the reception doors with a look of curious surprise. *He* was normally the one to say that he was too busy to chat. Up until that moment, that was all he thought Sally did, that and her nails, of course. OK, that wasn't entirely true, but he'd never known her to pass up the opportunity to catch up with the latest gossip, especially when the subject would have been about weddings, honeymoons, and even more fascinating – babies!

Watching her carefully nudge her way through the doors, he glanced into the kitchen to see Vicky, focussed on making herself a coffee. 'Morning Vicky!' he said, wondering if she, too, would be too busy to chat.

'Oh, hi boss,' she replied, offering him a surprised, if not brief smile. 'I wasn't expecting you back for at least another week.'

'Sorry, but…why wouldn't I be back for another week? I've already been away for two, or didn't you notice?'

'You did have a baby, didn't you?'

'Ah, right, I see what's happened. You're confusing me with Christine. She's the one who had the baby. Not that I didn't want to, of course. Nothing would have given me greater pleasure than to spend four-and-a-half hours stuck inside a Spanish hospital, screaming in agony whilst trying to work out what the word empujar meant.'

Unsure if she was even listening, he watched her continue to make her drink, before adding, 'It means push, by the way. Just in case you were wondering.'

'How's Christine?' Vicky eventually asked to glance spasmodically up.

'Exhausted!'

'And the baby?'

'Full of beans. And milk, of course.'

'Looks like you've got some of that on your tie.'

'Actually, I think that's toothpaste,' Tanner replied, glancing down.

'Are you sure?'

'Uh-huh. I tasted it on the way in.'

'You do know that's disgusting, don't you?'

'Well, yes, or at least it would have been, if it had been baby vomit. Talking about my journey in, and the mile-long tail back all the way through Wroxham, are the news vans blocking up the road outside the same ones that were there when I left?'

'They're not piling up already, are they?'

'Why? Has something happened that I should be aware of?'

'It's the Adlington case,' Vicky replied, spinning around to pull some milk out from the fridge.

'Er...I thought that was a done deal.'

'Another story broke over the weekend. According to the Norwich Reporter, the Adlingtons were only a small part of a much larger child prostitution ring. We're currently trying to establish just how much of it is true, but judging by the number of emails and calls we've been taking, it would appear to be, at least in part.'

'Is that where Sally was going, with the coffees?'

'Er...no. That's something else.'

'Something else, as in...?'

'A young man walked into the station about half an hour ago. He was covered in mud, and what would appear to be a large amount of blood. We're currently trying to establish if the blood is his, which is proving difficult, as he won't let us anywhere near him, certainly not close enough to take a sample.'

'I presume there's a reason for you to think that it might not be?'

'Apart from the knife he had with him at the time, and the fact that he keeps trying to convince everyone that he hasn't killed someone? Not really.'

'He hasn't killed *who?*'

'That's what we're trying to figure out.'

'He hasn't said anything else?'

'Not yet.'

'Does he have any injuries?'

'A few.'

'Enough to warrant the blood?'

'Possibly, but again, we're not sure.'
'What about a name?'
'Well, we presume he has one.'
'But he hasn't said?'
Vicky shook her head. 'He doesn't appear to have any ID, either.'
'Is someone with him?'
'Cooper and Townsend.'
Tanner raised a concerned eyebrow. 'Any reason why it's not you?'
'Forrester wants me to focus on the child prostitution story.'
'Well, OK, but I thought I left you in charge to make such decisions for yourself?'
'You did, but you know what Forrester's like.'
Tanner rolled his eyes. 'I suppose he was phoning you up every five minutes to see how you were getting on?'
'Actually, he only called once.'
'Oh...right!'
'But that was to tell me he was moving into your office.'
'What?'
'He's still there, if you want to speak to him.'
'He's in my office?'
'Uh-huh.'
'You mean...now?' Tanner continued, staring past all the desks to where he could see the handle of his closed office door.
'He moved in the day after you left.'
'For Christ's sake!' he exclaimed, shaking his head in frustrated consternation. 'Why didn't you tell me?'
'I thought I just did.'
'I meant, when I was in Spain?'
'Well, I would have, of course, but I wasn't exactly sure what you could have done about it.'

'I could have phoned him up to ask what the hell he was doing, for a start!'

Having finished making her drink, Vicky took a sip to smile sheepishly up at him.

'Right! I suppose I'm going to have to have a word with him, being that I don't have a bloody desk to work from.'

About to storm off, he heard Vicky call out behind him, 'Before you go, I don't suppose you could go a little easy on him?'

Tanner stopped in his tracks to turn around. 'Why on Earth would I go easy on him? He's never trusted me! Nor anyone else, for that matter!'

'It's just that...' Vicky continued, in a low, conspiratorial tone, '...well...he seems a little depressed. That's all.'

'Isn't he always?' Tanner huffed, turning to head off again.

'Possibly more so than normal,' he heard Vicky continue. 'According to Sally, his wife just kicked him out.'

Her words brought Tanner grinding to a halt.

'I was told in the strictest confidence, so if you could keep that to yourself,' she added.

'Yes, of course. But he can't live here.'

'He's not sleeping here. At least, I don't think he is.'

'Then where's he staying?'

'A hotel down the road.'

Tanner turned his head to look surreptitiously away. 'OK, but just because his wife kicked him out, doesn't mean he can waltz in here to take over both my job *and* my office.'

'Oh, I'm sure that's not his intention.'

Tanner let out a world-weary sigh. 'I suppose I'd better go in to see if he's alright.'

'I think he'd like that, but if you could keep what I told you to yourself. I'd hate for Sally to get into trouble for telling me.'

'Yes, of course. Although, if he'd planned on keeping it a secret, Sally was probably the *last* person he should have told!'

- CHAPTER TWO -

'MORNING, SIR,' SAID Tanner, knocking gently on his own office door to poke his head around the corner.

'Ah, Tanner!' Forrester exclaimed, offering him a beaming smile as he climbed quickly to his feet. 'I wasn't expecting to see you for at least another week!'

'Thank you, sir but there was no need for any more time off. Apart from the fact that it's more peaceful here than at home, I wouldn't have been so presumptuous as to assume that I could take paternity leave without actually asking for it.'

'There's no need to ask, Tanner. It wasn't as if the baby was expected, at least, not smack bang in the middle of your honeymoon.'

'True,' Tanner replied, stepping inside to close the door.

'How's Christine?'

'Exhausted, but that's hardly surprising.'

'And the baby?'

'Full of beans,' Tanner replied, wondering just how many times he was going to be asked the exact same questions.

'For a minute there, I thought you were going to say milk!' laughed Forrester.

A little miffed to have had his joke stolen, Tanner forced himself to smile. 'Most amusing, sir.'

'Speaking of milk, it looks like you have some on

your tie.'

Regretting not having exchanged it with the one in his car, he replied as he'd done before. 'I think it's actually toothpaste, sir.'

'Are you sure? It looks more like baby vomit to me.'

'Quite sure, thank you,' Tanner replied, deliberately casting his eyes down at his desk, the one Forrester was still standing behind.

Forrester awkwardly followed his gaze, as if suddenly remembering that the desk Tanner was looking at wasn't his. 'I suppose you'd like your desk back?'

'If that's OK with you?'

'Yes, of course!' he continued, beginning to retrieve numerous items from the top to start placing them into various pockets. 'I was just filling in, whilst you were away.'

Unable to help feel sorry for him, Tanner waited for him to collect his personal items before asking, 'Can I make you a coffee?'

'I'm OK, thank you,' Forrester responded, shifting himself around the desk to allow Tanner to take his place.

'It's no problem. I was going to make myself one anyway. Actually, I'm probably going to make myself about half-a-dozen between now and when I leave tonight.'

'Then, if you wouldn't mind?'

'Not at all!' Tanner exclaimed, spinning around to begin wrestling with the coffee machine. 'Whilst I'm doing that, perhaps you can tell me what's been going on around here since I've been away.'

'Oh, nothing much, at least, not until the last couple of days.'

'I assume that's when the story broke about the alleged child prostitution ring.'

'You've heard about that, have you?'

'Vicky told me, when I came in.'

'We've already been inundated with calls.'

'What about the people behind it?'

'Fortunately, the newspaper that broke the story didn't go so far as to actually name anyone, but they do have a list, at least they say they do. They've already reached out to us, asking if one of their senior editors can drop by to discuss what they've found. I think someone is due at around half-past nine tomorrow.'

'You'd have thought they would have done that before breaking the story.'

'I'm not sure that's how investigative journalism works, I'm afraid. I was going to meet with them myself, but now that you're back, perhaps I can leave that with you?'

'Yes, of course.'

'Then there's the man who came in earlier.'

'The one covered in mud and blood, adamant that he hasn't killed someone?' queried Tanner, turning to hand Forrester a cup of freshly made coffee.

'Cooper and Townsend are with him now,' Forrester nodded, taking a tentative sip. 'Maybe you could pop your head around the door, to see how they're getting on at some point?'

'Has anyone been reported missing?'

'Not yet. Nor do we know if the blood is his or not, and as he won't let us take a sample, it's going to be challenging for us to find out.'

A knock at the door was followed by Townsend's head, appearing from around the other side.

'Ah, Townsend!' Forrester exclaimed. 'We were only just this minute talking about you.'

'Sorry to bother you,' the handsome young DC began, exchanging uncertain glances between the two senior police officers, as if unsure as to which one he should be addressing. 'The man in the interview room,' he continued, his eyes eventually resting on Forrester. 'He's becoming increasingly agitated. Cooper was wondering if it may be useful for him to see a psychiatrist before we go any further.'

'I think that's my cue to leave,' Forrester muttered, ditching his hardly drunk coffee onto the desk to catch Tanner's eye. 'Before I go, I don't suppose there's a desk I could borrow for a few hours? I'm viewing a property down the road this afternoon, so I'd rather not have to drive all the way back to HQ.'

'Yes, of course! There must be an empty one around here somewhere. Maybe you could ask Sally?'

'Will do,' Forrester replied, stepping around Townsend to leave them both with a cheerful smile.

'He seems happy,' commented Townsend, making sure the door was closed.

'I suspect it's more of a projected façade.'

'A what?'

'Putting on a brave face,' Tanner translated.

'You mean, because his wife kicked him out?'

'Sally's told you?'

'I think she's told everyone!' he laughed. 'I wouldn't be surprised if she's posted something about it on Instagram, to help increase the reach.'

'It's not funny, Townsend.'

'What, that Forrester got kicked out by his wife, or that my ex-girlfriend doesn't understand the meaning of the word discretion?'

'What do you mean, your *ex*-girlfriend?'

Townsend gave his shoulders a depressed shrug. 'She broke up with me, whilst you were away.'

'I wouldn't worry about it if I were you. Judging by your past history, you'll be back together in no time.'

'I'm not so sure. She's already started seeing

someone else.'

'That was quick!'

'He's a friend of a friend.'

'Well, at least you know how Forrester feels.'

Townsend glanced up to offer Tanner an acrimonious scowl. 'Is that supposed to make me feel better?'

'No, Townsend, it was supposed to help you to become a little more aware of how challenging relationships can be, especially ones that are supposed to last a lifetime, as opposed to those that only seem to last until a person's next drunken meander down to the local nightclub.'

'I don't think they met at a nightclub.'

'I was speaking figuratively, Townsend.'

'Oh, right,' the young DC replied, with a confused expression.

'Anyway,' Tanner exhaled, 'you came in to ask something about the witness you've been speaking to?'

'Not me. Cooper. He thinks the guy's at least three sandwiches short of a picnic, and wants permission to have him carted off to the nearest mental asylum.'

'Has he said anything that's been of any use?'

'Cooper, or the witness?'

Tanner sent Townsend an unamused scowl.

'Not really,' Townsend continued, straightening his face. 'He just keeps repeating the same thing, over and over again.'

'You are still referring to the witness?' Tanner queried.

Townsend smiled back in response. 'Good to have you back, boss!'

'I wish I could say it was good to *be* back,' Tanner replied, glancing out of the window to see yet another news van pulling up onto the pavement outside.

'Anyway,' he continued, draining his cup, 'I suppose I'd better have a chat with this deranged lunatic of yours. Let me just grab another coffee, and I'll be straight over.'

- CHAPTER THREE -

KNOCKING ON THE door to Wroxham Police Station's unimaginatively named Interview Room One, Tanner poked his head around the corner to see Townsend and Cooper sitting on one side of the table, with a particularly dishevelled looking man slumped on the other. 'Is it alright if I come in?' he asked, catching Cooper's eye.

'Help yourself!' Cooper huffed, standing up to face him. 'But you'll be wasting your time. The man needs professional help, and I don't mean from us.'

Stepping to one side as Cooper shoved his way past, nearly spilling his freshly made coffee as he did, Tanner muttered, 'Good to see you, too,' watching him leave before closing the door.

'So, what do we have here?' he continued, smiling first at Townsend, then at their guest's closely shaved, blood-smeared head. 'Or should I say, who?'

'He still hasn't told us his name,' Townsend replied, as Tanner took the vacated seat next to him.

'Right, well, my name's Detective Chief Inspector Tanner,' Tanner began, making himself comfortable as he studied the person opposite. 'May I ask who you are?'

'I didn't kill him,' the man mumbled quietly back in response.

'It would help if I knew how to address you. Mr...?'

'I didn't do it. It wasn't me.'

Tanner leaned forward to rest his mug on the table. 'Has anyone offered you a drink? A coffee, perhaps?'

The man's blood-shot eyes darted up to look at Tanner's steaming mug, before returning to stare down at the table's uncluttered surface.

'Would you like mine?' Tanner offered, somewhat reluctantly.

There was no response.

'Tell you what. How about I give you my specially blended, piping hot, freshly made filtered coffee, in exchange for you telling us your name?'

Keeping a firm hold of it, Tanner nudged the mug over the table towards him.

A prolonged silence followed, before the man eventually whispered something unintelligible.

'Sorry, what was that?' Tanner asked, leaning his head forward.

The man drew in a juddering breath, before eventually whispering, 'Joe.'

'I don't suppose you have a surname as well, Joe?' Tanner continued, nudging the coffee a little closer.

'Miller. Joe Miller.'

'OK, thank you, Joe,' he continued, offering Townsend the briefest of smiles before pushing his mug all the way over. 'Can we get you anything to eat as well?'

Shaking his head, Miller wrapped his filthy hands around the cup to take a tentative sip.

'Are you sure? We could probably rustle up some biscuits?'

He shook his head again to begin staring down into the mug.

'OK, well, let us know if you change your mind. Meanwhile, perhaps you can tell us a little more about this person you said you found?'

'I didn't kill him!' the man repeated, lifting his eyes to meet with Tanner's for the first time.

'Nobody's suggesting you did, Joe, but it would certainly help if we knew who this person was.'

Silence returned, as his gaze fell back to the mug.

'Did you know him?'

Miller glanced briefly up, as if he wanted to say something, but was too afraid.

'It's OK, Joe. We're not going to assume you had anything to do with whatever took place just because you knew who the person was.'

Miller continued to remain silent.

'Then perhaps you can tell us *how* you knew him?'

More silence followed.

'Maybe through a friend?'

He shook his head.

'Had you seen him somewhere before? On TV, perhaps?'

As he returned to his previous state of staring unblinkingly down at the mug, as if in some sort of catatonic trance, Tanner let out a frustrated sigh. 'Listen, Joe, if you're not prepared to tell us what you know, you'll leave us with little choice but to assume that you *have* killed someone, accidentally or otherwise. That will mean we'll have to arrest you, which will involve taking your fingerprints, together with a DNA sample, whether you want us to or not. So, let me ask you again, if you do know this man, then can you please at least tell us how?'

'I just do,' came his mumbled reply.

'But in what context?' Tanner demanded, unintentionally raising his voice.

Drawing in a slow, deliberate breath, the man lifted his blood-shot eyes to fix them dementedly onto Tanner's. 'Because I'm the one who dug his grave. That's how I know him!'

- CHAPTER FOUR -

A KNOCK AT the door had Tanner and Townsend glancing around to see Vicky's mop of dark red hair appear from around the other side.

'Sorry to bother you, boss,' she whispered, her eyes flickering between the two detectives, 'but...may I have a quick word?'

'Now's really not a good time,' Tanner replied.

'It's rather important,' she replied, sending him an insistent glare.

Tanner let out an exasperated sigh before pushing himself away from the table. 'Very well. Townsend, you better stay here.'

'I think it's better if you both come,' Vicky continued.

Exchanging a curious glance, they both stood quickly up to navigate themselves out into the corridor.

'OK, Vicky, you have our attention.'

'I've just taken a call,' Vicky continued, leaning between them to close the interview room door.

'Yes, and...?'

'A body's been found near Dereham, on the other side of Norwich.'

'But – that's miles away!'

'Twenty-six point three miles away, to be exact,' Vicky replied. 'I just looked it up on Google.'

'I don't think it matters exactly how many miles away it is, Vicky, it's not in our jurisdiction.'

'Sorry, boss, but Forrester seems to think otherwise.'

'You've told Forrester?'

'I didn't have a choice. He's sitting at the desk opposite mine. He overheard the entire conversation.'

Tanner rolled his eyes up to the ceiling. 'Anyway,' he eventually continued, 'why does he think we should cover it?'

'Because a man was seen running away from the scene in the early hours of the morning.'

'Yes, and...?'

'He was reported as carrying a knife, and was said to have been covered in mud and blood. He was also ranting and raving about having *not* killed someone.'

Tanner glanced back at the closed interview room door. 'Where was this place again?'

'A village by the name of Swanton Morley. The body was found at the local church, lying at the bottom of an open grave.'

- CHAPTER FIVE -

WITH VICKY IN the passenger seat, Tanner rounded a corner of the quiet, peaceful town of Swanton Morley to see a robust rectangular church tower, looming up into the overcast sky ahead.

'I assume that's it,' he enquired, leaning forward to peer at it through his Jag's sloping windscreen.

'There are enough cars there,' Vicky replied, following his gaze, 'so it must be.'

Eventually turning into a narrow, gravel-lined carpark to find every available space taken by either police vans or squad cars, Tanner was forced to bring his XJS to a stop immediately behind an ambulance, parked in the middle at the furthest end.

Climbing out to stretch his back, he glanced up to see a chubby, red-faced uniformed police constable come running down a short series of steps towards them.

'Oi!' the young man called out, waving an arm erratically above his head. 'You can't park there!'

'Oh, sorry,' Tanner replied, glancing around. 'I couldn't find anywhere else.'

'Then you'll have to park on the road outside,' the constable demanded, gesturing to the road in question as he came wobbling to a breathless halt.

Tanner turned to look back, first at his car, then at the road he was being directed to. 'If it's all the same to you, I'll think I'll just leave it where it is, thank you.'

'You can't do that! You're blocking everyone's way! The ambulance in particular!'

'I shouldn't worry. From what I've heard, the person I presume the ambulance is here for doesn't have anywhere in particular he needs to be. Not urgently, at least. Besides, with any luck, we won't be long.'

The rotund police officer lifted his clean-shaven double-chin to study Tanner's face with a dubious eye. 'May I ask who you are, exactly?'

'DCI Tanner,' Tanner replied, producing his formal ID, 'and my colleague, DI Gilbert.'

The moment the officer's eyes saw Tanner's ID, he leapt to attention, as if he'd been electrocuted. 'I'm most dreadfully sorry, sir,' he instantly apologised. 'I thought you were from the press.'

'Don't worry, it's hardly your fault. We've been sent here from Wroxham Police Station.'

'Oh, right.'

With the young officer remaining exactly where he was, his eyes fixed to a point just beyond Tanner's ear, Tanner was left to clear his throat. 'Would it be alright if we could take a look at the body?'

'Yes, of course, it's just that...'

'It's just...what?'

'I'm sorry, sir, but my boss has given me strict instructions not to allow anyone to park here.'

'And your boss is who, may I ask?'

'Well, at the moment it's DI Haverstock, sir. Our DCI is off sick.'

'Tell you what,' Tanner continued, leaning forward to whisper in a low conspiratorial tone, 'I won't tell him if you won't.'

'Er...right, sir.'

'If someone does need to get out,' he continued,

nudging his way past, 'just give me a shout, and I'll be happy to move it.'

- CHAPTER SIX -

FOLLOWING THE YOUNG constable up a series of steps dug into a steep incline, they passed a thick line of shrubs and trees to see Swanton Morley's church, sitting on top of a hill above them, its robust perpendicular stone tower presenting an imposing sight.

After being led up to the church's arched stone entrance, they were taken along a path around the back, where they discovered a vast sweeping graveyard, littered with dozens upon dozens of lopsided headstones, tumbling down the other side of the hill like discarded dominos. At the furthest end could be seen a small group of overall-clad forensic officers, near to what looked to be an open grave. Surrounding them were six or seven uniformed police personnel, intermixed with a smaller number of suited and booted men, who Tanner automatically assumed to be the local CID team.

Leaving the path, they were led past the moss-covered gravestones, all the way down to the bottom of the hill, to be eventually met by the group they'd seen from the top, most of whom had stopped whatever they'd been doing to stare at them with similar expressions of quizzical hostility.

'Sorry to bother you, Haverstock, sir,' began the young constable they'd been following, bringing himself to attention in front of a stocky, sombre-faced man in his mid to late thirties, dressed in a pressed grey suit with a dark blue tie, 'but there are a couple of detectives from Wroxham Police Station here to see you.'

'We didn't actually come to see you,' corrected Tanner, offering the man an affable enough smile. 'More the body that we've been told has been discovered here.'

'May I ask why?' Haverstock queried, looking Tanner up and down with a resentful air.

'We think we may have a witness to the incident, back at the station,' Tanner courteously replied.

'Back at *your* station, you mean?'

'Er, yes, sorry. *Our* station.'

'Then don't you think it would have been more useful to have had this so-called witness driven to *our* station for us to talk to, instead of you coming all this way to look at a body that frankly has nothing to do with you?'

'To be completely honest, I couldn't agree more!'

Haverstock folded his arms. 'Then why, may I ask, did you come?'

'Because Superintendent Forrester told us to,' shrugged Tanner.

The mention of their superior's name had Haverstock presenting Tanner with an embittered frown. 'Fair enough, I suppose, but I've been given the lead on this, which means it's my crime scene. It's therefore my decision as to who is, and isn't, allowed to enter.'

'I'm simply following orders.'

'As am I.'

'Then perhaps you'd better speak to Forrester?'

Narrowing his eyes at Tanner, Haverstock tugged out a phone to begin swiping impatiently at the screen.

'Whilst you're doing that,' Tanner continued, 'I don't suppose we could take a very quick look at the body?'

'Not until I've confirmed who you are with Forrester,' he replied, lifting the phone to his ear. 'Besides, I can't risk contaminating the crime scene.'

Tanner glanced curiously around at the dozen or so people milling about, half of whom didn't seem to be doing anything more productive than to continue staring at them with their hands shoved into their pockets. 'You mean, any more than it already has been?'

'Excuse me, but just who the hell do you think you are?' Haverstock suddenly demanded, his crumpled face quickly darkening.

'Sorry, I must have forgotten to introduce myself,' Tanner replied, presenting his ID. 'DCI Tanner. This, here, is my colleague, DI Gilbert. And you are...?' he continued, taking gleeful pleasure in watching the man end his attempted call to shift his weight from one foot to the other.

'DI Haverstock,' the man eventually muttered, in a tone of obvious reticence.

'Then I assume it *is* OK for us to take a quick look at the body?'

'I'm not sure that I can stop you, *sir*,' Haverstock replied, stepping to one side to allow both Tanner and Vicky past.

'No, I suppose you can't,' Tanner said quietly to himself in response. He'd never had a chance to pull rank on someone before, and was unable to prevent himself from enjoying the moment.

Nudging through the small crowd of people, Tanner led Vicky over a series of raised aluminium platforms towards the open grave they'd first seen from the back of the church.

Nodding politely at a forensics officer, stepping gracefully out of their way, Tanner stopped to stare down into the grave to see the slim, athletic figure of someone with short, brown, neatly cut hair crouched at the bottom.

'Good morning!' Tanner called down, in an overtly cheerful tone. 'Am I to assume you're the medical examiner?'

'I have been known to be called that,' came a female voice.

'Oh, you're a...' Tanner heard himself say.

'A woman?' the person in question responded, turning her head to present Tanner with a look of rueful disdain.

'Sorry,' Tanner grimaced. 'It's just that – with the hair – and everything, I assumed you to be a... a...'

'A mongoose?'

'No... a...'

'A meercat?'

Tanner could feel himself blush with embarrassment.

'Oh, you mean a *man!*'

Unable to think of anything to say in response, Tanner just stood there, opening and closing his mouth like a breathless goldfish.

'Don't worry,' the woman eventually laughed, 'ever since I had my hair cut, everyone seems to automatically assume I'm a man. Even my husband was a little confused.'

'Well, look, I'm sorry again.'

'Don't be. Besides, it was my fault. I should have put a sign out saying Woman At Work, like you men find it necessary to do.'

Keen to change the subject, Tanner directed her

attention to the body he could see, covered in reddish churned-up mud at the bottom of the open grave. 'May I ask what we have?'

'May I enquire as to who's asking?' the woman shot back, in an insistent tone.

'DCI Tanner,' he replied, 'Also my colleague, DI Gilbert. She's a woman as well, you know!'

'You don't say!' the medical examiner exclaimed, taking a moment to study Vicky's face, as if she was an alien species from some distant planet.

Smiling a hello down to her, Vicky leaned forward to whisper, 'Believe it or not, he's not some sort of brainless misogynist. He's just a normal man.'

Replying with an understanding nod, she returned to looking at Tanner. 'I assume you're new here?'

'Sort of,' Tanner replied. 'We've been sent over from Wroxham. May I ask your name?'

'Alison Westwood,' she replied. 'Please forgive my appearance. I look better when I'm not crouched at the bottom of an open grave, except in the mornings, of course, or just after my daily spin class.'

'How about the victim?'

'Oh,' she replied, glancing down, 'he's probably looked better as well, certainly before someone went to the trouble of murdering him.'

'Has that been established; that he was murdered?'

'Unless he decided to drag himself down here from the back of the church, stab himself eleven times in the chest, to then cover himself with a thin layer of earth, possibly as part of a rather macabre game of hide-and-seek.'

'So, you're not sure, then?'

Alison returned an amused smile. 'I'll be able to give you a more accurate assessment when I've had him hauled back to the lab. I assume you'd like a copy of my report?'

'To be honest, I'm not sure that I do.'

'You're not heading-up the investigation?'

Tanner shook his head. 'We've only been sent over to take a quick look. We have someone back at Wroxham who says they found the body. We're just trying to establish if he's anything more than just a witness.'

'OK, well, if it's of any use, I'd say it was quite a frenzied attack. There's no other reason for him to have been stabbed quite so many times.'

'Do we know who he is?'

'Not yet, but I still need to go through his pockets.'

'Can you tell me anything about how he died, apart from being stabbed multiple times in the chest, of course?'

'There's an indentation in the back of his skull, but it didn't kill him. When you take into account the parallel lines we've found in the grass, leading from the back of the church all the way down to the side of the grave, I'd say he was knocked unconscious at the top of the hill. There hasn't been any blood found anywhere else, so I'm assuming the main attack took place once he was here.'

'Do you think it would be likely that his assailant would have left the scene with some mud on him?'

'I would have thought so,' Alison replied, taking a moment to glance around at the vertical walls surrounding her. 'To be honest, I'd be surprised if he wasn't covered in the stuff.'

Tanner glanced briefly around at Vicky. 'Time of death?'

'Approximately nine to twelve hours ago.'

'Do you know who alerted the police?'

'The vicar, apparently.'

Tanner lifted his head to begin glancing about. 'I

don't suppose you know if he's around?'

'I'm sorry, I don't. Try asking Haverstock. He should know.'

'Ah...that *could* be a problem,' Tanner replied, staring over at the man in question, in the middle of sharing a particularly hilarious joke with his subordinate chums.

'I wouldn't worry about Haverstock. His bark is worse than his bite. Not sure about his jokes. Apart from that, I'd have thought you would have outranked him?'

'In theory, I do,' Tanner nodded, 'but it's his investigation, and I have zero jurisdiction here.'

'What would you like me to do about my report? I'm more than happy to send you a copy.'

'I don't want to get you into any trouble.'

'I'd only get into trouble if I'm told *not* to send you a copy, which doesn't seem very likely.'

'OK, well, I suppose it wouldn't do any harm,' Tanner replied, digging out one of his business cards to pass surreptitiously down to her. 'My email address is at the bottom, together with my phone number.'

'Sorry, but...why would I want your phone number?' she asked, reaching up for it.

'Oh – er – just in case you discover anything unexpected, I suppose,' came Tanner's flustered response.

'I'm winding you up,' she laughed, tucking the card into one of the pockets of her black cargo trousers. 'But just in case you were thinking about asking me out to start some gloriously sordid affair; with one husband, three children, two dogs, four cats, and a pregnant gerbil, I wouldn't have the time, even if I wanted to.'

- CHAPTER SEVEN -

LEAVING THE MEDICAL examiner to continue her work, Tanner led Vicky back over the raised aluminium platforms, offering a respectful nod to Haverstock and his team as they passed.

Once out of earshot, he stopped to first stare up at the church, then back at the grave.

'I think she liked you,' he heard Vicky comment beside him.

'Huh?'

'The medical examiner,' she continued, following his gaze. 'I think she liked you.'

'Doesn't everyone?'

'Not in that way.'

'I'm fairly sure she had other things on her mind, as should you, young Vicky.'

'Is that why you gave her your phone number?'

'I was under the impression that I gave her my business card.'

'Which had your phone number on it.'

Tanner turned to stare at her. 'Please stop trying to wind me up.'

'I wasn't *trying* to wind you up, boss. I *was* winding you up.'

'Then can you please stop.'

Vicky shrugged her shoulders whilst suppressing a whimsical smirk. 'I was only trying to find out why you gave her your phone number.'

'I don't suppose we could bring our attention back to the investigation instead?'

'I thought we only came to have a look?'

'We did.'

'And that it wasn't our investigation?'

'It isn't.'

'Then why would we need to bring our attention back to it?'

'Because, there's a man back at our office covered in mud and blood, pleading with us that he didn't murder the person at the bottom of the grave behind us, when all the evidence is telling us the exact opposite.'

'OK, so we have him driven over here to let Haverstock interview him, as Haverstock himself suggested.'

'Well yes, I suppose we could.'

'But you're not going to.'

'Not yet, no.'

'May I ask why?'

'Because, I haven't finished.'

'Oh, right.'

'Apart from that, from what I've seen here so far, I'm inclined to believe him.'

'And what have you seen so far that's made you think that?'

Tanner shrugged as he glanced ruefully about. 'It just seems a little too pre-meditated a crime to have been carried out by a man who's as mentally unbalanced as our suspect would appear to be. You don't bash someone over the head, drag them all the way down to the far end of a graveyard, dump them into a grave you'd just happened to have already dug, to then set about stabbing them to death in a so-called "frenzied attack", not without having thought a little about it first. You certainly don't then start running around the countryside in the middle of the night, telling everyone that you *didn't* murder the person you must have spent some time planning on murdering, as if it was a complete surprise that you actually did.'

Vicky raised a sagacious eyebrow. 'Fair enough, I suppose, but it doesn't alter the fact that this isn't our investigation. Nor should it be, given its location.'

'Well, Forrester told us to come over to take a look, which is exactly what we're doing.'

'And having done so, I assume we can go?'

Tanner's attention returned to the church's tower, looming up above them. 'Sure, no problem. I'd just like to have a very quick chat with the vicar before we do.'

'For what purpose?'

'Just to say hello.'

Vicky replied with a disapproving scowl.

'Tell you what,' Tanner continued, 'why don't you stay here to see if you can find out anything else.'

'And how do you propose I do that?'

'Just see what you can overhear.'

'You want me to *spy* on them?' she questioned, her voice becoming a whispered tone of harsh disapproval.

'I wouldn't say *spy*, exactly. Just stand here for a while,' Tanner added, beginning to slink his way back up the hill, 'and let me know if there are any developments.'

- CHAPTER EIGHT -

LEAVING VICKY STARING after him like an abandoned puppy, Tanner ploughed his way back up the hill, endeavouring to look as nonchalant as possible whilst doing so. When he reached the path leading around the church, he glanced over his shoulder to see his detective inspector had started to inch her way backwards, towards the group of men still surrounding Haverstock, her head angled towards her phone. 'Good girl,' he said to himself, shoving his hands down into his pockets to start ambling his way around the high stone walls. Before rounding the furthest corner, he glanced quickly back to notice the medical examiner climbing out of the grave to beckon Haverstock's attention. Intrigued to see what she'd found, he continued to watch as she presented something to him, suspended at the bottom of a clear plastic bag.

'Are you alright?' came a loud, abrupt voice from directly behind him.

'Jesus Christ!' he exclaimed, leaping around to find himself staring into the kindly grey eyes of a vicar.

'Er...no,' the elderly man replied, gazing wistfully away, 'at least, I don't think I am.'

'I'm most dreadfully sorry,' Tanner began, horrified by the words that had come out of his mouth. 'I didn't mean to say what I just said.'

'Don't worry young man. It was entirely my fault. I should never have crept up on you like that. Can I help you at all? You look a little lost.'

'I was actually looking for you.'

'Oh, right!'

'My name's John Tanner,' he continued, pulling out his formal ID. 'I'm with Norfolk Police.'

'Detective *Chief* Inspector!' the vicar read, in an impressed tone, as he studied the proffered ID. 'How may I help?'

'I understand you're the person who found the body?'

'Unfortunately, I am. It's always such a shame when something like this happens. My first thought was that the poor chap must have fallen into the grave by accident, but the other police officer I spoke to said it looked more likely that he'd been left there by someone else.'

'May I ask how you found him?'

'*How* I found him?' the vicar repeated, returning to Tanner a perplexed expression.

'It's just that the grave is at the very bottom of the hill.'

'Oh, right. I see what you mean. I think it was the car I saw, when I arrived this morning.'

'The car?'

'The one left in the carpark. It's only supposed to be for church visitors, and it's rare for one of the local residents to use it for anything else. So I had a look around, just in case anyone was waiting to see me. That's when I saw the tracks leading down to the grave.'

'So, you naturally decided to walk all the way down to the very end of the graveyard to take a look?' Tanner enquired, struggling to keep the suspicion out of his voice.

'I must admit, I don't think it would have been something I'd have normally done. It was a conversation I'd had with the groundskeeper on Saturday that made me think something may have been amiss.'

'Which was...?'

'Oh, nothing really. We have a funeral on Wednesday. A burial, instead of a cremation, which is fine, of course. It just requires more work. I normally ask the groundskeeper to make the necessary preparations, either the morning of the service, or the day before, but he said he couldn't do either. So we agreed that he'd do it on Saturday afternoon, on the condition that he covered the grave with plywood, to make sure nothing could accidentally fall in.'

'Was anything likely to?'

'Well, no, but I've had an instance when a cat fell into one once. The poor thing was trapped there for several days before it was eventually found, so it's something that's always played on my mind.'

'I assume he forgot to cover it?'

'Not at all! I watched him do so. It was also covered yesterday, before the morning service. It was only afterwards, late in the afternoon, when I realised it wasn't.'

With his curiosity piqued, Tanner gazed back down the hill to see Vicky, stomping her way up towards them.

Waving briefly down to her, he returned his attention to the vicar. 'This groundskeeper you've been talking about. His name isn't Joseph Miller, by any chance?'

'It is, yes! Why, do you know him?'

'If it's the same Joseph Miller we have sitting inside Interview Room One, back at Wroxham Police

Station, then yes, I believe I do.'

The vicar stared at Tanner with an incredulous expression. 'You don't think it was him who...who...?'

'At this stage, we don't know. All we do know is that he walked into the station this morning, telling everyone that he *didn't* do it.'

'Well, there you are then. I must admit, I was struggling to believe that he could have done anything even remotely as horrific as this this.'

'I'm – er – not sure it's quite as straight forward as that. He was in quite a state at the time. As far as I know, he still is. He was also covered from head to foot in both mud and blood.'

The vicar looked miserably down at the path. 'Unfortunately, I think that could be my fault.'

'*Your* fault?'

'When I saw the plywood covering the grave was missing, I phoned him up to tell him. He said someone must have taken it, so I asked him to come down to re-cover it. He then went on to say that he didn't have time, at which point I'm afraid we had a bit of an argument.'

'May I ask what the result of the argument was?'

'He somewhat reluctantly agreed to come over in the very early hours of this morning to cover it again. That must have been when he discovered the body. But please don't think he had anything to do with it just because he's in a bit of a state. He's always had problems of the mind. I've known him all his life. I can assure you, he wouldn't hurt a fly.'

Hearing Vicky, puffing her way up the hill behind him, he turned to take her in with a concerned expression. 'Are you OK?'

'Just a little – out of breath,' she replied, coming to an unsteady halt beside them.

'This is my colleague, Detective Inspector Vicky

Gilbert,' said Tanner, 'someone who's clearly in need of a good personal trainer.'

'Nice to meet you, Vicky.'

'The vicar, here...' Tanner began, by way of introduction.

'Father Graham,' the elderly man smiled back in return.

'Father Graham has just been telling us a little more about our witness, back at the station. Apparently, he came here in the early hours of the morning to cover the grave with plywood, at which point he must have discovered the body.'

'About that,' said Vicky, still catching her breath, 'the medical examiner just found a wallet. Assuming it belongs to the victim, then it would appear to be a man by the name of William Greenfield.'

'I hope you don't mean old *Bill* Greenfield?' Father Graham interjected, with an expression of acute concern.

'I take it you knew him?' asked Tanner.

'Well, yes, of course. He's a teacher at our local school. He has been for years.'

'Was he here on Sunday?'

'I think so,' the vicar replied, looking thoughtfully away. 'Yes, for the evening service. I remember seeing him talking to someone afterwards.'

'I don't suppose you saw *who* he was talking to?'

The vicar suddenly glanced down at the path with a look of reticent guilt. 'I'm – er – I'm not sure.'

'Then perhaps you heard what they were talking about?'

'I didn't – but...'

'But...?' Tanner repeated.

'Look, I don't want to get anyone into any trouble, or anything.'

'If you know something, Father, then I'm afraid

you have both a moral and legal obligation to tell us.'

The vicar began wringing his hands as his eyes glanced fitfully about. 'I didn't hear what they were talking about, but the discussion did appear to be fairly acrimonious.'

'Are you sure you didn't recognise the person he was arguing with?'

'Well, yes, I did, but I can assure you, Chief Inspector, he can't possibly be the person you're looking for.'

'*Who* isn't the person we're looking for?'

'George Elliston.'

'I assume you've known him all your life as well?'

'Well, no. He's only been coming here for a few months, but he's just such a nice chap. I can't imagine him doing anything untoward to anyone. Certainly nothing like what happened to poor Mr Greenfield. He's also running in the forthcoming by-election, of course. If he had suddenly decided to murder someone, I can't think of a worse time for him to have chosen to do so.'

- CHAPTER NINE -

Hearing approaching footsteps, Tanner glanced around to see DI Haverstock, creeping to a gradual standstill behind him.

'You all look like you're having fun,' the detective inspector commented, beaming an exaggerated smile around at the three of them. 'Anything you'd like to share?'

'We were just having a chat with the vicar, here,' Tanner replied.

'Yes, of course. Hello, Father Graham. We did speak earlier, didn't we?'

'Indeed we did, Detective Inspector. I was just telling your colleague here about how I found the body.'

'*How* you found the body?'

'About seeing the car, and then noticing that the plywood was missing, yesterday afternoon.'

Haverstock exchanged a confused expression between Tanner and the vicar. 'I'm sorry, but I thought you said you found the body this morning?'

'That's right, I did.'

Tanner cleared his throat. 'Father Graham was just going over the details as to what led him to look inside the grave, being that it's all the way down at the bottom of the hill, at the furthest end of the graveyard.'

'Oh, I see.'

'He was saying that the groundskeeper excavated the hole on Saturday, after which it was covered over with sheets of plywood, for safety reasons, but when he saw it on Sunday, he noticed the plywood was missing.'

'That's when I asked the groundskeeper, Joe,' the vicar added, 'if he could pop by at some point to cover it again.'

'Right, yes, of course,' Haverstock responded. 'And all this is relevant, because...?'

'Only in that it helps to explain who our witness is, back at Wroxham Police Station, the one I mentioned to you earlier,' Tanner replied.

'The groundskeeper, presumably?'

'It would appear so.'

'And with that cleared up, I assume you'll be heading back?'

'Absolutely!'

'Great! Then may I wish you a safe journey home.'

Nodding goodbye to them, Haverstock skirted around to continue his way to the other side of the church, leaving Tanner, Vicky, and Father Graham staring a little awkwardly around at each other.

'I take it you're not working on the case together?' the vicar eventually asked, glancing surreptitiously over his shoulder to see the detective inspector disappear around the bell tower's furthest side.

'Not exactly,' Tanner replied, 'but we are working towards the same objective.'

'Well, I hope so,' the vicar replied, sending Tanner a questioning frown. 'Anyway, I must be getting on. If you could let me know what happens with Joe, I'd be very grateful.'

'Will do.'

'And if he needs a character witness, I'd be more than happy to oblige.'

Tanner waited for the vicar to shuffle away before turning to look at Vicky. 'Did you make a note of the man the vicar said he saw the murder victim arguing with?'

'You mean, the one you neglected to mention to Haverstock, the person who's leading the investigation?'

'Are you questioning my memory, or my apparent unwillingness to share information with my esteemed colleague.'

'Both, I think,' Vicky replied, digging out her notebook.

'Well, I've never been very good with names.'

'And your esteemed colleague?'

Tanner shrugged. 'If he was doing his job properly, he'd have discovered for himself that the victim was seen arguing with someone only a few hours before his body was found. I take it you *did* make a note of the person's name?'

'I'm afraid I didn't.'

'Oh, right.'

'But my memory is clearly far better than yours,' she added, scrawling something down.

'Are you going to tell me, or not?'

'George Elliston. I've actually met him before, you know.'

Tanner cast a curious eye over at her.

'He came knocking at my door a few days ago,' she continued. 'He was trying rather hard to get me to vote for him.'

'Dare I ask how he was doing that?'

'With his natural charm and devilish good looks. He had a leaflet as well, of course.'

'Sounds like he has your vote already!'

'We'll see,' she replied. 'He doesn't represent the party I normally vote for, but I might be willing to make an exception.'

'Because of his looks?'

'Not just his looks. He also had broad shoulders, a narrow waist, and a great sense of humour.'

'Sounds like quite a catch. Maybe we should pop over to see if we can have a little chat with him?'

'Well, I don't mind, obviously, but I'm fairly sure Haverstock will.'

'Then I suggest we don't tell him.'

'Shouldn't we at least let Forrester know?'

'Oh, I'm sure he won't mind.'

'But he might, though.'

'Then I suppose we'd better find out.'

'By phoning him up, to ask him?'

'No, by going around to see the suspect.'

Vicky shook her head from side to side. 'It's logic like that that put the Great into Britain. Have you ever thought about going into politics yourself?'

'Between a bouncing baby girl, and the slightly less bouncy body of some dead guy, I'm not sure I'd have the time. C'mon. You can dig out his address whilst I drive us over there.'

- CHAPTER TEN -

SURPRISED TO FIND George Elliston's address was all the way over in Acle, over twenty miles from the church he'd apparently been attending for the last few months, Tanner and Vicky arrived outside the door of a modest, semi-detached house, set within a quiet cul-de-sac, to ring the doorbell.

Waiting for someone to answer, Tanner looked again at the two cars they'd squeezed their way past in the driveway, a Porsche 911, and an enormous Bentley Continental, both dark grey, both spotlessly clean, and each with its own private numberplate.

'I reckon the cars are worth more than the house,' Tanner remarked, in a clandestine tone, as the muffled sound of footsteps could be heard from the other side of the door.

Standing back as the door was opened, Tanner found himself looking into the attractive green eyes of a stylish middle aged woman, dressed from head to foot in black. 'Mrs Elliston?

'Yes?' she replied, with a flustered, demanding look.

'DCI Tanner and my colleague, DI Gilbert. I don't suppose your husband is in?'

'Who is it?' came a man's voice, calling out from somewhere inside.

'It's the police!' she yelled back in response. 'Here to see you, apparently.'

'The police?' the voice repeated, in an incomprehensive tone.

Grabbing a set of keys from off a side table, the woman turned to look at Tanner. 'Forgive my husband. He's always been a little slow on the uptake.'

'What do they want?' came the voice again.

'I've no idea. You haven't gone and robbed a bank, again, I hope?'

Hearing the sound of footsteps, stomping over the floor above, she turned back to offer the two detectives a mischievous smile. 'He'll be down in a sec.'

Taking hold of the edge of the door, they watched her lever on a pair of stilettos and grab a black leather Gucci bag from off the same shelf, only to knock over a framed photograph of a pretty teenage girl, smiling awkwardly at the camera.

'Shit,' she muttered, picking it up to replace gently back on the shelf. 'Right, sorry, but I've got to go.'

They stood to one side to allow her out for her to stop on the driveway to check through her handbag. 'Oh, by the way,' she continued, glancing back at them, 'if he did rob a bank, can you let me know how much he took. I could really do with a new kitchen.'

Watching her smile at them before pulling open the car's door, Tanner turned back to find himself staring into the face of a handsome man with a thin, chiselled face, glaring out at them whilst endeavouring to do up his tie.

'May I help you?'

'George Elliston?'

'Yes, why?'

'Detectives Tanner and Gilbert, Norfolk Police. May we come in?'

Watching him glance fitfully down at a stylish

Omega watch, Tanner added, 'We'll only be a minute.'

'You can have ten, but then I really must be off. I'm giving a lunchtime talk at a local library.'

'Ten minutes will be fine,' Tanner smiled.

'And you'll have to take your shoes off, I'm afraid,' Elliston added, gesturing down at a steel rack, on top of which sat a half-dozen or so neatly positioned shoes. 'My wife is very strict about that sort of thing.'

Trying not to show his irritation, Tanner stepped inside to slip his off.

Once Vicky had done the same, they proceeded to shuffle their way inside.

'I do hope you know that my wife was joking,' they heard Elliston say, 'about me robbing a bank?'

Tanner turned to catch Vicky's eye. 'I think we assumed she was.'

'OK, good. She's always had rather an odd sense of humour.'

As they entered a modest, tired-looking kitchen, Elliston reached the furthest counter to pull open a cupboard. 'I would offer you a coffee,' he began, dragging out a mug, 'but I've barely got enough for myself.'

'We're fine, thank you,' Tanner replied, glancing inquisitively around to see a number of framed photographs dotted about, each one featuring the same teenage girl whose picture had been knocked over in the hall.

When Elliston eventually turned back, a steaming mug clasped in his hand, Tanner gestured over at them to enquire, 'Your daughter?'

The man stopped where he was to stare over at him, his eyes immediately filling with a caustic mix of desperation, sadness, and pure blinding rage.

'She is,' he eventually replied. 'She passed away.'

Tanner instantly regretted having opened his

mouth. 'I'm sorry to hear that.'

'Hit and run,' Elliston added, his body visibly wilting as his eyes drifted away.

'Again, I'm sorry,' Tanner replied, his mind picturing his own.

'Anyway,' the man continued, pulling himself up straight. 'How can I help?'

'We actually came to talk to you about something that happened yesterday.'

'Yesterday?' he repeated.

'At the church at Swanton Morley. I understand you were there?'

'In the evening, I was, but – why would you want to talk to me about that?'

'The vicar said he saw you having what he described as an acrimonious discussion with someone.'

'I suppose I did. What of it?'

'Are you able to confirm who that person was?'

'The person I was talking to?'

'Was it a man by the name of William Greenfield, by any chance?'

Elliston's eyes shifted between Tanner's and Vicky's.

'Is that a yes?'

'Look, what's all this about?'

Tanner drew in a breath. 'In the early hours of the morning, the body of a man who we believe to be Mr William Greenfield was found hidden at the bottom of an open grave.'

'You mean – he's – he's dead?'

'As it's possible that you were the last person to see him alive, and that you were seen having an argument with him not all that far from the place his body was found, we're naturally keen to find out what you know about the incident.'

'I didn't kill him, if that's what you're implying.'

'We're not implying anything, Mr Elliston. We're simply trying to establish what happened?'

'What do you mean, what happened?'

'Well, for a start, could you tell us what you were arguing about?'

'It was nothing.'

'It must have been something?'

'If you must know, he scraped my car in the carpark. I simply asked for his contact details to send to my insurance company when he went ballistic.'

Tanner raised a curious eyebrow. 'And why, may I ask, did he go "ballistic"?'

'You'd have to ask him!'

'Under the circumstances, that might be difficult.'

Elliston snapped his mouth closed to stare down at the floor. 'Sorry. That was unforgiveable. He basically denied going anywhere near my car, but as I saw him do it, with my own eyes, I knew he wasn't telling the truth.'

'That's what you were arguing about?'

'Pretty much.'

'And how was the discussion resolved?'

'I had no choice but to let it go. No one else saw the incident, so it would basically come down to his word against mine. Besides, the damage was minimal.'

'You didn't get into a fight over it?'

'Er...I'm not the fighting type,' he smiled. 'Sorry.'

'May I ask which car you were driving?'

'It was the Bentley. The one parked outside.'

'Yes, we saw it on the way in. Nice car, by the way.'

'Thank you!'

'I was saying to my colleague that I thought it was probably worth more than the house!'

Elliston laughed. 'I suppose that's the idea, that it looks expensive, but sadly, it isn't. Neither is the

Porsche. I bought them both at auction. They might not look it, but they've each done well over a hundred thousand miles.'

'Fake it till you make it,' smiled Tanner.

'Something like that. It's a similar story with my watch, I'm afraid,' he continued, casting an admiring eye down at it. 'My wife's Gucci handbag, as well. We managed to pick them both up for next to nothing on eBay. I can't say we used to be quite so pretentious, but since I decided to stand in the fast-approaching by-election, we both thought I'd stand a better chance if the entire population of Norfolk didn't think we were completely broke.'

Finishing his coffee, Elliston looked again at his watch. 'I'm sorry, but, if there's nothing else, then I do really need to be getting on.'

'Yes, of course,' Tanner replied, turning to leave. 'Actually, sorry, but there was just one more thing.'

As Tanner turned back, he saw Elliston force a smile at him.

'I was wondering why you go to a church that's all the way on the other side of Norwich?'

Elliston shrugged with indifference. 'That's where we got married. We used to live nearby. It's the only church I feel I have any sort of a connection with.'

'The vicar said you'd only been going there for a few months?'

'It's been a little longer than that. It was after what happened to our daughter that I started going again.'

'And your wife?'

Elliston shook his head. 'Just me, I'm afraid.'

Tanner watched the man place his empty mug in the sink before turning to look at Vicky. 'Right!' he eventually said. 'I think that's about it. Shall we go?'

Seeing her nod, he gave her a moment to put her notebook away before following her back down the hall. When she crouched down at the front door to lever her shoes back on, Tanner pulled out one of his business cards to hold out to the man following behind. 'Thank you again for your time, Mr Elliston. If anything else comes to mind, something you think may be relevant, please don't hesitate to give me a call.'

'Yes, of course.'

Remembering his own shoes, he turned to find Vicky staring at him with a peculiar expression. As her eyes darted down to the shoe rack, he followed her gaze to see a pair of muddy walking boots, neatly lined up next to some brand new ones. Looking back at her with a questioning shrug, she glared dementedly back at the boots again.

With it obvious she was trying to tell him something, he knelt down to put his own shoes on. It was only then that he could see what she'd been so determined to bring his attention to. On the toes and laces of each boot were what appeared to be drops of dried-up blood.

- CHAPTER ELEVEN -

STEPPING OUT OF the house, Tanner waited for Elliston to close the front door before whispering to Vicky, 'Was that what I think it was?'

'I don't know. What did *you* think it was?'

Glancing around to make sure the front door was definitely closed, he shifted his gaze over to the Bentley. 'Wait there a sec,' he eventually said, ambling his way over to start surreptitiously examining its bodywork.

'Can you see anything?'

Having navigated himself all the way around, he shook his head to pull out his phone.

'Who are you calling?' she asked, keeping her voice as low as possible.

Without replying, Tanner lifted the phone to his ear.

'Forrester, sir,' he eventually began, 'it's Tanner.'

'Ah, Tanner! I've just been chatting to DI Haverstock about you. I assume you're on your way back?'

'Sort of.'

'What do you mean, sort of?'

'We made a slight detour.'

Tanner heard Forrester exhale down the end of the line.

'We're currently standing outside the house of a

man by the name of George Elliston,' Tanner continued.

'Dare I ask who George Elliston is?'

'His name was given to us by the vicar over at Swanton Morley. He mentioned something about seeing him having an argument with the murder victim yesterday evening.'

'I'm assuming that you didn't bother to mention anything about this to Haverstock?'

'Sorry, sir, I must have forgotten.'

'And when you say you're standing outside this person's house, is that because you finished talking to him, or because you're about to?'

'We've just come out.'

'And...?'

'Well, apart from what I just told you,' Tanner began, leading Vicky away from the house, 'about him being seen arguing with the murder victim the evening before the body was found, he's also been driving all the way to Swanton Morley from his home in Acle, just to go to church.'

'Is that it?'

'Not quite. As we were leaving, Vicky noticed a pair of muddy walking boots in the hallway. The mud appeared to be a similar reddish colour to the mud at the murder scene, but what was most interesting were the drops of blood on the toes and laces.'

The line fell momentarily silent.

'Did you ask him about it?' came Forrester's eventual response.

'I wanted to speak to you first, sir.'

'That makes a change. What about the argument? I suppose he denied it?'

'Not at all. He said it was about an incident in the church carpark; that the victim scraped his car. But I've just had a look at the car in question. There doesn't appear to be a mark on it.'

Tanner gave Forrester a moment to respond.

'Did he see you examining the boots?'

'I don't *think* so, but I'm not sure we can take that risk.'

'No, I suppose we can't.'

'So, I was wondering what you wanted us to do?'

'I'm not sure we have any choice. If he did see what you were looking at, he'd be an idiot not to try to immediately destroy the evidence, long before we'd be able to obtain a search warrant.'

'We could ask politely if he'd like to come down to the station for an informal chat?'

'But that still wouldn't give us the right to take his boots in as evidence. Tell you what, why don't you go back inside to ask him about them, in particular about the blood. It may be that he has a perfectly valid reason for it being there.'

'And if he doesn't?'

'Then I suppose we won't have any choice. You'll just have to arrest him.'

- CHAPTER TWELVE -

ENDING THE CALL, Tanner turned to look at Vicky.

'What did he say?'

About to answer, he saw Elliston emerge from his house from out of the corner of his eye, a coat over one arm, and a shopping bag at the end of the other.

'Mr Elliston!' he called, lifting a hand to help garner his attention.

The moment Elliston saw them, marching their way back up the drive, he seemed to hesitate before closing the door.

'Sorry,' he eventually said, offering Tanner an affable smile. 'I thought you'd gone.'

Thinking that was a particularly odd sort of thing for him to say, as if he'd been waiting for them to leave before doing so himself, Tanner returned to him a smile of his own. 'If you don't mind, we just had a couple more questions.'

'I'm sorry again, but it really isn't a good time. As I think I mentioned, I'm giving a lunchtime talk at the local library, and I'm already late.'

'We won't be a minute,' Tanner replied, deliberately blocking his way to his car.

As Elliston moved to walk around, Vicky stepped up to stand beside Tanner, leaving him exchanging a frustrated glance between them. 'As I said, I really need to get going. Maybe you could come back later, when I have a little more time?'

'And as I said,' Tanner continued, still smiling, 'we only need a minute.'

'Then would you mind if we go back inside the house?' he requested, his eyes darting about at the surrounding semi-detached houses.

'Don't worry, your neighbours will probably think you're explaining why we should vote for you.'

Elliston's eyes returned to Tanner's. 'Then perhaps if you could speed things up a little?'

Tanner turned his attention to the man's Bentley Continental. 'I was just having a look around your car.'

'Right.'

'This *was* the one you took to church, yesterday evening?'

'Uh-huh.'

'The one you said Mr Greenfield drove into.'

'I don't think I said that he drove into it. I think the word I used was scraped.'

'It's just that I couldn't see a single mark on it.'

'It was the offside corner, near the grille,' Elliston commented.

'Do you mind showing me?' Tanner asked, standing to one side.

'There really isn't all that much to see.'

'If you could show us anyway?'

'Of course, sorry,' he capitulated, throwing his coat over the arm carrying the bag to nudge his way past.

Following after, Tanner watched him crouch down to run a hand over the bumper's smooth curved surface.

'You can see there's a slight indentation, here,' he eventually said, glancing up.

Tanner crouched down beside him to run his hand over the same area. Having done so, he climbed quietly to his feet, taking a moment to cast his eyes along the length of the car before returning to look at Elliston. 'When we were leaving your house earlier, my colleague noticed a pair of boots covered in mud that had been left in the hallway.'

Elliston's eyes flickered from Tanner's to Vicky's.

'We were wondering if they belonged to you?' Tanner continued.

'They're my old walking boots.'

'I don't suppose you wore them to church, yesterday?'

'Er, no,' he replied, glancing down. 'I wore the shoes I have on now.'

Tanner followed his gaze to see a pair of polished, black office shoes.

'Did you wear the same suit and tie?'

'Same suit, different tie, I think. I assume there's a reason *why* you're asking me all these questions?'

Tanner looked over Elliston's shoulder, towards the front door of his house. 'No reason in particular. It's just that we thought we saw what appeared to be blood on the walking boots under discussion.'

'Very possibly. I cut myself, a few days ago.'

'You cut yourself where?'

'On my wrist.'

'May I see?'

Once again, Elliston seemed to hesitate. 'Of course,' he eventually responded, placing the bag onto the drive with the coat draped on top of it.

Tanner waited for him to tug up the sleeve of his jacket to undo the button of his shirtsleeve's cuff.

'It's here,' he said, bending his elbow to show Tanner a long jagged scar, running underneath his forearm from his watch's brown leather strap.

'Looks nasty,' Tanner commented. 'When did that happen?'

'It was a few days ago. I caught it on a bramble, doing a spot of gardening. I didn't even notice until I came inside.'

Tanner stepped back to take in the coat, in particular the plastic shopping bag lurking underneath it. 'May I ask what's inside the bag?'

'Just some old clothes. Nothing of any importance.'

'May we look inside?'

Elliston fixed his eyes onto Tanner's as he re-buttoned his cuff. 'To be honest, Chief Inspector, I'm not entirely sure you have the legal right to.'

Tanner raised a spurious eyebrow at him.

'From what little I know,' Elliston continued, 'you'd only be allowed if you had reasonable grounds to believe that I was carrying either illegal drugs, a weapon of some description, stolen property, or something which could potentially be used to commit a crime.'

'Are you some sort of a lawyer, Mr Elliston?'

'So, may I go now?' he smiled.

'Only if you show me what's inside the bag.'

Holding Tanner's gaze, Elliston shoved his hands down into his pockets.

'Tell you what,' Tanner continued, 'either you voluntarily show me, or I'll be forced to arrest you, at which point I'll have every legal right to not only search your bag, but your pockets, car, house, and everything inside it.'

The man's face flecked with colour.

With Tanner continuing to stare at him with a look of ragged determination, Elliston eventually opened his mouth. 'It's not what you think,' he began, crouching down to lift first the coat, then the crumpled shopping bag. 'My wife told me to take them to the charity shop. I wasn't trying to hide evidence, or anything.'

Tanner only had to cast his eyes briefly inside the bag before opening his mouth. 'Mr George Elliston, I'm arresting you for the murder of William Greenfield. You do not have to say anything, but it may harm your defence if you do not mention something you later rely on in court. Anything you do say may be given in evidence.'

- CHAPTER THIRTEEN -

'THERE'S CLEARY BEEN some sort of misunderstanding,' Elliston muttered, as Tanner calmly took the man's bag and coat to hand over to Vicky. 'My new boots arrived yesterday. You can see them in the hall. That's why I was taking these down to the charity shop.'

'If you can turn around for me, please?' Tanner requested, taking the handcuffs Vicky was holding out for him.

'You're not going to handcuff me?'

'I do hope you're not going to be any trouble, Mr Elliston?'

'But – I haven't done anything wrong!'

'If that's the case, then you'll have nothing to worry about.'

'What about my talk at the library?'

'I think that may need to be re-scheduled.'

'Can I at least call a solicitor?'

'You'll have plenty of time to do that when we get you down to the station. Now, if you don't allow me to handcuff you, I'll be forced to charge you with obstruction, as well.'

Elliston stood staring incredulously at Tanner for a moment longer. 'Alright, alright!' he eventually said, pivoting himself reluctantly around, 'but can I at least ask one thing?'

'You can ask,' Tanner replied, beginning to secure

the handcuffs around the man's lightly tanned wrists.

'Can you at least keep my name out of the papers? If word gets out that I've been arrested, I haven't got a chance in hell of winning the election.'

'If I were you, Mr Elliston, I'd be slightly more concerned about being convicted of murder, than whether or not you're elected to become Norfolk's next MP.'

'This is ridiculous!' he stated, as Tanner began frogmarching him down the driveway. 'How can you possibly think that I could have murdered someone?'

'I don't know,' Tanner pondered, 'but I think it might have had something to do with those walking boots of yours.'

'But – I've already told you about the blood. I cut myself when I was gardening!'

'Yes, I remember. You also told me it happened a few days ago. Unfortunately, I'm no expert, but I'd say that cut is at least two weeks old, whilst the blood on your boots looks relatively fresh. Then there's your story about having an argument with the murder victim the evening before his body was found, because he scraped your car in the church carpark.'

'He did!'

'I'd be more willing to believe you if there was a single mark on it, which there isn't, no matter what you say. Then there's this idea that you suddenly decided to start going to church after what happened to your daughter.'

'You couldn't possibly know how difficult it's been for us.' Elliston continued, his voice quivering with emotion.

'Unfortunately I can, being that something similar, if not worse happened to my own.'

Reaching his car, Tanner brought Elliston stumbling to a halt. 'I can subsequently understand why someone would turn to God to help steer them through it,' he continued, turning the man around to stare into his panic-stricken eyes. 'What I don't understand is why you'd pick a church on the other side of Norwich.'

'I already told you! It was the church I got married in!'

'Maybe,' shrugged Tanner, opening the passenger door to lever the back of the cream leather seat forward, 'but as I mentioned before, the main reason I decided to arrest you goes back to your walking boots, the ones we caught you trying to sneak out of your house. Even if the blood on them *is* yours, which I doubt, the colour of the mud covering them is *extraordinarily* similar to that found in the graveyard at the back of Swanton Morley church. On top of that, I can't seriously imagine anyone taking a muddy old pair of walking boots down to a charity shop whilst on their way to giving a talk at a local library, one that they're already late for, at least not before making some sort of an effort to give them a bit of a clean first.'

- CHAPTER FOURTEEN -

WITH VICKY SITTING beside him, and Elliston jammed into the XJS's cramped back seat, Tanner let him know to keep his head down as he drove sedately past a steadily growing number of over-sized news vans, still piling up outside Wroxham Police Station.

Turning in, he parked around the back to climb casually out. There he remained for a moment, his hand resting on top of the open door, whilst making sure there were no reporters, camera men, or members of the general public milling about.

Once happy that the coast was clear, he leaned in to tip the back of his seat forward against the Jag's black leather steering wheel. 'Right, out you get!'

'Are you sure nobody's around?' Elliston queried, casting a furtive eye through the car's narrow back window, between its two curving rear buttresses.

'There's nobody here *now*,' Tanner replied, 'but that could change at any moment.'

Helping him out, he escorted him through the station's rear access door as Vicky followed behind, to leave them waiting in the dimly lit hallway whilst he headed through to reception.

With the room virtually empty, he stepped quickly over to the duty sergeant to find him slumped behind the plastic security screen, staring at a newspaper. 'Afternoon, Taylor!' he said, taking sadistic pleasure in watching him jump with a start.

'Oh, er, afternoon, boss. I was just, um...'

'Working hard?'

'I was actually doing the crossword,' he replied, presenting Tanner with a sheepish grin.

'So I can see.'

'It was very quiet, so I thought it would be alright.'

'As long as it's not the one in the Norfolk Herald, I'll let you off.'

Seeing him glance guiltily down at the paper, Tanner angled his head to see that it *was* the one in the back of the Norfolk Herald. 'C'mon, Taylor! You can do better than that.'

'I've only just started doing them, boss, and I'm not very good.'

'No, me neither. Anyway, I've got some *actual* work for you to do!'

'Oh, right!' he replied, sitting up.

'Vicky's with a suspect in the hall leading out to the back. I was hoping you'd be able to process him to then have him escorted into one of the interview rooms, without anyone from either the press or general public seeing him?'

'Is it someone famous?' Taylor asked, climbing eagerly to his feet.

'He's one of the candidates in the forthcoming by-election. For both his sake and ours, I'd prefer his name to stay out of the papers. We've got quite enough press attention as it is.'

'Yes, boss. No problem!'

As Taylor made his way out from behind the security screen, Tanner glanced discreetly around. 'Is Forrester still here?'

'He's just coming in now.'

Tanner followed his gaze to see the man in question, closing the door of his black 7 Series BMW to begin marching towards the main entrance.

'Do you know where he's been?'

'Flat hunting, I think. His wife kicked him out, apparently.'

'Yes, I know,' Tanner replied, watching Taylor head out the back before pivoting around to see Forrester, heaving open the station's heavy glass entrance door.

'Afternoon, sir!'

'Ah, Tanner! How'd you get on?'

'We followed your instructions, sir.'

'And?'

'When we went back in to ask the suspect about the walking boots, we caught him creeping out of his house with this bag held in his hands, and guess what was inside?' Tanner asked, holding the bag open for him to see.

Forrester leaned forward to peer curiously down. 'What did he have to say about the blood?'

'That he cut his wrist a few days before, whilst doing a spot of gardening. But the wound was at least two weeks old. I don't know about you, but I'd say that blood looks relatively fresh to me.'

'I assume you brought him in?' Forrester asked, glancing about.

'He's with Vicky, out the back. I've just sent Taylor off to have him formally processed.'

'OK, good. I'll let Haverstock know. He'll probably want him transported over to their offices for questioning.'

'I was actually hoping to be able to interview him here, sir.'

Forrester narrowed his eyes at his DCI. 'I'm not making you the SIO for this investigation, Tanner.'

'Nor would I want to be, sir, but as we already have two suspects here, it would seem to make more sense for Haverstock to come to us, than for us to send the suspects to him, especially with the clock ticking on both.'

Forrester glanced pensively down at his watch. 'OK, I'll have a word with Haverstock,' he eventually responded, 'to see if he's amenable to the idea.'

'He won't be.'

'Probably not, but I think you're right. It does make more sense for him to come here than the other way round. However, with the body being where it is, it's only fair that he continues to lead.'

'Fine by me.'

'Which means you'll have to interview the suspect together.'

Tanner opened his mouth to protest, before asking instead, 'Whilst we're waiting for him, perhaps he could send over what they've already found?'

'Will do,' Forrester replied, digging out his phone.

'And maybe ask him if they have any recent updates?'

Forrester nodded. 'But I want you to wait for him to arrive before starting the interview.'

'Of course!' Tanner smiled. 'No problem at all!'

- CHAPTER FIFTEEN -

SLINKING AWAY TO leave Forrester to his call, Tanner was about to go through to the main office when he saw Vicky, entering reception from the back of the building.

'All good?' he asked, as she made her way towards him.

'Taylor's with Elliston now,' she replied. 'He said he'd let us know when he was done.'

'I don't suppose the suspect has decided against calling a solicitor?'

'Unfortunately not. He's on the phone to one now.'

'OK, but whoever he's calling had better hurry up,' Tanner replied, glancing down at his watch. 'I'm not letting this one go just because we run out of time.'

Vicky's eyes shifted down to the bag he was still holding. 'Do you want me to have those sent off to forensics?'

'Yes, please,' he replied, handing it over. 'We need to know if the blood matches the victim's, and the mud the crime scene.'

'Yes, I know.'

'Sorry, of course.'

'Do we have the victim's DNA?'

'Forrester's asking for everything to be sent over to us.'

'Does that mean we're taking the lead?'

'He wants them to stay on it, for now at least.'

'What about the suspects?'

'I've managed to convince Forrester that it would make more sense for Haverstock to drive over here to interview them, than for them to be driven over to him.'

'Haverstock will be thrilled.'

Tanner smiled. 'I've been told to wait until he gets here before speaking to Elliston.'

'You need to wait for his solicitor, anyway.'

'I suppose.'

'What are we going to do about the other suspect?'

'Oh, I think we can let him go.'

With her head baulking back in surprise, Vicky sent Tanner a dubious frown. 'Are you sure about that? I mean, we've barely found out his name. We don't even know how he was able to get here from Swanton Morley, or why he even wanted to.'

'Does it matter?' Tanner asked, with curt indifference.

'It will if he turns out to be the person we're looking for.'

'But he's not, though,' Tanner replied, his attention drifting away.

'You're one-hundred percent sure about that?'

'I'm as sure as I need to be.'

Seeing Vicky staring at him with a disapproving frown, he turned his head to face her. 'What?'

'Sorry, I was about to say, "you're the boss", when I remembered you weren't, at least, not in this particular instance.'

'If Haverstock wants to have Joe Miller back inside an interview room, then he can simply have him arrested. Don't forget, he was a walk-in. We won't lose anything by letting him go, unlike Elliston.'

'But what if he is the murderer, and immediately goes off to kill someone else? I mean, the guy's clearly got some mental issues.'

'We can't hold someone in custody just because they need psychiatric help.'

'We can if we suspect them of murder.'

'But we don't, though.'

'You mean – *you* don't,' she corrected.

Tanner folded his arms to glare over at her. 'I take it you do?'

'I didn't say that. I was simply suggesting that it may be sensible to keep him here for a little longer, at least until we're sure that Elliston is definitely our man.'

'I'm already sure Elliston is our man.'

'Why, because we caught him in possession of a pair of walking boots?'

'If it makes you feel any better, if Miller does head off only to start murdering half the population of Norfolk, I'll take full responsibility.'

'Can we at least take a sample of his prints and DNA before he does walk out the door?'

'OK, fine. But I want Elliston's sent off to forensics immediately. If they match anything found on the knife Miller was carrying, I want to know about it ASAP.'

Tanner waited for Vicky to pull out her notebook before continuing. 'Then we need to start finding out all we can about him, in particular about his relationship to the victim. When we find the connection, we'll find the motive, other than that he supposedly reversed into his car, of course.'

'Is it worth checking to see if there's a corresponding mark on the victim's car, possibly with traces of paint from Elliston's Bentley?'

'I suppose that would make sense, but I couldn't see a single mark on it, despite what he was saying. Oh, and another thing.'

'Uh-huh,' Vicky replied, glancing up from her notes.

'I want us to find out a little more about Elliston's daughter, specifically about the accident. If the man behind the wheel of the car that ran her over was the same person who's been found murdered at Swanton Morley, then I think we'll be able to have this wrapped up in record time, maybe even before Haverstock arrives!'

'You do know that it's not a competition, don't you?'

'I'm aware of that, thank you,' Tanner remarked, glancing over to see Forrester was still on the phone. 'Do you think Taylor's done yet?'

'I've no idea.'

'When he is, can you ask him to escort Elliston into one of the interview rooms? Then I'll meet you there.'

'To do what?'

'To start the interview, obviously!'

'But – I thought Forrester told you to wait for Haverstock?'

'He can join us when he arrives.'

'What about Elliston's solicitor?'

'Tell you what. I'll grab us some coffee whilst you update the team. If neither have shown up by then, I suggest we make a start.'

'Unless Elliston objects to not having his solicitor present, of course.'

'Let's see, shall we? Worst case scenario is that we'll have to spend a few minutes chatting about nothing more intriguing than the weather.'

- CHAPTER SIXTEEN -

'GOOD AFTERNOON, MR Elliston,' said Tanner, opening the door to the recently vacated Interview Room One to let Vicky inside. 'How's everyone been treating you?'

'Fine, I suppose,' the suspect mumbled, slouched in a chair on the other side of a table.

'I brought you a coffee. White, one sugar?'

'Has my solicitor arrived?' Elliston enquired, watching Tanner set a steaming mug down on the table in front of him.

'Not yet, but whilst we were waiting, I thought it would be nice if we could get to know each other a little more.'

'Good luck with that!'

'I thought that maybe we could start by having a little chat about those walking boots of yours?' Tanner continued, pulling out a chair for first Vicky, then himself.

A knock at the door had them turning to see Taylor's face appear from around the other side.

'Sorry to bother you, boss, but there's a solicitor here by the name of Ms. Heatherington to see Mr Elliston.'

As Tanner grimaced a smile back at him, he opened the door fully to allow a particular large middle aged woman to squeeze herself inside.

'They were trying to start without you,'

commented Elliston, staring over at Tanner with an accusatory glare.

'Oh, I'm sure they wouldn't have done anything quite so stupid,' the solicitor replied.

'May we get you a coffee?' asked Tanner, offering the woman a sheepish grin.

'I don't drink coffee,' she stated, wafting her way around the back of her client's chair to take the seat next to him.

'Peppermint tea?' Tanner continued, 'or maybe a vodka tonic with a twist of garlic?'

'Shall we just get on with it?' she replied, opening a briefcase to retrieve a large leatherbound notepad and pen.

'Hello Stephanie,' said Elliston, quietly offering the solicitor a friendly smile.

'George,' she replied, with a perfunctory nod.

'You two know each other, do you?'

'Ms Heatherington is our family solicitor.'

'Excellent!'

'Have they formally commenced the interview?' she asked her client.

'Nope! They just waltzed in with three cups of coffee to immediately start asking me questions.'

'Nothing you answered, I hope?'

'Fortunately, you arrived before I felt the need to.'

Heatherington took a moment to take Tanner in. 'You do know that you need to formally caution my client on tape,' she began, looking down to start taking notes, 'beginning with what he's been arrested for, *before* you can start to interview him?'

'As your client said, we came in to bring him some coffee.'

'He's lying,' Elliston muttered. 'They were asking about my boots, the ones they took from me, the moment I was arrested for doing absolutely nothing.'

'Then perhaps, Mr...?' the solicitor continued, her pen poised over her notebook.

'Detective Chief Inspector Tanner,' Tanner replied, offering her a fractured smile.

'Then perhaps, Mr Tanner, you could start that process now?'

'I'd be delighted to.'

Starting the recording device fixed to the wall, Tanner ran through the official procedures before turning to look at Elliston. 'Now, back to those walking boots.'

'Before my client *does* begin to answer your questions,' the solicitor interrupted, 'may I first ask *why* he was arrested?'

'For the murder of Mr William Greenfield. I thought I'd made that clear when I was ploughing my way through the legal formalities.'

'Yes, but you didn't go into detail.'

'Detail?'

'The reason for his arrest. I assume you do understand that you have to have reasonable grounds in order to do so?'

'I think the reasons will become obvious during the course of the interview.'

'Unfortunately, I'm not prepared to let you continue until you've been able to first demonstrate what those reasonable grounds were.'

Tanner drew in a frustrated breath. 'Your client was seen arguing with the victim – by a vicar no less – only a few hours before we believe he was killed.'

'Uh-huh,' she muttered, taking notes.

'His reasons for having that argument – that the victim just happened to scrape his car in the church carpark – seemed somewhat unlikely, being that the car in question doesn't have a single mark on it. Then there were the boots, of course.'

The solicitor glanced up from her notebook to offer Tanner a belittling smile. 'Please, do carry on.'

'We found blood on them.'

'The victim's blood?'

'We've yet to established that.'

'Do you have a murder weapon?'

'We believe we do.'

'And have either my client's fingerprints or DNA been found on that?'

'Again, we've yet to...'

'How about the murder scene itself? Has it been established that my client was there?'

'Well, no, but...'

'So I ask you again, Mr Tanner. On what grounds was my client arrested?'

Tanner could feel himself beginning to lose his temper. 'Because, we caught him in the act of trying to destroy evidence.'

'Sorry, but which evidence was that again?'

'The walking boots!'

'Yes, of course. And how, may I ask, was my client endeavouring to destroy them? Was he attempting to set them on fire, or maybe he was about to throw them into a nearby river?'

Tanner shifted awkwardly in his seat. He knew where this was going, and he didn't like it. 'He was carrying them out of his house, hidden inside a plastic bag.'

'To do what with them?'

'We don't know.'

'You don't know?' she repeated.

'Well, he *said* he was taking them to a charity shop.'

'And how do you know he wasn't?'

'Because it was obvious.'

'In what way?'

'They were still covered in mud.'

'I see. And do you think he would have been the first person to take a pair of shoes to a charity shop, without having taken the time to clean them first?'

'He'd told us he was already late for a talk he was giving, which made it even less likely.'

'Was there any particular reason why he wouldn't have been able to drop them in on the way back?'

Tanner ground his teeth as he glowered silently at the solicitor.

'So, the only evidence you *really* have is that a vicar said that he *may* have seen my client talking to the victim, a few hours before he was thought to have been killed.'

'The vicar didn't say it *may* have been him, he said it was definitely him. And they weren't having a pleasant chat, but a full blown argument.'

'That's all very interesting, Mr Tanner, but if that's the only evidence you had when you decided to arrest Mr Elliston, then I'm afraid you didn't have the grounds to do so. Bearing that in mind, and that my client is in the middle of an election campaign, I'd very much appreciate it if you could let him go.'

Leaning back in his chair, Tanner folded his arms over his chest to study the woman's round, miserable-looking face.

'Well?' she demanded.

'I suggest we take a break,' he eventually said, pushing himself up from his chair.

'Presumably to make the necessary preparations to have my client released?'

'Whether or not you agree that we had reasonable grounds to arrest your client is, frankly, neither here nor there. It's merely your opinion, as it is ours that we did. Of course, you're more than welcome to challenge that decision, but to do so will involve taking your complaint to court. Meanwhile, we have every legal right to hold your client for a period of up to thirty-six hours, whilst we continue the process of collecting evidence. So, bearing that in mind,' he continued, offering both the solicitor and her client a generous smile, 'I suggest you make yourselves comfortable.'

- CHAPTER SEVENTEEN -

PAUSING THE INTERVIEW, Tanner led Vicky out to mutter, 'Bloody solicitor. Who the hell does she think she is?'

'Er...I think you've just answered your own question,' Vicky replied, following him down the corridor.

Reaching the end, Tanner stopped to draw in a calming breath. 'I suppose,' he eventually sighed, 'but from my own personal dealings with them, most aren't normally quite so...'

'Intelligent?'

'I was going to say antagonistic.'

'Really? I thought that was their job?'

Tanner stood simmering by the door for a moment with his hand resting on the handle. 'The problem is,' he eventually continued, 'she's right. The only reason we dragged him in so soon was to prevent him from destroying evidence. Speaking of which... I don't suppose we've heard back from forensics?'

'You mean...about the boots?'

'Too soon?'

'Well, we did only send them off about half an hour ago. They probably haven't even arrived yet.'

'Then I suppose we'll just have to be patient.'

'Don't you mean *you'll* have to be patient.'

'Patience has never been one of my virtues.'

'You don't say,' she replied, under her breath.

Feeling a little more upbeat, Tanner pulled open the door leading through to reception to see Forrester, staring up at one of the many posters with his hands shoved down into his pockets.

Leaving Vicky to make her way back to the main office, he thought he'd wander over to see him, just to make sure he was OK.

'Ah, Tanner!' Forrester said, seeing him approach. 'Do you mind helping me with a bit of market research?'

'Market research, sir?' Tanner repeated, returning to him a confused frown.

'I was just wondering what you thought about this poster?'

Tanner took a moment to gaze up at the poster in question. 'It's...er...very nice, sir,' he replied, unsure what else he was supposed to say.

'The wording is fine, I suppose, and the design is alright. The question is, do you think they actually work?'

'This one in particular, or posters in general?'

'Ah, yes. Good question!'

It was? thought Tanner.

'What with government cutbacks, and everything,' Forrester continued, 'there's a lot of debate going on at the moment as to whether they're worth the money. You'd be surprised how much they all cost. Take this one for example. Does a poster telling people that crime doesn't pay really help to deter someone from committing one?'

'I suppose that depends on how much they're earning at their current job,' Tanner replied, suppressing a smirk.

'Yes, I suppose it would,' Forrester responded, folding his arms to rest a ruminating finger against his unusually stubbly chin.

'Er...I don't suppose there's been any sign of Haverstock?' Tanner asked, keen to move the subject onto something a little more pertinent.

'Haverstock?' Forrester asked, as if he'd never heard the name before. 'Sorry, yes, of course. He said he'd come over tomorrow.'

'*Tomorrow?*' Tanner repeated.

'Yes, I know. I did try to persuade him to come today, but he said he couldn't spare the time.'

'Are you seriously telling me that he doesn't consider interviewing the prime suspect of a murder investigation to be a priority?'

'I don't think it was that, necessarily. More that he doesn't consider Mr Elliston to be the prime suspect.'

'Does he have someone else in mind?'

'Not that he mentioned. Anyway, as he remains the SIO, I have to respect his decision.'

'Fair enough, I suppose,' Tanner replied, shaking his head.

'So anyway, with that in mind, you may as well start the interview.'

'Actually, sir, I already have,' Tanner announced, flinching in preparation for being on the receiving end of a tirade of abuse.

'OK, good,' Forrester said, his attention drifting back to the poster. 'So, how's it going?'

Staring at the side of Forrester's face, Tanner raised a bemused eyebrow. 'Not great, to be honest. His solicitor doesn't think we had sufficient grounds to arrest him.'

'No, well, we probably didn't. But as I remember, we didn't have much of a choice.'

By this stage, Tanner was beginning to seriously worry about his superintendent. He'd never known him to be quite so agreeable, nor lacking so much focus. 'Are you sure you're alright, sir?' he eventually asked, with genuine concern.

'Huh?'

'I was just asking if you were OK?'

'Yes, of course! Never better! So anyway, what's the next step?'

Tanner shrugged in response. 'I'm not sure there's all that much we can do. We just need to wait for more evidence.'

'There's nothing back from forensics?'

'Not yet, no.'

'Oh well. I suppose we'll just have to be patient,' he said, offering Tanner an encouraging smile.

'Patient, sir?'

'Yes, you know. When you're forced to wait for something that you really want, like a Christmas present, for example.'

'I'm – er – aware of what the word means, sir, I'm just not sure I've ever heard you use it before.'

'I suppose there's a first time for everything. Anyway, I'd better let you get back to work.'

'Yes, sir. Thank you, sir.'

As Tanner turned to leave, he heard Forrester call after him, 'Before you go, I forgot to mention something Haverstock told me.'

'Apart from that he couldn't be bothered to come down to interview the prime suspect?' Tanner muttered to himself, as he came grinding to a halt.

'That one of the Swanton Morley residents said they saw a car leaving the church carpark,' Forrester continued, 'at around eleven o'clock on Sunday night.'

'I don't suppose they saw what sort of car it was, by any chance?' asked Tanner, turning slowly around.

'Apparently, it was a Bentley Continental. I don't know if that's of any use to you?'

- CHAPTER EIGHTEEN -

HAVING POURED HIMSELF a much needed coffee inside the peaceful serenity of his own private office, Tanner was about to check through his emails when Vicky's head appeared around the door he'd forgotten to close.

'How's Forrester?'

'Not himself,' he replied. 'When I told him that we'd already started interviewing Elliston, after he'd told me to wait for Haverstock, he actually used the word "good"!'

'Good?' Vicky repeated.

'He also seemed to be more interested in the effectiveness of one of the posters on the wall than the current murder investigation,' Tanner continued, opening his email account to see over a dozen had come through since he'd last looked.

'Which one was that?'

'Crime Doesn't Pay,' he muttered, trying to determine which email he should open first.

'I suppose its messaging could be considered to be a little ambiguous.'

'And when I tried to bring his mind back to the matter at hand, to tell him that we were in desperate need of evidence, he told me to be patient.'

'And what's wrong with that?'

'Nothing. It just wasn't something I'd have expected him to say.'

'Sounds like he's been traumatised by his wife kicking him out.'

'No doubt. Anyway, something good did come of it. Two things, in fact.'

'Which were?'

'Haverstock's not coming down until tomorrow.'

Vicky raised a surprised eyebrow.

'Apparently, he said he had better things to do,' Tanner added, seeing her reaction.

'Do they have another suspect?'

'Not one he told Forrester about.'

'So…he just can't be arsed to drive over?'

'I think it's more to do with him being unable, or perhaps unwilling to believe that we've hopefully managed to find the person responsible. Which leads me on to the other thing Haverstock mentioned. One of Swanton Morley's residents said they saw a car leaving the church carpark at around the same time it's thought that the victim was murdered, and not just any car, either.'

'Not a Bentley Continental?'

'The very same!'

'OK. That puts him at the scene.'

'Well, it puts his car at the scene,' Tanner corrected, 'but it's at least a sign that we're on the right track.'

'I actually came in to see if you're ready to go back in?'

'I was going to check through my emails,' he replied, before shaking his head to close the screen's window.

'You can if you want?'

'It's fine. I'll look at them later,' he replied, standing up to take hold of his coffee. 'If I start now, I'll be here all day.'

About to follow Vicky out, Townsend's head

appeared around the still open door.

'Is now a good time, boss?' he asked, offering Tanner a questioning gaze.

'I suppose that depends on what it's about?' he replied, in a dubious tone.

'It's about the investigation.'

'Then fire away!'

'Vicky asked me to look into the death of Elliston's daughter, to see if the hit and run driver had been identified.'

'And were they?'

'That's the thing,' Townsend replied, glancing down at a document he was holding. 'She didn't die in a hit and run accident. At least, that's not what's written on her death certificate.'

'I don't think a death certificate necessarily says *how* a person dies.'

'This one does,' Townsend stated.

With his curiosity piqued, Tanner took the document to glance quickly through it.

'It says suicide,' added Townsend, directing Tanner's attention down to the relevant part.

Tanner had to read the word twice before passing it over to Vicky.

'But – why would he lie about something like that?' she asked, staring down.

'I've no idea, but I suggest we head back to see if we can find out.'

- CHAPTER NINETEEN -

'SORRY TO HAVE kept you,' said Tanner, leading Vicky back into the interview room to find the solicitor, deep in conversation with her client.

'I assume you've come to your senses?' she queried, glancing up.

'Er...sorry, but in what way?'

'That you've decided to let my client go?'

'Oh, I see. Er...no. Right! Shall we crack on?' he grinned, pulling out a chair for first Vicky, then himself.

'If we must,' she replied, picking up her pen.

Placing a file on the table in front of him, Tanner formally recommenced the interview. 'I'd like to start, if I may,' he eventually began, leaning forward to meet Elliston's wavering gaze, 'with the argument you were seen having with the murder victim, Mr Greenfield.'

'Has it been established that it was an argument?' the solicitor questioned.

'That was what the witness told us,' Tanner replied. 'It was also something confirmed by your client, when we first spoke to him.'

'I never said it was an argument,' Elliston interjected.

Tanner let out a capitulating sigh. 'Can we settle on it being a disagreement?'

'It was a polite discussion, about what happened in the carpark. Nothing more.'

'That's not what you said outside your house.'

'Maybe so, but I've since had time to think back to the discussion in question.'

'In other words, your solicitor has advised you to try and play down the fact that it was an argument.'

'You're lucky my client is even answering your questions!' the solicitor snapped.

Tanner shook his head. 'Anyway, going back to the discussion you were having with the man who was murdered a few hours later. You said it was because he'd scratched your car, in the church carpark.'

'At the time I thought he had,' Elliston replied, 'but I've since realised that I may have been mistaken.'

'You seemed very certain of it before. You even went to the effort of showing me where it had been scratched.'

'As I said, I must have been mistaken. Where I was standing at the time, it did look like he had.'

'So you're now saying that Mr Greenfield *didn't* scratch your car, and that you *didn't* then proceed to have an argument with him about it?'

'That's correct.'

Tanner sat back in his chair to fold his arms over his chest. 'Is there anything else you'd be willing to admit that you've been lying about?'

'I object to the accusation that my client has been lying, Mr Tanner,' the solicitor snapped, glaring up from her notes. 'He'd simply misremembered the events that had occurred.'

'Yes, of course,' Tanner replied, returning to her a thin smile. 'That must have been it. Anyway, going back to my previous question.'

'Sorry, which question was that?' Elliston queried.

'Is there anything else you've lied – sorry –

misremembered, since our conversation this morning?'

'I don't think so.'

'Nothing about your daughter?'

Elliston eyes hovered between Tanner's.

'May I ask what my client's daughter has got to do with this?'

'At this precise moment in time, we're not sure, but we would be very keen to know why your client told us that she'd been killed by a hit and run driver, instead of what really happened?'

The solicitor turned to look at her client as if she, too, was curious.

'Does it matter?' Elliston questioned, his hands fidgeting on the table in front of him.

'In my experience, it's just unusual for a parent to lie about how their child passed away. I can understand if you would choose not to say, especially given the nature of what did happen, but to just make something up like that does seem a little odd.'

The solicitor shifted her gaze from her client back to Tanner. 'If I'm going to allow this line of questioning to continue, then I think you're going to need to establish its relevance.'

'The relevance is that it proves your client lied to us about his daughter's death, which raises two rather important questions. Firstly, why he felt the need to, and perhaps more importantly, what else he's been lying about, apart from the incident with his car, and the discussion he had with the person who apparently *didn't* drive into it, of course?'

Elliston continued glaring over at Tanner as tears began creeping into the corners of his eyes. 'My wife and I tell people that she was hit by a car because it's easier to say that than what really happened; that she took her own life.'

'Then why not simply say that you'd rather not talk about it?'

'Because then people are left wondering what really happened, which automatically leads to rumours and conjecture, something I really don't need when I'm running in the local by-election.'

'So, you tell people she was hit by a car because you think it will help you to become Norfolk's next MP?'

Elliston glowered silently at Tanner as his face darkened with brooding rage.

'Is it alright if we move the subject along?' the solicitor requested.

'Yes, of course,' Tanner replied, opening the file in front of him. 'Going back to the argument – sorry – the discussion you were seen having with Mr Greenfield. Are you able to tell me what time that was?'

'It was about seven o'clock.'

'And what did you do after that?'

'I didn't kill him, if that's what you mean!'

'Apart from not killing him, what did you do?'

Elliston shrugged with apathetic indifference. 'I went home, like everyone else.'

'Which was when, exactly?'

'About ten minutes after the time I previously stated.'

'Are you sure about that?'

'Quite sure, thank you!'

Tanner took a moment to open the file. 'You mentioned before that you took your Bentley Continental.'

'That's right.'

'Are there any other church members who own such a prestigious car?'

'I doubt it!'

'How about one of the local residents?'

Before Elliston had a chance to answer, his solicitor placed a restraining hand on his forearm. 'Excuse me, Mr Tanner, but once again I find myself having to ask the relevance of this line of questioning?'

'I'm simply trying to establish if your client is aware of anyone who either goes to the church at Swanton Morley, or who lives nearby, who owns a car similar to his?'

'Yes, but for what purpose?'

'Is he aware, or isn't he?' Tanner repeated.

The solicitor studied Tanner's face for a moment before cupping her hand to whisper something in her client's ear.

'It's a very straight-forward question,' Tanner sighed.

As she leant back in her chair to reacquire Tanner's gaze, Elliston clasped his hands together on top of the table. 'I've no idea!' came his eventual reply.

'But you'd have to agree that the chances of there being two Bentley Continentals located within such a small geographical area would be rather unlikely?'

'Can you please get to the point!' his solicitor demanded.

'One of the local residents saw your client's car – or at least one that's remarkably similar to it – leaving the church carpark at around eleven o'clock that night, some four hours after he said he'd left, which is curious in itself, but what is even more curious is that it's exactly the same time the victim, Mr Greenfield, is thought to have been killed.'

- CHAPTER TWENTY -

'I'M SORRY, BUT – there must be some mistake!' Elliston exclaimed, his face draining of colour.

'I don't *think* so,' Tanner replied, re-reading the information in front of him.

'May I ask who this so-called witness was?' questioned the solicitor, leaning forward to pick up her pen.

'Unfortunately, I'm not at liberty to say.'

'It's just that the thought does occur to me that whoever it is might not be telling the truth.'

'Yes, that's it!' Elliston suddenly exclaimed. 'Someone's trying to make out I was there when I wasn't!'

Tanner returned to them both a look of confused perplexion. 'For what possible reason?'

'Isn't it obvious?' Elliston continued.

'Frankly, no, it isn't.'

'To make it look like I killed him!'

'You think someone murdered Mr Greenfield for no other reason than to frame you?'

'I think what my client is proposing is that after someone took the victim's life, they had the idea to make it look like my client was responsible. Perhaps they saw them arguing beforehand?'

'I thought they were only having a polite discussion?' queried Tanner.

The solicitor smiled back at him. 'If I were you, Mr Tanner, I'd have a bit more of a chat with this witness of yours.'

'I'll certainly consider it, thank you, Mrs Heatherington'.

'It's Ms, actually,'

No surprises there, Tanner thought to himself, watching Elliston whisper something into her ear.

As Elliston returned to staring down at his hands, his solicitor made a quick note before glancing back up. 'There's something else we think you need to consider as well.'

'Oh, really? Do tell.'

'That it could be one of my client's political rivals.'

'You're not seriously suggesting that one of them would have murdered Mr Greenfield for no other reason than to win the election?'

'I've no idea. Have you asked them?'

'Surprisingly, no, I haven't!'

'Then don't you think you should?'

'At this stage, I think I'd prefer to find out what your client was doing last night, between the hours of nine and twelve.'

'I'm sorry, but haven't you asked him that already?'

'Not yet.'

'You mean to say that not only have you not one single shred of material evidence to tie my client to the crime he's been arrested for, but you didn't even bother to establish if he had an alibi before doing so?'

'Which is why we're asking him now,' Tanner replied, shifting awkwardly in his seat.

'But – don't you think you should have done that *before* dragging him in here, not only damaging his good name in the process, but also completely derailing any chance he had of winning the forthcoming by-election?'

'We've taken every precaution to make sure his name stays out of the press.'

'These things always come out. You know they do!'

'As I said, we've done all that we can to make sure it doesn't.'

'You know, there's something else that occurs to me,' she continued, placing her pen down to narrow her eyes at him. 'That all this might be political.'

Tanner laughed out loud. 'I can assure you, Ms Heatherington, that my own personal political views have absolutely nothing to do with this.'

'I see. May I ask which party you voted for in the last election?'

'That's none of your business!'

'If it isn't the party my client is representing, then I think it may very well be my business. My client's business, as well!'

'My political interest in your client is such that I haven't even thought to ask which party he's representing. Nor do I intend to.'

'I'm sorry, but given how much publicity his campaign has received over the last few months, it doesn't seem very likely that you don't already know.'

'I can assure you that there isn't a political bone in my body, certainly not one I'd consider using my position in society to derail someone's chances of winning an election.'

'Can you prove that?'

'Can you prove that your client wasn't at the scene when Mr Greenfield was killed?'

'Er...I can't, no, but I don't have to. My client is innocent until proven guilty, or had you forgotten that?'

'Then maybe he'd be so kind as to tell us where he was?'

'I'd still like to know why you hadn't bothered to establish his whereabouts before now?'

'Probably because you've barely given him a chance to talk since the moment you walked in!'

A sterile silence fell over the room.

'Well?' Tanner demanded.

The solicitor slowly turned her head to look at her client. 'You may answer the question.'

'After church, I drove straight home.'

'Thank you.'

'No problem,' Elliston smiled.

'May I ask which route you took?'

'The same one I always do.'

'Which was…?'

'Along the A47.'

'What did you do when you got home?'

'I had dinner with my wife.'

'I assume she'll be able to vouch for that?'

'Of course!'

'And what did you do then?'

'We went for a walk together, by the River Bure. It's only about ten minutes from our house.'

'Did anyone see you?'

'Nobody we knew.'

Tanner took a moment to make a few notes of his own before glancing up. 'One more question, Mr Elliston. Did you wear a pair of walking boots when you went for this evening stroll of yours?'

His eyes flickered for the briefest of moments. 'Of course!'

'Your old ones, or your new ones?'

'The ones you took from me. I've yet to wear my new ones.'

Tanner quietly returned to his notes.

'Are we done?' the solicitor demanded.

'We are, yes. Thank you!' Tanner replied, smiling

up at them as he put his pen away.

'So, my client can go?' she queried, in a surprised tone.

'Oh, no. Sorry. We still need to wait for forensics to come back to us on the walking boots in question,' he said, glancing down at his watch, 'which probably won't be until tomorrow now. They still need to take a look at the murder weapon as well. We then need to check his alibi, of course, as well as to see if your client's car was picked up by any ANPR cameras along the A47 at the given time. As well as that, I need to have a chat with the witness who said they saw your client's car, driving out of Swanton Morley's church carpark, at a completely different time. Assuming everything still proves beyond a reasonable doubt that your client *wasn't* at the scene when Mr Greenfield was killed, he'll be free to go.'

- CHAPTER TWENTY ONE -

PAUSING THE INTERVIEW again, Tanner led Vicky back out into the corridor to close the door.

'At least we have something to be getting on with,' he whispered, leading her to the end, 'at least until forensics comes back to us.'

'What do you want me to do?' she asked, following after.

'Maybe if you could take a look at the ANPR cameras, both at the time Elliston said he left the church, and when the witness mentioned seeing him? Then I suppose we'd better find out who that witness is.'

'You're not going along with that ridiculous story of theirs: that one of his political rivals murdered Greenfield to derail Elliston's election?'

'Obviously not. But it is possible that someone with particularly strong political views lied about seeing his car in an effort to do so. Maybe you could ask Gina to check to see if that person has any obvious political allegiances? Perhaps she could give the witness a call as well, to ask if they know the suspect? But please make sure to remind her not to mention anything about Elliston having been arrested on suspicion of murder,' Tanner added, seeing Vicky pull out her notebook. 'Actually, second thoughts, it's probably better if I do it.'

'I'm fairly sure Gina is capable of being discreet,'

Vicky replied.

'Yes, of course.'

'What about Elliston's alibi?'

'You mean, his wife?'

'I can ask Sally to give her a call?'

Tanner thought about it for a moment. 'Tell you what, why don't you get Sally to check the ANPR. That'll leave you free to call Elliston's wife.'

'No problem.'

'Oh, and when you do, make sure to keep the questions open. Ask her what she did last night, rather than if to confirm whether or not she was with her husband. One of the benefits of dragging him in so soon is that hopefully they wouldn't have had a chance to concoct a story together.'

'Unless his solicitor has already spoken to her?'

'If that's the case,' Tanner shrugged, 'then there's not a whole lot we can do about it.'

'I suppose not.'

Pushing their way through the doors into reception, Tanner stopped in the middle to stare out at the carpark, and the news vans lining the road outside.

'I hate to remind you,' he heard Vicky whisper, following his gaze, 'but we still have to look into that child prostitution story.'

'Yes, I know,' Tanner muttered, 'but, unfortunately, the most recent events have to take priority.'

'I was thinking that maybe it would be an idea to get Cooper to head that one up?'

'To be honest, I'd rather you did,' Tanner replied, rubbing his eyes.

'I suppose that depends on who you'd like to work with on the murder investigation, Cooper or me?'

'Good point.'

'May I make another suggestion?'

'I suppose that depends on what it is?'

'That you sneak off early to see that baby of yours?'

'I must admit, it would be nice, but I still have about two-dozen emails to go through. Probably more like three-dozen by now.'

'Couldn't you go through them at home? We can call you if anything comes up.'

He turned to see her looking at him with a concerned, motherly frown. 'There's really no need to worry, Vicky. I'm perfectly OK.'

'I'm sorry, boss, it's just that – well – I don't mean to be rude – or anything – but you look exhausted!'

'You don't look so bad yourself,' he replied, offering her a weary smile. 'Anyway, you'd better be getting along. You'll find me in my office, if you need me.'

- CHAPTER TWENTY TWO -

BACK IN HIS office, Tanner made sure the door was closed before making a beeline for his coffee machine. Basking in the glorious silence, he slowly poured himself a cup. It was only when he sat behind his desk did he realise how tired he was. He didn't have a headache, fortunately, but his eyes felt sticky when he blinked, and whenever he did, his entire brain seemed to buzz like the fluorescent tube on the ceiling.

After trying to shake his head awake, he took a sip from his coffee to enjoy the delicious burning sensation as it slipped down his throat.

Feeling instantly refreshed, he opened up his email account to see even more had arrived than he'd feared.

He blinked again, only for his eyes to remain stubbornly closed.

Allowing them to remain so for a moment, he took a series of smooth, shallow breaths.

Before he knew what had happened, his head had slumped forward, causing him to sit up with a start.

Realising that he'd managed to fall asleep within about three seconds of closing his eyes, he took another sip of his coffee to force himself to stare at the screen. But the moment he blinked again he could instantly feel himself losing consciousness.

'For fuck's sake,' he cursed. 'I don't have time for

this.'

Thinking of the time, he swivelled his eyes down to the clock at the bottom of the screen. It wasn't even half-past one.

Wondering if Forrester was still there, he pushed himself up to take another look out at the carpark. 'Well, his car's gone,' he muttered, quietly to himself.

Reaching what he considered to be an executive decision, he headed back to his desk to turn off his computer, retrieve his laptop, keys, and phone to spin around towards the door.

Arriving home about half an hour later, Tanner crept his way inside, half-hoping Samantha was asleep, the other half desperate to see her.

'Honey, I'm home,' he whispered, determined not to wake her if she was.

'We're in the bedroom!' came Christine's voice, booming down the hallway, closely followed by a loud, gurgling squeak.

'She's awake, then,' he smiled to himself, ditching his keys on the hall's side table with scant regard for how much noise they made.

'I'm just getting Samantha ready for her afternoon nap. Do you want to see her before I put her down?'

'Well, I've only got about four million emails I need to go through, but I suppose I could spare ten minutes,' he muttered to himself.

'Was that a yes?'

'Er...yes please!'

'OK, but can you wash your hands first?'

With the prospect of seeing Samantha giving him a much-needed boost, he stopped at the bathroom before rapping gently on the bedroom door. 'Can I come in?' he asked, nudging it open to peer inside the cosy, dimly lit room.

'Look who's home?' said Christine, in a soft, high-pitched voice, kneeling beside a wicker Moses basket placed next to their bed. 'That's right, it's Daddy!'

Creeping inside, he followed her gaze to see Samantha's impossibly cute, chubby little face, peering up at him with a pair of large milky blue eyes. 'Hello little one,' he said, beaming a warm, loving smile down at her. 'I do hope you're going to try and get some sleep?'

Samantha gurgled a mocking laugh at him, to then kick herself out from the white knitted baby blanket she'd previously been wrapped in.

'I take it that's a no?' he groaned, lowering one of his hands to let her grab hold of his little finger.

'OK, time for bed!' stated Christine.

'I don't suppose I can pick her up, first?'

'Fat chance!' she replied, endeavouring to re-wrap the blanket around Samantha's tiny, wriggling body. 'You've managed to over-excite her quite enough as it is.'

'I must admit, I do tend to have that effect on people.'

'OK, say goodnight, Daddy.'

'Goodnight, Samantha. Sleep tight!'

Leaning forward to kiss her lightly on the forehead, Tanner left them to head into the kitchen. There, he took out his laptop to rest gently on the breakfast bar before pouring himself a glass of rum.

Determined to make some sort of a dent in his growing collection of unopened emails, he flipped the laptop open to begin scrolling down the list, cherry-picking only the most important ones.

About twenty-minutes later, he stretched his arms above his head. As he refreshed his glass, he heard the sound of the bedroom door being closed ever-so gently behind him.

'Is she asleep?' he whispered, as Christine came stumbling into the room like a tranquilised zombie.

'For now,' she replied, zig-zagging her way to the kitchen. 'Good to have you back early, for a change.'

'I snuck out.'

'Are you going back?'

'Not if I can help it.'

'Would you like some lunch?'

'I wouldn't mind,' he replied, feeling guilty for even asking.

'Ready meal?'

'Sounds good.'

'OK, give me ten minutes,' she replied, heading for the sink.

'How was your day?' he asked. Judging by the state of her, it couldn't have been good.

'It would have been fine if I'd been able to close my eyes for more than five minutes.'

'Didn't you manage to get *any* rest?'

Christine shook her head before spinning around to the fridge.

'How about Samantha?'

'Oh, she had a great day, at least I think she did. She even managed to get some sleep. How about you?'

'A little, at my desk, just before I came home, but that was only for a few seconds.'

'I actually meant how was your day?'

'Oh, um...let me think. It would probably be best described as being insanely busy.'

'First days back often are.'

'More so in this particular instance. I'd barely made it past the kitchen when I was told why there were so many news vans blocking the road outside.'

'Presumably to report on that child prostitution

story?'

'You've heard about that?'

'Uh-huh,' she replied. 'Is there any truth to it?'

'I've no idea. After that, I went through to my office to find Forrester had moved in.'

'Not seriously?'

Tanner nodded in response. 'Apparently, he arrived the day after we left for our honeymoon. He said he wanted to make sure everything ticked over smoothly in my absence.'

'I thought you left Vicky in charge?'

'I did.'

'Oh right. She must have been thrilled.'

'I'm not sure she minded too much, but only because of what Sally had told her, apparently in confidence, about her uncle.'

'Which was?'

'That Forrester's wife had kicked him out.'

'Oh, right. I'm sorry to hear that.'

'He's staying at a hotel down the road whilst trying to find something a little more permanent.'

'Not your office, though?'

'Not if I've got anything to do with it! Anyway, I'd barely had a chance to frogmarch him out when I had to deal with a guy walking in off the street, covered in both mud and blood, going around telling everyone that he hadn't killed someone.'

'He *hadn't* killed someone?' Christine repeated.

Tanner nodded whilst continuing to go through his emails. 'He was quite insistent about it, as well.'

'Do you know if he had?'

'Well, a body did turn up, at the bottom of a grave over in Swanton Morley, but we're fairly sure that he was only responsible for finding it.'

'Swanton Morley, as in the village on the other side of Norwich?'

'That's the one.'

'But...how did he end up all the way over in Wroxham?'

'Not sure.'

'He didn't say?'

'I didn't ask.'

Christine turned to offer him a quizzical frown.

'I let him go, before I had the chance to, but only because we found the person who I do believe *was* responsible.'

'You've made an arrest already?'

Tanner glanced up to offer her a modest smile before taking another sip from his drink.

'That must have been some sort of a record,' Christine commented, pulling a ready meal out of the fridge to stab to death with a fork before shoving it into the microwave.

'The church's vicar saw the guy having an argument with the victim only a few hours before he was killed. We then caught him trying to sneak a pair of muddy walking boots out of the house, the same ones Vicky discovered had blood on them a few minutes before. The nail in the proverbial coffin was when his car was seen pulling out of the church carpark, about three hours after he'd already told us he'd left.'

'I don't suppose you get a bonus for catching a murderer in record time?'

'Sadly, we don't work on commission.'

'That's a shame.'

'But I might get a gold star for good effort.'

'If it was made of actual gold, I suppose that would be alright,' she replied, leaning back against the kitchen counter as the microwave continued to whir. 'So, anyway, where do you want it?'

'I'm sorry?'

'Your lunch?'
'Oh – right – yes. Of course. Here will be fine, thank you.'

- CHAPTER TWENTY THREE -

Tuesday, 24th June

IT WAS ONLY when Derek Harvey was driving down a narrow, mist-shrouded country lane, in his brand new, but already filthy, vehicle recovery van, that he remembered it was his birthday. Unlike most people, the realisation that he'd somehow managed to forget didn't make him laugh out loud at how increasingly forgetful he was becoming, nor did it make him smile at the thought of all the cards and presents waiting for him at home. Instead, he took a firm hold of the van's plastic steering wheel to draw in a slow, miserable breath. He knew there wouldn't be any presents waiting for him at home because he lived alone. He doubted there'd be any cards, either. He didn't have any family, and he could count the number of friends he had on one hand, none being the sort to send him anything quite so sentimental. He doubted if any would even bother to post a birthday message on his Facebook timeline. They'd have struggled to, even if they'd felt the urge. He'd never told them when his birthday was, and Facebook wasn't going to do it for him. Although the social media giant had forced him to provide his date of birth when opening his account, he'd made sure it at least remained hidden from his public profile. That wasn't to help prevent identity theft. More because he didn't want anyone to be able to remind him, hence the reason why he'd become so annoyed at himself for having remembered. Like Christmas, it was the one day each year that seemed impossible for him to forget, no matter how much he wanted to. It was as if it had been burned into his subconscious mind from the moment he'd been born, never to be forgotten again. And ever since his tenth birthday, the day his mother told him that she was leaving his father, and that he was subsequently going to be dragged away from the man he loved with all his heart, to be forced to live with a self-obsessed alcoholic who used his so-called "special day" as an excuse to get even more drunk than usual before shouting and screaming at him until eventually passing out, he'd been desperate to forget.

With toxic childhood memories flooding his mind, he closed his tear-filled eyes to mutter, 'Fucking birthdays.'

The moment he re-opened them, he saw a deer streak across the road, right in front of him.

'Jesus Christ!' he exclaimed, swerving hard to avoid it.

Lurching the wheel back, just in time to prevent the van plunging down into an overgrown drainage ditch, he had to fight to bring the vehicle back under control before continuing on his way, albeit at a more sensible speed. The last thing he wanted was to write his van off. He'd only started his own vehicle recovery business a few months before, and was still barely making enough to cover the van's hire purchase payments, let alone the rent of his flat, and all the bills that came with it.

Realising his heart was beating far faster than he knew it was safe to, he recalled the words of his doctor; that if he wanted to live beyond fifty he was going to have to lose at least twenty kilograms and start taking regular exercise. He was also supposed to avoid stressful situations at all costs. 'I guess I shouldn't be doing sixty down a narrow country lane then, should I?' he laughed, nervously to himself.

Bringing his mind back to the task at hand; trying to find the person who'd called him about half an hour before, he checked his satnav. 'It should be down here, somewhere,' he muttered, slowing down once again to begin peering cautiously ahead.

As he rounded the next corner, he suddenly saw it, parked to the side of the lane in a short narrow passing bay. 'Bloody hell!' he said, with an envious whistle, instantly recognising the car's make and model. 'Someone's got some money!'

Unable to see the driver, he pulled up as close to it as he dared, to keep the road clear behind him. With nobody around, he gave his horn a short, friendly beep, before turning on the van's swirling orange recovery lights to haul himself slowly out.

Closing the door, he quickly checked to make sure he'd left enough room for other road users to get past, before turning his attention to the stranded vehicle, and its apparently missing driver.

With still nobody in sight, he crouched behind it to see which tyre had the reported puncture, hoping it wasn't on the nearside. If it was, he was going to have a hell of a job getting to it. 'What the hell?' he was soon muttering to himself, when he realised none of the tyres were even remotely flat.

Pushing himself slowly up, he took a moment to glance up and down the otherwise deserted road, wondering for a moment if it was possible that he'd come to the wrong place. But he couldn't have. The caller had been very specific; halfway down Ringland Lane, which was exactly where he was. It was *possible* that there were two stranded cars down the same stretch of road, but it didn't seem very likely.

It was only then that it dawned on him why he wasn't able to see anyone inside the car. The windows all had a slight tint to them, and in dawn's early light, he simply couldn't see through them. But then why hadn't anyone climbed out when he'd pulled up? He'd certainly made enough noise.

Stepping around to the driver's side door, he inched his shaved, anvil-shaped head slowly forward. The windows were definitely tinted, but that wasn't the only reason why he was struggling to see through them. They were all completely steamed up, which must have meant that someone *was* inside, probably asleep.

'Hello!' he called, timidly knocking on the window. 'Is anyone there?'

With still not a single sign of movement, he cupped his hands around his eyes to peer cautiously inside.

'Jesus Christ!' he exclaimed, jumping back with a start. There *was* someone there. Through the dripping condensation he could see the outline of a head, resting back against the headrest, its deathly pale face staring vacantly out through a pair of dark, unblinking eyes.

Breathing hard, he tugged at the door handle, but it was locked. 'Can you hear me?' he called, rapping his knuckles against the glass. 'Are you alright?'

It was a stupid question. It was obvious to anyone with half a brain that whoever was inside was far from being so.

Lurching back to his van, he fumbled frantically for his phone. The moment he found it, he dialled 999 to press against his ear, whilst desperately trying to control his breathing.

The moment his call was answered, he sucked in a

short, juddering breath. 'Ambulance, please! It's urgent! I'm about halfway down Ringland Lane, near Attlebridge – in Norfolk,' he added, just to be sure. 'There's someone trapped inside their car. I can't open the door. I think – I think they might be dead.'

Leaving his name and address, he was eventually allowed to end the call to place the phone back inside his grimy fluorescent yellow jacket, only to hear something move behind him.

'Hello?' he called, whipping his head around.

But there was nothing there. Just the car parked exactly where it had been when he'd arrived.

Shaking his head, he was about to heave himself back up into his van when he heard the unmistakable sound of a car being unlocked.

With his heart suddenly pounding inside his barrel-like chest, he turned again to see the driver's door creep slowly open.

Unable to breathe, he watched as first an arm, then a leg appeared, before the body that he could have sworn had been nothing more than a lifeless corpse was standing beside the car, grinning at him like a deranged Cheshire Cat.

'Hello, Derek,' the re-animated corpse eventually said, casually closing the car's door to begin making its way over. 'It's good to finally meet you.'

'B-but you're...'

'Dead?' the person queried, offering him a whimsical frown. 'Maybe a little, but I'm feeling much better now. Thank you.'

'But I've called an ambulance, and everything!' Derek continued, his brain unable to comprehend what his eyes were seeing.

'I must admit, I was hoping you would.'

'I – I don't understand? Why would you want me to call an ambulance?'

'To save me the trouble, of course.'

Derek's puce, sweating face began to tremble like a sour blancmange. 'But – you're OK! There's nothing wrong with you!'

'Oh, it's not for me, Derek,' the walking corpse continued, as the serrated edge of an elongated blade appeared from behind a long, elegant leg. 'It's for you.'

- CHAPTER TWENTY FOUR -

TANNER ARRIVED AT work so early the next morning that there wasn't a single reporter or cameraman in sight, nor were there hardly any cars in the carpark, giving him the rare chance to park exactly where he wanted to.

Choosing a space as close to the entrance as possible, he climbed wearily out to make his way through to reception. There, he gave the duty sergeant nothing but the most perfunctory of nods before making a beeline for his office.

Once he'd made himself a coffee, he slumped down into the chair behind his desk to stare vacantly at his computer monitor's blank grey screen, blinking occasionally whilst sipping at the scalding hot contents of the mug clasped around his fingers.

He'd lied to Christine when he'd crawled out of bed to start getting ready for work, and was feeling guilty for having done so. He'd told her he wanted to get in early to finish going through his emails, when in reality he was desperate for some peace and quiet. It had been another difficult night, with Samantha waking up on the hour, every hour, screaming for milk, or a nappy change, or a cuddle, or whatever it was that she seemed in desperate need of. Each time she had he'd been left lying awake, staring at the ceiling, hoping to God Christine would get up to attend to her need, but unable to ask her to for fear of being told to do it himself.

The bottom line was that he'd forgotten just how challenging a newborn baby could be. Yes, they were tiny bundles of euphoric joy that were so impossibly cute, and smelt so incredibly good, that you wanted to hold them forever and never let go. But there were other times when they didn't smell very good at all. In fact, there were times they smelt so bad, you wanted to throw up. They also seemed doggedly determined to prevent anyone living within a half-mile radius of them from getting any sleep.

As Tanner sat there, gazing at a hazy reflection of himself in the otherwise blank, empty screen, his mind drifted aimlessly around, first wondering if that's how the person who invented double-glazing came up with the idea, as a means of stopping him from being woken up by his neighbour's baby about twelve times a night, then drifting randomly to the method of torture that relied purely on sleep deprivation. Whoever came up with that idea had to have been a parent, at least at some stage in their sad, sadistic little life. No question!

Remembering he was supposed be working, he shook his head in an effort to clear it of its stupid, pointless thoughts, to glance down at his watch. It wasn't even seven o'clock, meaning that he had over an hour and a half before any of his CID team began drifting slowly in.

Reaching underneath his desk, he turned on his computer to listen to it begin whirring itself awake. Knowing it would take a good minute to become fully operational, he leant all the way back in his so-called "Executive's Chair" to lift his feet onto the corner of the desk. With his head resting back against its soft black leather, he folded his arms over his chest. 'I'll just rest for ten minutes,' he said to himself, closing his eyes to feel that increasingly familiar buzzing sensation sweep through his brain. 'Just ten minutes, and I'll *definitely* start going through all those bloody emails.'

- CHAPTER TWENTY FIVE -

HEARING A WOMAN'S voice, calling his name from some distant place, Tanner woke with a start to find he wasn't in a slowly sinking rowing boat, in the middle of some vast expanse of open water, but was instead lying almost vertically on his office chair, with Vicky peering at him from his office door.

'John?' he heard her say again, as she stepped cautiously inside.

'What?' he asked, his befuddled brain struggling to entangle his dream from reality.

'Sorry, boss. I was just seeing if you were awake.'

'Well, I am now,' he replied, slipping his feet off the end of his desk to begin rubbing at his eyes.

'I wasn't sure if you wanted to be woken up, or not.'

'What time is it?' he mumbled, his eyes endeavouring to focus on his watch.

'Just after half-past nine.'

'For fuck's sake!'

Trying to blink his eyes open, he glared out through the partition window. 'Is everyone in?'

'Cooper's running late.'

'What about Forrester?'

'He's out seeing a flat.'

'Well, that's something, I suppose.'

'There's also someone out in reception, from the Norwich Reporter, saying they're supposed to have a meeting with you.'

Remembering what Forrester had told him the day before, that he'd arranged for one of the newspaper's editors to come in to discuss their child prostitution story, he pushed himself up from his chair.

'Shall I ask him to come back another time?'

'No, it's fine. I'm sure it won't take long. By the way, next time you find me asleep at my desk, please don't wait until I have a meeting before waking me up.'

'Yes, boss, but it was fairly obvious you needed the rest.'

'Not when we have a murder suspect in custody, and only about – what – three hours left before we need to find a local magistrate willing to grant us a holding extension.'

'Speaking of Mr Elliston, we've had news back from forensics on the knife Joseph Miller walked in with.'

'Another reason to have woken me up.'

'It only came in about five minutes ago.'

'And...?' Tanner demanded.

'The blood found on it does belong to William Greenfield.'

'OK, so we have ourselves a murder weapon.'

'They also found Joseph Miller's prints and DNA.'

'But we knew they would, didn't we?'

'Elliston's, as well.'

Tanner smiled at her whilst shaking his head. 'Couldn't you have told me that when you first walked in?'

'I was building up to it,' Vicky replied. 'Sally's typing up the extension application as we speak. I've asked her to print it out for you to sign as soon as she's done.'

'Has anything else come in that you haven't told

me about?'

'Nothing of any importance.'

'What about those walking boots?'

'I've already chased forensics. They said they'd do their best to get the tests on both the mud and blood back to us by ten o'clock this morning.'

'OK, that gives me half an hour. If you could show that editor through, I'll have a quick chat with him in here.'

- CHAPTER TWENTY SIX -

'SIMON REYNOLDS, EDITOR-in-Chief of the Norwich Reporter,' announced Vicky, ushering a smartly dressed, intelligent looking man into Tanner's office a few minutes later.

'I take it you're Detective Chief Inspector Tanner?' the man enquired, stepping inside.

'Only when I'm at work,' Tanner smiled. 'Please, take a seat,' he continued, standing up from his own as Vicky left to close the door. 'May I get you a coffee?'

'That would be nice, thank you,' he smiled. 'Milk, no sugar, if that's OK?'

'Good choice,' Tanner replied.

'When I first phoned, I was told you were on holiday.'

'It was my honeymoon,' Tanner replied, in a conversational tone.

'Oh – right. I hope you didn't cut it short, just to see me?'

'Not at all,' Tanner laughed. 'I actually nearly had to have it extended.'

'You weren't ill, I hope?'

'Not exactly. We came back with a baby.'

Taking the coffee Tanner was holding out for him, Reynolds raised a curious eyebrow. 'Duty Free?'

'Well, she was free, although how much she'll cost us in the long run is anyone's guess. Anyway, you wanted to talk about the news item you recently ran in relation to the Adlingtons?'

Reynolds sat back in his chair to cross one leg over the other. 'We've spent the last four months researching a story about what we believe to be a predatory child sex ring, one that we think the Adlingtons were a part of.'

'Is this an alleged story, or did you have something to back it up with?'

'We had a reliable source.'

'May I ask who that person is?'

'Unfortunately, I'm not at liberty to say, but since the person came forward, we've been able to identify a number of victims going back over a ten year period.'

'Is your source one of them?'

Reynolds remained stoically silent.

Tanner pushed himself back in his chair. 'I'm sorry, Mr Reynolds, but if you're not prepared to share the information you have with us, then may I ask why you're here?'

'Because our source provided us with a list of names who are apparently currently active, but have never been caught.'

'Are you willing to share that list with us?'

'That's why I came,' he smiled, taking a sealed white envelope out from inside his suit jacket to place in the middle of the desk.

Tanner stared down at it without moving. 'I've been told that you've yet to publish their names? Is that correct?'

'We wanted to run them by you first.'

'Are any of them registered?'

'Unfortunately not.'

'Do you have proof that they've done the things your source has accused them of doing?'

'Not as such.'

'So, you don't, then?'

'None of the dozen or so victims who've so far come forward have been willing to identify the men who abused them. Unfortunately, they've all just been too scared. Anyway, we reached a point where we felt we were unable to go any further, so I decided to share their names with you, hoping you'd have more luck.'

'*After* publishing your story, of course.'

'We have a civic duty to bring such stories to the attention of the public.'

'Maybe so, but it would have been far better if you'd told us about this before doing so. All you've really done is to give those involved a heads-up that we're about to come knocking on their doors, giving them plenty of time to destroy any evidence there may have been, so making it virtually impossible for us to bring about any convictions.'

'But you can bring them in for questioning, which is something we're unable to do, for obvious reasons.'

'Not without evidence, we can't,' came Tanner's terse response.

'We're here to report the news, Chief Inspector, not to bring people to justice. If I'm not mistaken, that's your job.'

'Which would have been far easier if you'd come to us first.'

'No offence,' Reynolds continued, 'but if it wasn't for us, you wouldn't have even known about the problem.'

A brooding silence followed, broken by Reynolds, pushing himself up from his chair.

'Anyway,' he continued, 'as I said before, we've taken the story as far as it can go. You have the list of names. I'll let you decide how best to proceed.'

- CHAPTER TWENTY SEVEN -

AS SOON AS Reynolds had left, Tanner slipped the still sealed envelope off the desk to head out in search of Vicky.

'How'd it go?' she asked, glancing up from her monitor as he made his way over.

'We have a list of names,' he said, holding the envelope out.

Vicky sat up with interest to take the envelope from him. 'Anyone I know?' she asked, turning it over in her hands.

'I've no idea. I haven't bothered to look.'

'Oh...right. Any particular reason why?'

'Because...' Tanner began, perching himself on the edge of her desk, 'as I attempted to explain to our visitor, the fact that they've already gone and published the story means that those involved would have had plenty of time to destroy any evidence there may have been to bring about a conviction against them.'

'I thought the article said they had over a dozen victims?'

'So he said, but unfortunately, none of them are willing to identify the people who abused them, which is hardly surprising. I'm amazed they had the courage to come forward in the first place!'

'But...if we promise to keep the victims' identities a secret?'

'I'm not saying it won't be possible to find one or two who'd be prepared to testify against them, but it would have been a hell of a lot easier if the newspaper had come to us with the story before publishing it.'

'I'm not sure that's how the press works.'

'No, I suppose not,' he replied, shaking his head. 'Anyway, I don't suppose there's been any more news from forensics?'

'Nothing yet,' she replied, glancing up at the clock on the wall.

'How's Sally getting on with that extension request?' Tanner continued, turning to see her chair was empty.

'Er...she was there a minute ago.'

'OK, well, maybe you can leave her a message, asking her to find me when she's done. We really need to push on with Elliston. Do you know where he is?'

'He's waiting for us in Interview Room One,' Vicky replied, typing something out on her keyboard, 'with his solicitor.'

'OK. I'm going to head over. Join me as soon as you can.'

'I'm ready now,' she smiled, standing up to grab hold of a file.

'You've left Sally a message?'

'Uh-huh.'

'Oh, right. OK, then let's go.'

Spinning around, Tanner began leading the way out, only to see Forrester, charging in the other way.

With the forlorn hope of being able to avoid him, he was about to duck into the kitchen, under the pretence of making himself a drink, when he heard the superintendent bellow out his name.

'Oh, hello, sir!' Tanner replied, glancing over with a manufactured look of surprise. 'I didn't see you there.'

Coming to a standstill directly in front of him, Forrester began staring around the office with a look of turgid disdain. 'I just dropped in to tell you that I'm heading back to HQ.'

'OK. Right.'

'How's everything been going?'

Tanner glanced over his shoulder to see Vicky had managed to surreptitiously navigate herself over to Gina's desk. 'Yes, good. We were about to recommence the interview of our prime suspect.'

'You still think it's him, do you?' Forrester asked, sending him a dubious scowl.

'Yes, sir. I do. More so now that we have some physical evidence to help back it up.'

'And what physical evidence is that?'

'His fingerprints and DNA have been found on the knife that was used.'

Forrester's head jolted back in surprise. 'Are you sure?'

'One-hundred percent!' Tanner stated. 'The forensic report came in about twenty minutes ago.'

Forrester shoved his hands into his pockets to stare despondently down at the floor.

'Was there any particular reason why his fingerprints and DNA *shouldn't* have been found?' Tanner asked, with a curious frown.

'I've just had a call from Haverstock,' Forrester replied, glancing up. 'They've found another body; a man stabbed multiple times in the chest, very much like the other victim.'

Tanner felt his stomach tighten. 'Time of death?'

'This morning, at around seven o'clock. I assume your suspect was here at the time?'

Tanner's eyes drifted slowly away. 'He's been in the holding cell all night.'

'There's no way he could have escaped?'

'Well, I can check the security cameras, but it doesn't seem very likely, especially when he was still there this morning.'

'Where is he now?'

'Interview Room One, waiting for us with his solicitor.'

Forrester folded his arms to rest a pensive finger against his sagging chin. 'So, we now have two suspects, both here when this other guy was killed.'

'Two suspects, sir?'

'Huh?' asked Forrester, his attention drifting back to Tanner.

'You said two suspects.'

'Yes, of course. The one you seem to think is our prime suspect, and that other chap, going around telling everyone that he definitely hadn't killed someone.'

'But...we let him go, sir,' Tanner replied, swallowing in nervous expectation as to what Forrester was going to say in response.

'What?'

'The other man. The one with the psychological issues. We let him go.'

'Please God, tell me you're joking?' Forrester replied, his entire body trembling like a volcano that was about to erupt.

'I'm sorry, sir, but it wasn't him!' Tanner stated.

'You mean, the man who came wandering in off the street, covered from head to foot in mud and blood, going around telling everyone that he definitely didn't kill the person who was later found stabbed to death at the bottom of an open grave, the same person who was holding the knife that killed him. That's the guy you think *didn't* do it?'

'Er...yes, sir.'

'JESUS FUCKING CHRIST!' Forrester finally

bellowed, his face going as red as a boiled beetroot.

As the floor shook, Tanner glanced nervously around the office to find every other person there staring at them, each wearing similar expressions of anxious dread.

'Right!' Forrester continued, taking a series of short, shallow breaths, 'I want two things to happen. First, I want the man who you had the genius idea to release brought in for questioning.'

'That would mean having to arrest him, sir.'

'Really? How strange! I can't imagine why you'd want to do that.'

'Of course, sir,' Tanner replied, thinking it was probably best to keep his mouth shut.

'Second, I want you to drive over to see this other body, the one your original suspect probably killed as a way of celebrating his unexpected release. Maybe that will give you the opportunity to explain to Haverstock why he has yet *another* murder victim to deal with.'

'Yes, sir. Of course, sir,' Tanner replied, remaining where he was.

'Well?' Forrester demanded. 'What the hell are you waiting for?'

'Sorry, sir, but I was just wondering which one you wanted me to do first; find the suspect, or drive over to see the body?'

'Both, Tanner! It's called multi-tasking! Perhaps you've heard of it?'

'I have indeed, sir.'

'Excellent! Right! I'm heading back to HQ. Please make sure to call me the minute you've laid your hands on that missing suspect of yours.'

'Absolutely, sir.'

'And if you could refrain from fucking anything else up in my absence, I'd be extremely grateful.'

- CHAPTER TWENTY EIGHT -

AS EVERYONE IN the entire office seemed to hold their breath whilst waiting for Forrester to leave, Vicky came skulking over. 'Sounds like Forrester's feeling more like his normal self.'

'His wife must have taken him back,' mused Tanner, his ears still ringing.

'Do you have any idea how you're going to find the missing suspect, whilst taking a look at this latest murder victim at the same time?'

'Simple,' he replied. 'I'll drive over there whilst you look out the passenger window.'

'Me?'

'You don't expect me to go on my own, do you? Besides, four eyes are better than two.'

The sound of someone clearing their throat had them turning to see Sally, smiling coyly up at them. 'Sorry to bother you, boss. Is – er – now a good time?'

'Five minutes ago would have been a better time, preferably before your uncle saw me.'

'Yes. Sorry about that.'

'I'm not sure how it's your fault. Anyway, how can I help?'

'I have that extension request for you to sign,' she replied, holding out a clipboard in one hand and a pen in the other. 'That's assuming you still want to continue questioning Mr Elliston?'

'If it wasn't for the fact that we've just been told his

fingerprints are all over the murder weapon, then I'd probably have let him go. But then again,' he continued, taking the pen to scrawl his signature at the bottom, 'seeing what happens when I do allow someone to walk out the door, that probably wouldn't have been such a good idea.'

With Sally continuing to gaze anxiously up at him, Tanner handed the pen back to ask, 'Was there something else?'

'The forensics report just came in about the blood found on the suspect's walking boots.'

'OK. Go on.'

'It says they belong to the boots' owner, Mr Elliston.'

'But that doesn't make any sense!' Vicky exclaimed, as Tanner was left to curse quietly to himself. 'They've confirmed that his fingerprints and DNA have been found on the knife, and that it's definitely the murder weapon, but the blood on his boots belongs to him, not the victim?'

'Maybe he was wearing different shoes?' suggested Sally.

'Then why was he trying to sneak them out of his house, the moment he thought we'd left?'

'I suppose we're going to have to consider the possibility that Elliston was doing exactly what he told us he was doing,' muttered Tanner, in a reticent tone. 'Taking them to the nearest bloody charity shop!'

'Still covered in mud?'

'Maybe that's normal?' he shrugged.

'What about how determined he was for us not to look inside the bag he was carrying them out in.'

'Perhaps that was us, projecting our suspicions onto something that simply wasn't there,' Tanner continued.

'But if his fingerprints and DNA are on the knife?'

'Then maybe we need to see if there's similar evidence to suggest that Elliston murdered the second victim as well. If there is, then it looks likely that his theory is correct, that someone is trying to frame him.'

'By murdering someone else, when Elliston's locked inside a holding cell?'

'You're forgetting that apart from us, nobody knows he's been arrested. As far as everyone else is concerned, Mr Elliston is still very much on the campaign trail, working hard to become Norfolk's very next Member of Parliament.'

- CHAPTER TWENTY NINE -

LEAVING SALLY TO email the extension request to the local magistrate, Tanner gave Vicky a moment to find where the second victim's body had been found before leading her out to his car.

Half an hour later, they were pulling up alongside a police squad car, halfway down a quiet country lane, to step out and glance curiously about. Ahead was an ambulance, parked to the side of the road. Behind that was a grubby white van with a row of orange emergency lights on its roof, surrounded by a flickering line of blue and white Police Do Not Cross tape.

Looking for Haverstock, Tanner eventually saw him, stepping out from behind the ambulance to stare immediately over.

'Chief Inspector Tanner!' the detective inspector called out. 'What an absolute honour!'

Waving a response, Tanner whispered to Vicky, 'If we can establish that the person responsible for this is different from the suspect we have back at the station, then we still have ourselves a murder suspect.'

Seeing her nod discreetly back, he looked up to offer the detective inspector a beaming smile. 'Good morning, Haverstock! I hear you have another murder victim on your hands?'

'And I hear you're missing a murder suspect, after having made the rather peculiar decision to let him walk out the door?'

'You heard about that, did you?' Tanner asked, electing to take a more humble, self-deprecating approach, instead of simply pulling rank on him.

'Forrester called me about half an hour ago.'

'That must have been about five minutes after he bawled me out in front of my entire office,' he laughed. 'I must admit, I did deserve it. I shouldn't have let him go so soon.'

'We all make mistakes.'

'Some more than others,' he laughed again, before turning to beckon Vicky forward. 'Have you met my colleague, DI Gilbert?'

'Only briefly,' Haverstock responded, presenting her with a respectful nod.

'She's the one who advised me against letting the suspect go. I didn't listen, of course.'

'He rarely does,' Vicky said, offering Haverstock a friendly smile.

'Anyway,' Tanner continued, 'I was really hoping you'd be able to walk us through the crime scene?'

Tanner watched Haverstock hesitate.

'Are you hoping to find anything in particular?'

'Forrester mentioned something about there being similarities with the previous victim. I was hoping you'd be able to explain to us what those similarities were.'

'I think I mentioned what they were to Forrester.'

'Would you mind showing us?'

'If you insist,' the DI responded, reaching down to lift the fluttering tape.

Ducking underneath, they followed him around the ambulance to see the body of a large, obese man, sitting against the side of the van, his face the picture of bewildered shock as he stared unblinkingly at the hedgerow on the opposite side of the lane.

'You can see the stab wounds,' Haverstock remarked, gesturing down. 'Fifteen in total.'

'Do you know who found him?'

'The paramedics.'

'And who called them?'

'We think it must have been the victim. At least, the call was made from his phone.'

'Have the paramedics given a statement?'

'They have.'

'Which was…?'

'That they were called to attend someone who was supposedly locked inside their car, but when they arrived, they found the victim, as he is here.'

'There was nobody else?'

Haverstock shook his head.

'Did they drive past anyone on the way down?'

'Not a soul.'

Tanner thought for a moment. 'What about the emergency call? Have you had a chance to listen to it?'

'Not yet, but we're proceeding on the basis that the victim was lured here by someone pretending to have broken down, being that it's a vehicle recovery van.'

'So I can see,' Tanner replied, casting his eyes over it. 'Do we know the victim's identity?'

Haverstock took a moment to dig out his notebook. 'The name on his driver's licence is Mr Derek Harvey. At the moment, all we know about him is that he lives in Billingford, not far from here, and that the van is registered in his name.'

'He doesn't have a criminal record?' Tanner questioned, crouching down to examine the body, and the surrounding area more closely.

'Not that's on the system.'

'How about the murder weapon?'

'We're still looking.'

Pointing to a mark on the van's door, just below the handle, he asked, 'I assume you've seen this fingerprint?'

'Forensics have already logged it for analysis.'

'Anything else?'

'Nothing so far. But as I said, we're still looking.'

Glancing over to see the medical examiner he'd met the previous day, deep in conversation with an overall-clad forensics officer on the other side of the ambulance, Tanner pushed himself up. 'Well, thank you for your time, Haverstock,' he said, with an affable smile. 'It's very much appreciated.'

- CHAPTER THIRTY -

BACKING AWAY FROM the body, Tanner lifted the tape for Vicky to whisper, 'Before we go, let's just have a very quick word with the medical examiner.'

Seeing her nod as she ducked underneath, he followed her around the ambulance to see the woman in question.

'Mrs Westwood,' he called out quietly, raising a hand as he did.

'Ah, Mr Detective Chief Inspector Tanner. You're back!'

'Please, call me John.'

'Please, call me Alison,' she smiled. 'I hope you haven't come all the way over here to chase me up on that post-mortem report?'

'We were actually wondering if it would be possible to have a quick word about the body.'

'Any body in particular?'

'This one, at least for now.'

Returning an accommodating smile, she pulled out a tablet out from under her arm to begin swiping at the screen. 'Right. Here we are. He's an overweight male in his mid-to-late forties, in desperate need of some deodorant. Oh, and he was stabbed fifteen times in the chest. Is there anything else you need to know?' she asked, glancing up.

'How likely do you think it is that his assailant is

the same person who killed the previous victim?'

'On a scale of one to ten, I'd probably say a nine. Apart from the previous victim being stabbed only eleven times, the modus operandi would appear to be the same. The difference in the number of stab wounds may be down to something as innocent as the attacker simply losing count. The only other difference is that the previous victim was hit over the head first, but that was probably down to the circumstance; that the attacker needed to get the victim away from the church before finishing the job.'

'Do you know if the previous victim was stabbed whilst he was still unconscious?'

'Well, there was no sign of a struggle, so it's certainly a possibility. Do you think it's important?'

'I was just thinking about the motive. With this one appearing to be a similar emotionally charged attack, I'd have thought the assailant would have wanted the victims to have known what was going on.'

'OK, well, unfortunately, there's no way for us to know. We can only tell if wounds are inflicted after someone is dead, not if they were either asleep or unconscious.'

'Assuming the same person is responsible for both, is there anything to indicate if they are male or female, tall or short, right or left handed?'

'Again, the circumstances of each attack were different. The previous body was stabbed when he was already lying at the bottom of a grave. It looks like the victim here was attacked when he was standing up, so it's going to be difficult to make a direct comparison, certainly in relation to the assailant's height. I *can* tell you that both were probably right handed, or at least the knife was held in the right hand.'

'Do you have any idea how tall the attacker was, at

this location?'

'I'd say roughly the same height as the victim.'

'Which is?'

'I don't know. I've yet to measure the body, but I'd guestimate him to be about average height, for a British male, at least.'

'So, about five-nine?'

'There abouts.'

'OK, thank you.'

'Was there anything else?'

'No. Actually, yes. Sorry. There's a fingerprint on the van's door, just beneath the handle. I don't suppose you know if it belongs to the victim?'

'Not yet,' she replied, returning to her tablet's screen. 'I assume you have the victim's name?'

'We do, thank you,' Tanner replied, glancing around to see Vicky looking sheepishly back.

'Sorry, boss, I forgot to make a note of it.'

As Tanner rolled his eyes, Vicky fished her notebook out from the depths of her handbag, accidentally pulling out a plain white envelope as she did.

Seeing it flutter to the ground, she stooped to pick it up, whilst Alison read from her tablet.

'Derek Harvey, of 42, Castleview Terrace, Billingford, which I believe isn't too far from here.'

Making sure Vicky had been able to make a note, Tanner turned back to the medical examiner. 'Could you give us an idea as to when we'll be able to see the post-mortem report for this one?'

'Probably sometime after I've finished the first. Am I officially allowed to send a copy to you this time?' she queried, peering discreetly around the ambulance to where Haverstock could be seen staring idly down at his phone.

'Probably not, but if you could send it anyway?'

'OK, well, I was hoping to get the other one done and dusted by lunchtime, but I can't see that happening now. How about the first by three o'clock, and this one by sometime tomorrow?'

With time fast running out on how long they'd be able to hold Elliston for, Tanner didn't need a calculator to know that her proposed schedule wasn't going to work. 'I don't suppose there's any chance we could have an interim report back on both by end-of-play today? Maybe something from forensics, as well? It's just that we have a suspect back at Wroxham Police Station who I can only hold until midnight before I either have to charge him, or let him go.'

'Is that the witness you mentioned yesterday?'

'Er...no. I made the mistake of letting that one go.'

'You made the *mistake* of letting him go?' she repeated, offering him a curious frown.

'That was according to my boss, Superintendent Forrester,' Tanner replied.

'Do you think that person is responsible for what happened here?'

'I hope not!' he laughed, somewhat nervously. 'But if another body turns up, and he's caught pulling the knife out, whilst telling whoever found him that he's innocent, then I'd probably have to add him to a list that seems to be either growing, or shrinking, depending on the time of day.'

- CHAPTER THIRTY ONE -

WITH THE MEDICAL examiner agreeing to do the best that she could, Tanner thanked her for her time before turning away.

'If we can get something back from both by five o'clock today,' he whispered to Vicky, as he began leading her back to his car, 'then we should at least know if we can let Elliston go. At the moment, it's looking increasingly likely that someone *is* trying to frame him, especially if that fingerprint turns out to be his.'

Reaching the car, Tanner glanced around to realise that he'd been talking to himself. Vicky wasn't there. She was still standing next to the ambulance, staring down at an unfolded piece of A4 paper.

'Vicky!' he shouted, lifting his chin. 'Are you coming?'

Seeing her nod, he watched her tuck the piece of paper back into its envelope to start jogging over.

'Sorry, boss,' she eventually said, handing the envelope to him, 'but I think you need to see this.'

'What is it?' he asked, taking it from her.

'It's that list of names the newspaper editor gave you. It fell out of my bag when I was pulling out my notebook.'

Tanner removed it from its envelope to see five names, each with a corresponding address, telephone number, and email.

'I think the last two should be of particular interest,' Vicky continued, pointing down.

'Jesus Christ!' Tanner exclaimed. 'Five people, two of whom are dead!'

'Have you seen who the remaining three are?'

'Charles Fletcher, Marcus Thornton, and Robert Hanson,' Tanner replied, reading from the list with vague indifference.

'Sorry,' Vicky said, 'I meant *who* the remaining three are?'

'I've never heard of any of them!'

'Then I really think you need to get out more,' she said, taking the list from him. 'From the bottom up; Robert Hanson is the founder of Hanson Fashion. He was in the papers last year. They accused him of using child labour camps in Indonesia. He lost his entire business six months later.

'Marcus Thornton is of Thornton Computers. He used to have a chain of high street shops. That was until he was caught using them to sell stolen merchandise.

'And Charles Fletcher is *Sir* Charles Fletcher, the guy going up against our very own George Elliston in the forthcoming by-election, the same guy who reportedly lost the bulk of his family's fortune thanks to an out-of-control gambling habit. It's like a Who's Who of Norfolk's most dodgy residents. I'm not surprised the Norwich Reporter didn't want to publish their names. I can imagine they'd have been inundated with defamation law suits about three seconds later. And if two of them are already dead,' Vicky continued, 'then it doesn't require much imagination to think that someone may have started working their way through them, taking them out, one at a time, and I don't mean to dinner.'

Tanner began tapping a pensive finger against the

back of the paper. 'And as they're all accused of being paedophiles,' he added, 'it could also mean that the person responsible for their deaths could well be one of their victims.'

'Or perhaps,' mused Vicky, 'the murderer is someone on the list. If you think about it, this all started when that story came out in the newspaper.'

'You think someone might be keen to make sure nobody talks?'

'Well, without naming names, or anything, if I was a knight of the realm, someone who perhaps was endeavouring to become Norfolk's next MP, and I just happened to find out that one of my paedophile chums had started talking to the press, I might be keen to permanently silence them all as well.'

'I assume you're referring to this Sir Charles Fletcher character?'

'He would appear to have the most to lose if his name did come out in connection with a child prostitution ring. He would also appear to have the most to gain if it didn't. He becomes an even more likely candidate when you factor into the equation that there's a strong possibility that his main political rival is currently being framed for murder.'

'Sounds like we need to have a word with him. I suppose my only question is whether or not we should tell Forrester?'

'About the people on the list, or about us interviewing a knight of the realm?'

'Both, really, especially when we're supposed to be out looking for the man he seems to think is responsible, Joseph Miller.'

With Tanner remaining stoically silent, Vicky was left to ask, 'What's the plan, boss?'

Handing the piece of paper back, Tanner drew in a fortifying breath. 'We're going to have to do something to help manage Forrester's expectations, whilst continuing to pursue more pertinent lines of enquiry. I think the most effective way to do that would be to hold a press conference; firstly to address the story in the Norwich Reporter, then to mention the fact that we're looking to speak to a man by the name of Joseph Miller in connection with an ongoing murder investigation, preferably without the entire British population immediately jumping to the conclusion that he must therefore be a deranged serial killer.'

'And just how are you going to do that?'

'Hopefully by omitting to use the M word.'

'Is it possible to hold a press conference about a murder investigation without it?'

'It is if I replace it with the one beginning with P.'

'I sincerely hope you're not considering the idea of telling the entire British population that Joseph Miller is a suspected paedophile?' questioned Vicky, staring at him as if he'd completely lost his mind.

'You're right, that is probably worse.'

'Probably?'

'Which means I'm going to have to give it a little more thought.'

'What about the remaining people on the list? Shouldn't we warn them that there could be someone trying to bump them off, one at a time?'

Tanner glanced thoughtfully down at his watch. 'OK, here's what we're going to do. Ask Sally to organise a press conference for two o'clock this afternoon. Then tell Cooper to round up a handful of uniformed officers to start looking for Miller.'

'He'll love that!'

'Maybe suggest that he takes Townsend with him, as well.'

'Two happy customers!'

'Then give the three remaining names on this list to Gina and Henderson. We need to find out everything we can about them, and as quickly as possible, especially if any are already on the police database. If they are, then we need their fingerprints and DNA sent straight over to Haverstock's forensics team for them to check against anything found at the crime scenes.'

'And what are *we* going to do?'

'See if we can visit the remaining three people on the list before the press conference starts. But unlike our murderer, I suggest we start at the top.'

- CHAPTER THIRTY TWO -

WITH VICKY STILL on the phone to the office, Tanner was soon driving them through a pair of open wrought iron gates to see a resplendent white house, sitting on top of a modest hill ahead.

Following a winding single-track road, they passed overgrown lawns on either side to eventually find themselves entering a large gravel-lined courtyard encircled by numerous cars, one of which turned out to be a dark grey Bentley Continental.

Climbing out to take note of a series of identical posters, stuck to every single one of the ground floor windows with the words VOTE FLETCHER printed in bold, capital letters, Tanner began making his way towards the steps leading up to the pillared entrance when he saw a slim, elegant man, edging his way back through the open doors carrying something large, square, white, and seemingly rather heavy.

With Vicky emerging from the other side of his car, he silently directed her attention towards him. It was only when the man turned slowly around did they see what he was carrying; an enormous computer monitor, with the box containing the hard drive balanced precariously on the top.

'Good morning!' Tanner called out, as the man inched his way down the worn stone steps. 'Need a hand?'

'I'm fine, thank you,' he muttered, his sharp blue eyes peering at them from around the bulky computer. 'Are you here for this afternoon?' he queried, staggering his way slowly towards the rear of the Bentley.

'What's happening this afternoon?' Tanner enquired, following behind.

'You're not here for the canvassing?' the man continued, reaching the back of the over-sized car to ease the monitor down into its already open boot.

'We're actually from the police,' Tanner remarked, in a casual, off-hand manner.

The man seemed to hesitate for a moment before standing straight to glance around.

'The police?' he eventually queried, as if stuck for anything else to say.

'Detective Chief Inspector Tanner, and my colleague, Detective Inspector Gilbert,' Tanner replied, each holding out their respective IDs.

'And what brings you all the way out here?' he asked, closing the boot.

'We were hoping to have a word with the person whose name appears to be on all the posters,' Tanner continued, gesturing around at them.

Glancing down at the still proffered IDs, the man followed Tanner's gaze. 'May I enquire as to what it's in connection with?'

'Unfortunately, that's something we can only discuss with Mr Fletcher.'

'Well, it's no secret. That's my name on the posters, at least I hope it is,' he chuckled. 'So anyway...how can I help?'

'We were wondering if you'd be able to tell us where you were on Sunday night, between the hours of nine and twelve?'

'Why? What am I supposed to have done?'

'At the moment, we're simply trying to establish your whereabouts.'

'This isn't about that body, the one found over at Swanton Morley, by any chance?'

Tanner shot Vicky a glance before turning slowly back. 'May I ask how you know about that?'

'I have my connections,' the man replied, lifting his narrow chin to stare down his nose at them.

'I don't suppose you could be a little more specific?'

The man held Tanner's gaze for a moment longer before his face cracked into an amused grin. 'Sorry,' he laughed, 'I'm winding you up. I read about it in the Norfolk Herald. I have a copy here, if you'd like to see it,' he added, navigating his way around the car to remove it from the passenger's seat. 'It's utter nonsense, of course, but great fun all the same.'

Waiting for the man to hand it to him, Tanner stared down at the headline with furious disdain.

"Deranged Lunatic Sought in Connection with Grisly Church Murder."

'I assume that *is* what you're here to ask me about?'

Scanning quickly through to see that not only had they mentioned the victim's name, but also Joseph Miller, who the article seemed to be suggesting was responsible, Tanner passed it to Vicky. 'As accurate as I'm sure the story is, we'd still like to know your whereabouts?'

'Yes, of course. I was here all night. My wife will be able to confirm that.'

'Is she around, by any chance?'

'She's inside, sorting through about two million leaflets. We just had rather a large delivery. That's why I was throwing some of our old junk away; to try and make a little more space.'

Tanner gazed up at the enormous Palladian mansion. 'I must admit, it's hard to believe you'd need to.'

'Oh, you know how it is. You never seem to have enough, no matter how large your house is, especially when you have five generations of your family's junk to contend with. Anyway, was that it?'

'Sorry, just one or two more questions.'

'OK, then fire away!' he replied, folding his arms to lean back against his car.

'Do you read any other newspapers, other than the Norfolk Herald?'

'I periodically glance through the F.T. Then we have the Sunday Times, of course.'

'You don't happen to read the Norwich Reporter, by any chance?'

'Er...no, sorry. My wife tells me I should, to help keep me up-to-date with the local news – the *real* local news, that is – but unfortunately, if I'm to be completely honest, I just can't be arsed.'

With Vicky tucking the Norfolk Herald under her arm to pull out her notebook, Fletcher pushed himself off the car. 'Oh, sorry, but... would you mind not making a note of that? I doubt it would go down well if my future electorate were to find out that I didn't actually give a single shit about them.'

Vicky glanced up with a narrow smile, before clicking the top of her ballpoint pen to begin taking notes anyway.

'Oh well,' Fletcher shrugged, refolding his arms to smile back at Tanner. 'I suppose I can always deny it.'

'If you don't read the Norwich Reporter, then is it safe for me to assume that you haven't heard about the alleged child prostitution scandal they recently published a story about?'

'I think my wife may have mentioned something

about it. Why?'

'And the man whose body was found at Swanton Morley? I don't suppose you know him, by any chance?'

'You mean – the story's true!' he exclaimed. 'Well, that's a first!'

'If you could answer the question, Mr Fletcher.'

'Actually, my name's Sir Charles Fletcher, but you can call me Sir Charles, if you prefer.'

'If you could answer the question, Sir Charles.'

'Sorry, what was it again?'

'I was asking if you knew the victim?'

'I didn't recognise his name, if that's what you mean?'

Tanner pulled out the list provided by the Norfolk Reporter's Editor-in-Chief. 'How about someone by the name of Robert Hanson?'

'Isn't he that fashion designer, the one who fell from grace when it was discovered that his clothes were all made by Indonesian sweat shops?'

'Does that mean you do know him?'

'Not personally, but I suppose it's possible that we've met. Maybe at a charity event?'

'Another name I have is Marcus Thornton?'

'Of Thornton Computers?'

'I believe so.'

'OK, well, again, I know *of* him.'

'And last, but by no means least, Derek Harvey?'

'Derek Harvey?' he repeated, looking wistfully away. 'I'm sorry, but the name doesn't ring a bell.'

'His body was found this morning,' Tanner added, glancing up. 'He was killed in very much the same way as the previous victim, Mr William Greenfield.'

'I'm sorry to hear that, but I'm still struggling to see what all this has to do with me?'

'We were given this list of names by the Editor-in-

Chief of the Norwich Reporter,' Tanner continued, holding the piece of paper up. 'It's in relation to their previously mentioned story, about the alleged child prostitution ring.'

'Uh-huh.'

'All the people on the list have been implicated by an unknown party.'

The sound of a car, making its way up the winding drive, had Fletcher glancing over his shoulder. 'Is this leading anywhere, Detective Inspector?'

'It's actually Detective *Chief* Inspector,' Tanner corrected, returning to him an accommodating smile.

'Sorry. Is this leading anywhere, Detective *Chief* Inspector?'

'Only that two of the people on the list have turned up dead. The bottom two, in fact, which makes me wonder if there's someone out there busily working their way up, which is where you come in. You see,' he continued, turning the piece of paper around for him to see, 'for some as yet unknown reason, the name at the top would appear to belong to you.'

- CHAPTER THIRTY THREE -

AS THE APPROACHING car began crunching its way over the drive, Fletcher pushed himself off his Bentley to wave at the driver, before leaning forward to catch Tanner's eye. 'May I see that list?'

'By all means,' Tanner replied, handing it over.

'You say this was given to you by the Editor-in-Chief of the Norwich Reporter?' he continued, casting his eyes over it.

'At just after half-past nine this morning.'

'And that two of them have been found dead?'

'The bottom two,' Tanner smiled.

'OK, well, I've no idea why my name's on here, but if you've come to warn me that there's some deranged lunatic wandering around Norfolk, with the intention of murdering me in my sleep, then I shouldn't worry. I have a twenty-four hour motion sensitive surveillance system surrounding the entire estate, each camera being monitored by myself, my secretary, and an outsourced private security firm. So if so much as a squirrel farts without asking permission beforehand, it wouldn't be long before I was told.'

Tanner took a moment to glance around the outside of the building, spotting various security cameras as he did. 'Even so, it may be wise for us to leave a police squad car at the end of your drive, especially as the gates were wide open when we arrived.'

'That won't be necessary,' he replied, as the sound of people climbing out of their car could be heard. 'The gates are normally closed. They most definitely are at night, but I'd certainly like to thank you for your concern. Now, if you'll excuse me.'

'There was just one more thing.'

'OK, but can you hold on for one second,' he replied, looking beyond Tanner's shoulder to call out, 'Steven! Mary! Thanks for coming! If you could go through to the conservatory, everyone's meeting up there.'

Tanner glanced around to see a smartly dressed couple wave back before making their way into the stately home.

'Sorry about that,' Fletcher continued. 'Please, do go on.'

'We couldn't help but notice what you were carrying out of your resplendent mansion when we arrived.'

'You mean, a twenty-year-old computer, one that hasn't worked in years?'

'May I ask why you've decided to throw it away?'

'Er...I thought I'd already said.'

'Only a few days after a newspaper article came out, together with evidence suggesting that you may have had something to do with a child prostitution ring?'

'Ah, I see what you're getting at. You think I'm throwing it out because it contains two decades worth of pictures featuring half-naked children. Well, it might have some, but they'd be of my own, probably when they were having a bath together at the age of three. You're quite welcome to it if you want. It would certainly save me a trip to the dump.'

'I also wanted to ask about your car?'

'Right, yes,' he replied, turning around to cast an admiring eye at it. 'Rather nice, don't you think?'

'I assume you know of another Norfolk resident by the name of George Elliston?'

'Of course! Why? He's not on this list as well, is he?' he asked, glancing back down.

'He isn't, but he does have a car that's remarkably similar to yours.'

'Does he, indeed! Then he's got more taste than I'd given him credit for.'

'May I ask how long you've had it?'

'Three years? Something like that. Speaking of cars,' he continued, gesturing at Tanner's, 'I used to have an XJS myself. Blue, instead of black. You don't see them very often. Not anymore. How do you find it? I always thought the steering was a little light, especially when you got above sixty. Thirsty buggers, as well.'

'It gets me from A to B,' Tanner replied. 'Going back to yours, if I may?'

'Yes, of course.'

'There was one just like it seen leaving Swanton Morley's church carpark at around the time we believe the victim, Mr Greenwood, was killed.'

Fletcher turned slowly back to meet Tanner's continuing gaze, his cold blue eyes set within his pale, triangular face making him look like a predatory wolf. 'I think you'll agree, Detective whatever your name is, that I've been just as nice as pie to both you and your lady policewoman friend,' he began, his unsettling gaze resting briefly on Vicky, 'despite what you've been insinuating; that I'm some sort of disgusting child sex offender. And now you're suggesting that I'm a psychotic serial killer as well! I'm sorry, but this really is too much. Thank God my children aren't around to hear what you're accusing me of. You should certainly be very grateful that my wife isn't! Did you know that her father is none other than Lord Jeffrey Hewitt? He could probably have you demoted down to the rank of traffic warden with just the click of a mouse. So anyway, I suggest you either arrest me for whatever it is that you think I've done, or get the fuck off my property, before I set the dogs on you.'

Tanner raised a curious eyebrow at Vicky. 'Sounds like it might be time for us to leave.'

Seeing her smile nervously back, he returned to find Fletcher, still glaring ominously at them. 'Thank you for your time, Sir Charles. We really do appreciate it.'

Within the blink of an eye, the man's expression changed from that of predatory wolf, to charming by-election candidate. 'No problem at all. The way out is the same way you came in. Just follow the road down. The gates should still be open.'

Beginning to lead Vicky away, Tanner stopped to spin suddenly around. 'Sorry, I almost forgot. Do you mind if we have that list back?'

'Be my guest,' he replied, handing it over.

'Actually, there was just one more thing.'

Fletcher presented Tanner with a malevolent snarl. 'You really are beginning to test my patience.'

'Would it be OK for us to send over a forensics team, to take a sample of your fingerprints and DNA?'

The man's demeaner remained unchanged.

'Inconvenient, I know,' Tanner continued, 'but it would at least allow us to eliminate you from our enquiries.'

'Of course, sorry! Would you like me to come down to the station?'

'No, that's fine. We'll send someone around. Would three o'clock this afternoon be convenient?'

Fletcher glanced down at a slim, sophisticated gold watch. 'Do you think they could make it four? I should be back from my canvassing by then.'

'Four o'clock it is, and thanks again!'

- CHAPTER THIRTY FOUR -

'DO YOU THINK they do have dogs?' Vicky queried, whispering over Tanner's shoulder as she followed him back to his car.

'I've no idea, but to be honest, I can't say that I was particularly keen to find out.'

'No. Me neither.'

'Nice chap, though,' Tanner added, reaching his car to look back at the house.

'I thought so.'

'I suppose hearing what he had to say for himself only left one real question.'

'Which was...?'

'Are you going to vote for him?'

Vicky stopped beside him to follow his gaze. 'I suppose that depends on if he's prepared to do something about all the bloody potholes down our road.'

'Not if he turns out to be a deranged, psychotic, serial-killing paedophile?'

'He's a politician with links to the British Aristocracy,' she shrugged back in response. 'What else were you expecting?'

'Good point.'

'I must admit,' Vicky continued, 'I am a little surprised that you didn't arrest him?'

'Why? Because he's a politician, or because he has links to the British Aristocracy?'

'More because of what we saw him hauling out of his over-sized house, and his reaction when he realised that he'd been caught doing so.'

'Unfortunately, I wasn't prepared to make the same mistake I made with Elliston. At the moment, the only evidence we have that he has anything to do with either the murders, or the paedophile allegations, is that his name is on that list. Speaking of which...' he continued, holding the piece of paper towards her from the edge of one of its corners, 'I don't suppose you have an evidence bag, lurking inside that handbag of yours?'

'You mean, just in case he isn't back by four o'clock?' she replied, rummaging around.

'Something like that. If it doesn't have his DNA on it, then it should at least have his fingerprints. I was about to ask if he wanted to take a look at it, wondering if he'd really be that stupid, when he asked to see it anyway.'

'Maybe he's not stupid,' Vicky replied, fishing out a large clear evidence bag to hold open for Tanner. 'Maybe he's simply innocent, and doesn't have things like fingerprints and DNA samples weighing heavily on his mind.'

Tanner looked wistfully away for a moment before saying, 'Nah! I'm fairly sure he's just stupid,' slipping the list carefully inside the bag. 'It's amazing how many things people go around touching without thinking about it. But just in case that doesn't bear fruit, if you could arrange for a forensic team to pay him a visit anyway, that would be useful.

'It may also be sensible for us to apply for a search warrant for his house and car. If he *was* throwing that old computer away because it did have two decades worth of child pornography stored on it, then there's every chance his other more up-to-date computer devices have something similar.'

'Then there's that car of his,' he continued, waiting for Vicky to replace the evidence bag with her notebook. 'Our forensic bods should be able to tell if it was the same one seen driving out of Swanton Morley carpark on Sunday night, simply by comparing mud samples taken from either the tyres, or under the wheel arches.'

'It still could have been Elliston's,' Vicky remarked.

'Very true, but he isn't the one who denied having been anywhere near the place.'

'Forensics should also be able to tell if Sir Charles's car was parked up next to that vehicle recovery van as well.

'After that, we need access to his phone records, email, computer, and social media accounts. Has he had any contact with the other people on the list, in particular the two that are already dead? If that second victim *had* been lured out to attend to a broken down vehicle, then someone must have called him to do so.'

As Vicky finished her notes, Tanner was about to open the door when he heard his phone ring from the depths of his sailing jacket.

Tugging it out to see it was the office, he answered it to place against his ear. 'Tanner speaking!'

'Hi, boss, it's Sally.'

'Ah, Sally! I assume you're calling to let me know that you've managed to organise that press conference?'

'I have. It's all set for two o'clock. But I was actually calling about Mr Elliston's holding extension. We've just heard back that it's been approved.'

'Christ! I'd almost forgotten about him.'

'You do still want us to keep him?' she queried. 'It's

just that his solicitor has been kicking up an awful fuss.'

'Unfortunately, I think we have to, at least until we hear back from forensics. How long can we keep him for now?'

'Until half-past eleven tonight.'

'OK, that should be long enough. Maybe you can keep them entertained until then.'

'Right. Actually, sorry, boss, but how would you like me to do that?'

'Just make them a coffee every now and again. That should suffice.'

'That's what I've been doing, which is how I know that the solicitor isn't happy. Neither is the suspect, for that matter.'

'Oh well, never mind. Whilst you're on the phone, I'm going to pass you over to Vicky. She's got a few more things for you to be getting on with.'

About to hand the phone over, he heard Sally call out, 'Before you go, my uncle asked you to call him.'

'Shit,' Tanner whispered, pulling the phone away from his mouth to grimace over at Vicky. 'Forrester's trying to get hold of me.'

'You sound surprised.'

'He probably wants to know if we've found Joseph Miller.'

'Or maybe he wants to know what you want for Christmas?'

Tanner thought for a moment. 'No. It's too soon. If it was November, maybe.'

'Hello?' came the tiny sound of Sally's voice. 'Are you still there?'

'Sorry, Sally. I was just discussing something with Vicky. I don't suppose you know what your uncle wants, by any chance?'

'Only that it had something to do with the Norfolk

Herald.'

Tanner removed the phone to once again stare over at Vicky. 'Sounds like he's seen that story.'

With Vicky doing nothing more useful than to shrug back at him with a particularly unhelpful expression, Tanner returned to his telephone conversation. 'I assume Cooper and Townsend are out looking for Joseph Miller?'

'They've just left.'

'They've *just* left?' Tanner repeated.

'They had to have lunch, first.'

Tanner slowly shook his head from side to side. 'Anyway, I'm going to hand you over to Vicky.'

'What should I say if my uncle calls again?'

'I don't suppose there's any chance you could say that you haven't been able to get hold of me?' Tanner asked, wincing as he did.

'You want me to lie to my own uncle?'

'If you wouldn't mind?' Tanner bravely continued.

'Sure! No problem!' came her eventual, and surprisingly agreeable response.

'Oh – right. Thank you!' Tanner replied, with a relieved smile. 'Here's Vicky for you now.'

- CHAPTER THIRTY FIVE -

WITH VICKY BUSILY chatting to Sally on Tanner's phone, they climbed back into his car to do a quick U-turn before heading back down the drive.

Reaching the end, Tanner pulled up just beyond the gates to whisper, 'What's the address for the next one?'

'The next one what?' Vicky replied, covering the mouthpiece.

'The next paedophile on that list.'

'You mean *alleged* paedophile,' she corrected, delving back into her handbag.

'Here you go,' she eventually said, holding out the evidence bag with the list inside.

Taking it from her, Tanner held it up to begin peering through the crumpled plastic. 'Is that *Magnus* Thornton or *Marcus* Thornton?' he eventually asked.

Vicky leaned towards him to take a look. 'It's Marcus.'

'And is that a four, or a seven?'

Vicky let out a forlorn sigh. 'Hold on, Sally. I'm going to have to call you back.'

'Sorry,' Tanner apologised, 'my eyes aren't what they used to be.'

'Apparently, neither is your brain,' she retorted.

Tanner stared back at her with a look of mock

reproach.

'Too much?' she queried, going a little red around the edges.

'A little,' he replied, 'but don't worry. My ego isn't such that I can't take a gentle ribbing.'

'Sorry, boss. Sometimes words just come flying out of my mouth without having asked permission before doing so.'

'As I said, it's fine. Besides, you're probably right. I'm fairly sure my brain hasn't been working properly since I turned forty. Less so since I became a father, again! Apparently, sleep deprivation does little for one's cognitive ability.'

'Anyway, I think it's a four.'

'Sorry, what's a four?'

'The postcode,' Vicky continued. 'NR4, which means he lives on the other side of Norwich.'

Tanner glanced down at the clock set within the varnished wooden dashboard. 'And that means we won't have time to drive all the way there, interview him, and then come back, not if I'm going to make the press conference.'

'Could someone else do it?'

'I could drop you off on the way?'

'Anyone apart from me?'

'Don't worry, it's fine. We can see him afterwards. But that does give us half an hour to kill. Do you think we'd be able to drop this list off at forensics on the way back?'

Vicky glanced down at her own watch. 'It will probably depend on traffic.'

'OK, well, I suggest we have a go. Otherwise, we'll probably end up having to wait for forensics to drive all the way up to Sir Charles's house, only to find he's not there, simply because he doesn't have any real intention of giving us his fingerprints and DNA, not unless he absolutely has to.'

- CHAPTER THIRTY SIX -

FORTY-FIVE MINUTES later, Tanner swung his XJS into Wroxham Police Station to see a veritable hoard of reporters, bustling between a line of cars on one side of the station's carpark, and the main entrance on the other.

Feeling his stomach instantly tighten, he steered his car discreetly around the back to haul himself unsteadily out.

'Are you ready for this?' asked Vicky, climbing out the other side.

'Not really,' he replied, making his way around.

'Do you have any idea what you're going to say?'

'Something about there being a deranged, serial-killing paedophile on the loose, but that there's no need to panic?'

'Sounds about right, but maybe leave out the part about him being a deranged serial-killing paedophile.'

'So, just that there's some random person missing, and that the panicking part is optional?'

'Um...' Vicky continued, stopping by the station's rear entrance door, 'perhaps keep the word deranged, but leave out everything else.'

'You mean... it's our belief that there's a particularly deranged individual, roaming the Norfolk countryside, with the diabolical intention of doing nothing in particular?'

'Sounds good to me!'

Tanner scowled at her to wrench the door open. 'When I become internationally famous, could you remind me *not* to ask you to write my speeches?'

'No problem!' she smiled, nudging her way past. 'Oh, and by the way, you're late!'

Following her inside, Tanner made himself a quick coffee before heading for the building's main entrance.

The moment he stepped outside, his eyes were blinded by an explosion of flash photography, whilst his ears were bombarded with a deafening deluge of incomprehensible questions.

Taking a calming sip from his scalding hot drink, he placed it down onto a table that had been left out to slowly hold up his hands.

After waiting for what seemed like an eternity, the endless questions eventually subsided to leave a hollow, restless silence, marred only by the rumble of cars, nudging their way past the journalists' collection of badly parked news media vans.

'Good morning, everyone,' he was eventually able to say.

'It's actually the afternoon,' someone corrected at the back, signalling a peel of laughter to ripple through the group.

As someone took yet another photograph, Tanner imagined the headline to accompany such a picture. "Senior Norfolk Police Officer Mistakes Morning for Afternoon."

'Thank you all for coming,' he continued, endeavouring to keep his mind focussed on the task at hand. 'I understand that some of you may have seen the recent story published in the Norwich Reporter over the weekend.'

'I think we're more interested in the one that came out in the Norfolk Herald this morning,' someone else called out, this time a woman at the front, with fierce green eyes and flaming red hair.

'If I could come back to that in a minute.'

'The one about the body over at Swanton Morley, found stabbed to death at the bottom of an open grave?' she continued.

'As I said, if I could...'

'Is it true that you had the culprit in custody?'

'No, it's not true,' Tanner stated, already feeling his blood pressure beginning to rise. 'The person who I believe you're referring to came into the station entirely of his own accord.'

'But you did let him go, though?'

'Yes, we did, but only because there was no evidence to support the theory that he had anything to do with what took place at Swanton Morley.'

'Apart from the fact that he was covered from head to toe in the victim's blood?'

'That is a gross exaggeration!'

'But he *did* have the victim's blood on him, though?'

With the realisation that he honestly didn't know the answer to that, as he'd never bothered to test it to see if it was the murder victim's blood or not, Tanner endeavoured to side-step the question. 'Just because a person has someone else's blood on them, doesn't automatically mean they're guilty of having done anything malicious to them.'

'Is it true that he was covered in mud as well, the exact same as was found at the bottom of the grave where the victim's body was discovered?'

'Again, if it was true, it wouldn't mean...

'And that he was carrying a knife, once again covered in the victim's blood?'

'Jesus Christ,' Tanner muttered to himself, wishing he'd had the foresight to read the Norfolk Herald's article *before* stepping out to face the nation's press.

Beginning to wonder where the newspaper in question had been getting their information from, or, more pertinently, who, he drew in a fortifying breath. 'Unfortunately, none of this means the suspect you're referring to is responsible.'

'Joesph Miller,' the same woman called out again.

'I'm sorry?'

'The suspect's name is Joseph Miller,' she repeated.

'Right, yes, thank you, but firstly, I'd appreciate it if you could stop bandying his name about all the time, and secondly, if you could think for a moment before automatically assuming that he's guilty. Thankfully, we live in a country where people are innocent until proven otherwise.'

'Did you know that he'd been diagnosed as a paranoid schizophrenic?'

'None of this is relevant,' Tanner stated, wondering how the hell they'd been able to miss that one.

'Did you also know that he'd been sexually abused as a child?'

As the entire carpark fell into an uncomfortable silence, Tanner opened his mouth, only to close it again as the reporter's words began to seep slowly down into his conscious mind. It was only then that he knew, with absolute certainty, that he'd made an unforgivable error of judgement. He'd allowed himself to become so closely embroiled in the investigation that he'd been unable to see the wood for the trees. He should have had his team do a full background check on Joseph Miller the moment he'd walked through the door, certainly before letting him go. There was a reason why the rank of DCI was supposed to be less hands-on; to ensure such amateurish, unprofessional mistakes like this didn't happen.

Standing there, gazing out at the slew of reporters, each and every single one of them waiting with bated breath to hear what he was going to say next, his thoughts turned to Christine, and their newborn baby. If he openly admitted to having not known about the suspect's medical condition, or what had happened to him as a child, he may as well go home to await a police tribunal. More so now, as it was clear that the troubled young man was most likely to have been the prime suspect after all, and that his decision to release him had indeed led to another person being brutally killed.

With his family, and the self-preservation of his career at the forefront of his mind, he knew he had no choice. He was simply going to have to deny the fact that he didn't know.

'We've been aware of the individual's troubled history for some time, thank you,' he blatantly lied, only to feel instantly guilty the moment he had, 'but please don't presume to know all the various ins-and-outs of this on-going murder investigation. There are a number of pertinent facts that you are simply unaware of. There are also other suspects we're in conversation with.'

'Can you tell us who they are?'

'Unfortunately, I can't, but as we didn't tell you who the first suspect was, I'm not exactly sure what difference it would make.'

His comment was received with a welcome round of laughter.

'That said,' he continued, 'thanks largely to the

Norfolk Herald's insightful article, we *would* like to invite Mr Miller back into the station, but for no other reason...' he was immediately forced to add, raising his voice above the sudden barrage of questions, '...for no other reason,' he repeated, 'than to make sure that he remains unharmed, especially with so many loyal and enthusiastic Norfolk Herald readers who are probably already roaming the streets looking for him.'

With the press pack becoming more settled, another voice arose from somewhere to the right. 'What about the story in the Norwich Reporter?'

'Yes, thank you. As I was about to explain earlier, we are of course aware of the article, and have already launched our own inquiries, a part of which was to meet with the newspaper's Editor-in-Chief, which proved to be particularly useful. As I'm sure you can appreciate, at this early stage, we don't have any details that we're able to share, but we are already having conversations with certain key individuals who may, or may not, be involved. Rest assured, the moment we have any more information for you, we will be back in touch.'

- CHAPTER THIRTY SEVEN -

LEAVING THE PRESS pack as he'd found them, bawling questions at him whilst taking pictures of what must have been nothing more interesting than the back of his head, Tanner marched back inside to find Vicky, appearing to be waiting for him in reception.

'How'd it go?' she asked, in a curious tone.

'Didn't you hear?' he asked, glancing furiously about.

'I was making myself a coffee.'

'Well, you didn't miss much. Any news from Cooper?'

'About what?'

'Joseph Miller!'

'I'm – er – not sure,' she replied, her forehead creasing into a questioning frown.

'What about Townsend?'

'I think he's still with Cooper.'

'OK, I want every available officer out looking for him.'

'Who? Cooper?'

Tanner turned to stare dementedly over at her. 'Why the hell would I want us to find Cooper?'

'Because, you just asked me where he was.'

'I asked if you'd heard from him, not if you knew where he was!'

'I'm sorry, boss. I'm confused. You want every

available officer out looking for Joseph Miller?'

Tanner glanced anxiously over his shoulder to see the duty sergeant, DS Taylor, skulking within earshot behind the reception's security screen.

Taking a firm hold of Vicky's elbow, he led her towards the doors leading through to the main office. 'The press have managed to unearth a couple of things about our Mr Miller which I should have made sure to have discovered *before* having allowed him to walk out the door,' he began, keeping his voice as low as possible, 'first, that he's a diagnosed paranoid schizophrenic, and second, he was sexually abused as a child.'

'Right,' Vicky replied, 'but...why does that suddenly mean we need to find him?'

'Because of that list of names, that there would appear to be someone steadily working their way through it, and that the person responsible could well be one of their victims, deciding to take his own form of justice.

'Even if it doesn't turn out to be Miller,' Tanner continued, 'and he has nothing to do with any of this, I simply can't afford to take that risk, not when I was the one stupid enough to let him walk out the very door he'd only shuffled his way through a few hours before, looking every bit as if he *had* stabbed the first victim to death at the bottom of an open grave.'

'OK, yes, I see your point.'

'I'm also not prepared to take the chance that he's not already on his way to pay a visit to those remaining on the list. Who do we have left to see?'

Vicky pulled out her notebook. 'Marcus Thornton and Robert Hanson. We were on our way to see Thornton before we made the detour to come here.'

'Then I suggest we revert back to our original plan. When you get hold of either Cooper or Townsend, give them Robert Hanson's address, and tell them to head straight over there. Meanwhile, I'm going to get everyone else out looking for Miller.'

'What should I tell Cooper to do when they get there?' she asked, replacing her notebook for her phone.

'Just tell them to make sure Hanson is OK, and that we'll be with them as soon as we can.'

'What about Sir Charles Fletcher?'

'We've already warned him of the potential danger. It's up to him if he decides to heed our advice.'

- CHAPTER THIRTY EIGHT -

AS VICKY SPOKE on the phone with both Cooper and Townsend, relaying Tanner's orders for them to head straight over to Robert Hanson's house, Tanner quickly briefed the office, instructing them that Joseph Miller needed to be found as a priority, before meeting her at his car. There, they continued on their way to where Marcus Thornton supposedly lived; what turned out to be a dishevelled, average-sized Edwardian house, located along a quiet tree-lined avenue on the other side of Norwich.

Parking on the road outside, they made their way up a lopsided concrete footpath to eventually ring the bell of a badly painted front door.

After a minute or two of hearing nothing in response, Tanner rang the bell again.

'It doesn't sound like he's in,' commented Vicky, stepping back to stare up at the windows.

'Do we know where he works?'

'Well, he doesn't sell computers anymore. I know that much!'

'OK. Let's try once more, then I suggest we ask a neighbour.'

About to press the bell again, they heard the sound of someone closing a car door behind them.

Glancing around, they saw a robust, elderly woman, staring at them from beside a beaten-up Fiat

Uno.

'Are you looking for Mr Thornton?' she called out, far louder than was necessary.

'We are indeed,' Tanner replied. 'I don't suppose you know if he's in?'

'He should be,' she called back, shuffling around to open the car's creaking boot.

Hauling out a shopping bag filled with groceries, she gazed back at them to ask, 'Is he not answering?'

'He doesn't seem to be.'

'Then he's probably watching TV,' she replied, closing the boot to begin trundling up the path towards them. 'Are you friends of his?'

'Er...not exactly.'

Reaching the doorstep they were standing on, she stopped to take each of them in with narrowing eyes. 'You're not here to sell him something, I hope?'

Tanner and Vicky glanced around at each other.

'If you are, then he's not interested!' she stated, with categorical certainty.

'We're not trying to sell him anything, Mrs...?'

'Larkin. I'm Mr Thornton's domestic help.'

'Nice to meet you, Mrs Larkin. I don't suppose you have a key, by any chance? We're just keen to make sure he's OK.'

'Oh, I'm sure he's fine!' she replied, barging between them like a miniature tank.

Forced off the step, they watched her lift the doormat to retrieve a key, lurking underneath.

'Impressive security,' muttered Tanner, quietly to Vicky.

'What was that?' she demanded.

'I was just saying that's a very nice key,' Tanner replied, lifting his voice to match her own.

'There's no need to shout! I'm not deaf!'

Tanner turned to find Vicky wagging a scolding

finger at him.

Realising the elderly lady had opened the door and was already halfway through, Tanner called after, 'I assume it's OK for us to come inside?'

Just when he thought she hadn't heard him, he was about to go in anyway, when she turned on her heel to fix his eyes with a questioning glare.

'Are you sure you're not here to sell him anything? It's just that he finds it very difficult to say no. The last time I came round, I found an entire front door, propped up in the hallway, which he definitely didn't need, being that he's already got one.'

'It must have been someone selling doors, door-to-door,' Tanner commented, under his breath.

'What was that?'

'I promise we're not here to sell him anything, Mrs Larkin,' he replied. 'We've simply come around to see if he's in, and to make sure he's OK, of course.'

'Oh, he's in, alright,' she continued, turning back. 'I can hear the television from here.'

Following her inside to hear the muffled sound of the afore mentioned TV, blaring out from somewhere, Tanner looked to the right to see that there was indeed a brand new door, resting against a badly stained, mould-covered wall.

Looking ahead, he saw the old woman come grinding to a halt, shaking her head at a large potted plant, lying discarded on its side.

'Mr Thornton!' she yelled, glancing at a door behind her. 'You know that plant in the hall? When you do happen to knock it over, could you at least make the effort to pick it up again?'

Hearing nothing back in response, she turned to beckon them forward. 'If you go through, I'll pop the kettle on.'

As she disappeared through a door to the left, they

proceeded inside.

'Can I make the two of you a cup of tea?' they heard her bellow.

'Er...' Tanner began, glancing at Vicky to find her vigorously shaking her head. 'No thanks!' he called back, beckoning Vicky to follow him towards the door they'd been directed to.

Unsure whether it was really alright for them to simply walk in, he decided to at least knock first. 'Hello, Mr Thornton? Is it alright if we come in?'

Still unable to hear anything apart from the blaring TV, he gingerly placed his hand on the handle to nudge the door open.

'Mr Thornton?' he repeated, lifting his voice above the sound of explosions, gunshots, and men yelling at each other in thick German accents.

As he leaned his head cautiously inside, he saw what was causing the ruckus. In the far corner of a musty-smelling room was an enormous widescreen television, lighting the area with intense flashing black and white images from what appeared to be an old World War Two film.

'Mr Thornton?' he enquired again, taking a cautionary step inside to see the place was filled with all manner of junk, either piled high against the walls, or simply left lying in heaps in the middle of the room.

Noticing a thick pair of curtains, blocking virtually every shard of sunlight from outside, he found a light switch on the wall to turn it on.

With the room filling with yellow, unnatural light, he was forced to blink at the image of a man's pale, bloated, half-naked body, appearing on the carpet in front of him, a blood-soaked white vest covering his huge, barrel-like chest, whilst his trousers were caught around his ankles.

Finding himself unable to move, his eyes struggled

to take in the full horror of the scene being presented to him.

The sound of a tea tray, rattling its way down the hallway behind him, had his eyes jolting up from the man's ugly bare feet to notice something he'd failed to see, or had deliberately chosen not to. Where the man's exposed genitalia should have been, hanging between his wide hairy thighs, was a lump of congealed blood. It took him a full moment to realise that the missing part of his male anatomy wasn't missing at all. It was hanging half-out of his twisted, crooked mouth.

Hearing the tea tray rattle again, he wrenched his eyes off the body to spin quickly around, hoping to stop the old lady from seeing what was left of her former employer. But he was too late. She'd already barged past Vicky to station herself between the door and him, gawping open-mouthed at the body he'd only just been looking at himself.

'Mrs Larkin,' he began to say, doing his best to block her view, 'if perhaps you could make your way back to the kitchen?'

But she didn't move. She didn't even blink. Only her eyes could be seen drifting first up, then down, much as Tanner's had been doing just moments before.

As Tanner re-opened his mouth to try to persuade her to move away, the tea tray slipped from her withered hands to clatter against the floor, her trembling lips inching slowly open for her to eventually let out a terrifying scream.

- CHAPTER THIRTY NINE -

IT TOOK OVER fifteen minutes for the first police squad car to finally arrive. During that time, Tanner and Vicky extracted themselves from the scene whilst making sure to neither touch, nor disturb anything they hadn't already.

When the first squad car eventually arrived, Tanner left Vicky with Mrs Larkin, trying to calm her down, to greet the two unfamiliar police constables stepping out. Once he'd introduced himself, he ordered them not to go inside, but instead to begin sealing off the property, from the front door, all the way down to the gate at the end of the path.

When the ambulance came a few minutes later, he was forced to spend a further few minutes dissuading the paramedics from entering the property as well, explaining that it was now an official crime scene, and that the victim inside was a long way past saving.

It was only when Haverstock arrived did the situation change from one of professional control to hostile aggression.

'May I respectfully ask what the hell you're doing here?' the detective inspector demanded, the moment he saw Tanner strolling towards his car.

Knowing full well that he didn't have the authority to be anywhere near the place, Tanner hesitated before answering. 'We were chasing a lead,' he eventually replied.

'Relating to which investigation?'

'The alleged child prostitution.'

Haverstock wrapped his arms over his chest. 'Did Forrester give you permission to be here?'

'Well, no, but...'

'But you thought you'd come anyway?'

'I suggest you take a moment to remind yourself as to who you're speaking to, Detective Inspector Haverstock.'

'I apologise, Detective Chief Inspector Tanner, but may I take a moment to remind you that this isn't your jurisdiction. You're more than welcome to come over here, of course, but not before having acquired the necessary authorisation first. At the very least, you could have given us a call before doing so.'

'I apologise once again, but unfortunately, there simply wasn't time.'

'I see. And how long did it take for you to drive here? Long enough to pick up the phone, surely!'

With Tanner remaining silent, Haverstock was left to continue.

'Maybe you should consider how you would feel if you arrived at one of your crime scenes to find *me* traipsing all over it?'

Tanner knew Haverstock was right. However, the man didn't know the circumstances behind his decision to drive over. Why he didn't was simple: because Tanner hadn't told him!

'I've asked your men to seal off the area,' Tanner eventually responded, deliberately changing the subject.

'That's exceptionally kind of you.'

'I also told the paramedics not to enter the property, to help preserve the crime scene. However, you will unfortunately find my fingerprints inside, possibly my colleague, DI Gilbert's, as well.'

'I assume you've seen the body?'

Tanner nodded in response. 'He's a man in his mid-to-late sixties, probably around six-foot, weighing upwards of a hundred kilograms.'

As he began to answer, Haverstock reluctantly pulled out a notebook and pen.

'From my brief examination of the scene,' Tanner continued, 'I'd say he opened the door to his attacker. At that point, there may have been a struggle, possibly knocking over a houseplant in the hall. From the location of the blood, I'd say the main attack happened just beyond the door of the room he can be found in, where it looked as if he was stabbed several times in the chest, very much like the previous victims.'

'Was it you who found the body?'

'It was,' he replied, with solemn reverence. 'We rang the doorbell, but there was no response. That's when the victim's domestic help arrived, who invited us in. She found a key hidden under the doormat, proceeding to direct us through to a room at the back of the house, from where the sound of a TV could be heard. I think we all assumed him to be alive and well, and simply hadn't heard the doorbell, thanks to the television's excessive volume.'

'Has the victim been identified?'

'We believe his name is Mr Marcus Thornton,' Tanner confirmed. 'At least, that's who the domestic help seemed to think it was.'

'Has she given a formal statement?'

'Not yet, but she's in quite a state.'

'OK,' Haverstock sighed, forcing a smile at Tanner as he put his notebook away. 'With the formalities out the way, may I ask what brought you here in the first place?'

'As I said, we were following a lead.'

'I don't suppose it would be possible for you to be a little more specific?' he politely asked.

Tanner drew in a reticent breath. He really didn't wish to have to spend half an hour explaining the ins-and-outs of what he really did feel had become *his* investigation. However, he also knew that he should have been sharing what he'd learnt from the moment he'd shown up at Swanton Morley's church graveyard.

Deciding to only tell him what he felt was necessary, Tanner opened his mouth. 'I sat down with the Editor-in-Chief of the Norwich Reporter yesterday, regarding the child prostitution story they ran over the weekend. He provided me with a list of five names, all of which were accused of being involved by some unknown source. As it currently stands, three of them have now turned up dead.'

'May I ask who the remaining two are?'

'One's none other than Sir Charles Fletcher, who's currently running in the forthcoming by-election. The other is someone by the name of Robert Hanson, who I believe used to be something in fashion. I've got two members of my CID team currently sitting outside his house as we speak, making sure he remains unharmed, which reminds me...' he muttered, digging out his phone to check for messages.

'Does any of this relate to the story that came out in the Norfolk Herald this morning?'

'You've seen that, have you?' Tanner replied, relieved to see nobody had called.

'Well yes, of course. Certainly everyone over at Westfield Station has. It's become compulsory reading, if for no other reason than for its pure entertainment value.'

'I must admit,' Tanner replied, 'I used to dislike it

with a passion, but it's recently begun to grow on me.'

'You mean, like a tropical skin disease?'

Tanner found himself laughing. Against his better judgement, he was beginning to warm to the man standing in front of him.

'Anyway, I suppose I'd better get on,' Haverstock continued, offering Tanner an affable smile. 'If you think I can be of any help in any way, just give me a call. Oh, and if you are able to let me know the next time you're planning on coming over this way, it would be appreciated.'

- CHAPTER FORTY -

ALLOWING HIM TO pass, Tanner turned to see Vicky, chatting to Alison Westwood, the medical examiner they'd only been talking to a few hours before, heaving out various items from her car.

'Afternoon, Alison!' he said, stepping over to join them.

'Ah, you're here as well?' she queried, glancing up.

'Wherever I go, bodies seem to follow.'

'You should get a job as an undertaker,' she laughed. 'You'd make an absolute fortune!'

Tanner looked wistfully away. 'Now, why hadn't I thought of that?'

'DI Gilbert was just telling me that the modus operandi would appear to be the same as the previous two; an adult male with multiple stab wounds to the chest, the only difference being that his genitalia had been removed, with the anatomical items in question left hanging out of the poor man's mouth.'

'That did *appear* to be the case, although I can't say that I spent a huge amount of time examining the anatomical items in question to be sure that was what they were.'

'Assuming they are, for the victim's sake, let's hope they were removed after he died.'

'Quite!' Tanner agreed, full-heartedly.

'Vicky and I were actually discussing if the fact that

they had could shed some light on the assailant's gender?'

'In what way?'

'That it was something perhaps more likely to have been done by a woman than a man?'

Tanner paused to consider the idea.

'It was just a thought, really,' Alison continued, with an apologetic shrug. 'I've certainly never heard of a man mutilating another in such a horrific manner. In most instances, it's a woman, normally after having been raped by the man in question.'

'Well, it's certainly an interesting thought,' Tanner mused. 'The only problem is, we don't have any female suspects.'

'Maybe it's someone you don't know about yet?'

'Very possibly, but at this stage, I'm more interested to find out why whoever did this didn't do something similar to the other two victims. If they hadn't done before, why start now?'

'Maybe the opportunity wasn't there?' proposed Vicky. 'Or maybe it's a question of them becoming more confident?'

Tanner turned to face her. 'Or maybe we should be looking for two people, instead of one?'

With the question left hanging in the air, Alison closed the boot of her car. 'I'd better leave you two to it.'

'Sorry, before you go,' Tanner said, catching her eye, 'I hate to ask, but...I don't suppose you have any more news on those other two post mortems?'

Alison stopped where she was to offer him a guilty grimace. 'I seem to remember promising to have something over to you by end-of-play today.'

'I believe you did,' Tanner sheepishly confirmed.

'OK, well, we'll have to see, but to be honest, when I agreed to that, I wasn't expecting to have yet another body to deal with, only about four hours later.'

- CHAPTER FORTY ONE -

'SHE SEEMS ALRIGHT,' commented Vicky, as they watched the medical examiner march her way towards the house with a large black holdall swung over her shoulder that was almost as big as she was.

'Better than grumpy-old Johnstone,' Tanner muttered.

'I like grumpy-old Johnstone!' Vicky exclaimed, staring back at him with an accusatory glare.

'Me too. He's great. The best medical examiner ever. He'd be even better if he was around to help. Maybe I could give him a call, and they could take a body each?'

'But – that would leave one of them with two, which hardly seems fair.'

'Then perhaps we could cut each one in half? They could then be divided more evenly.'

Vicky took a moment to stare at him. 'I do hope you're joking?'

'Only in part. Six parts, to be precise.'

Vicky shook her head to look back at the house. 'I don't suppose you read anything into where the victim's genitalia were placed?'

'In relation to what?'

'That it may have been for a reason?'

'The reason being that the man enjoyed giving oral sex to other men, whether they wanted him to or not, so why shouldn't he enjoy the taste of his own, before shuffling off this mortal coil?'

'Er…I was actually thinking that it may have been a message, warning others to keep their mouths shut.'

'Oh, right. Yes. That does make more sense.'

'Or maybe,' Vicky continued, 'the reason why he was the only victim to have had it cut off to be left hanging out of his mouth was because he was the one who'd leaked all their names to the press?'

Tanner tilted his head to take Vicky in with a quizzical expression. 'Tell me, Vicky, have you ever considered a job in the police? Maybe working for CID as a detective inspector?'

'Not really,' she smiled.

'OK, well, let me know if you change your mind. You've clearly got a knack for it.'

'So…what do you think?'

'I think I'm going to give that Editor-in-Chief chap a call,' he replied, digging out his phone. 'We've reached a point where we need to know who gave him those names, whether he wants to tell us or not.'

'I thought journalist didn't have to reveal their sources?'

'I think that depends,' Tanner replied, lifting the phone to his ear.

'On what?'

'On whether or not he wants to have a couple of bags of heroine planted behind his fridge.'

'Er…I could be wrong, but I think that could be described as witness intimidation.'

'Only if I meant it.'

'I'm not exactly sure that would matter.'

Tanner lifted his hand as someone answered the phone. 'Hello, is that Simon Reynolds?'

'Yes, speaking!'

'Sorry to bother you,' Tanner began, putting the

call onto speaker phone. 'It's Detective Chief Inspector Tanner, Norfolk Police.'

With the line falling silent, Tanner glanced curiously at Vicky. 'We met the other day?' he added. 'When you came over to see me?'

'Sorry, yes, of course! You had me worried there for a minute,' he laughed. 'How can I help?'

'It's about that list of names you gave me.'

'Uh-huh.'

'You told me that they'd come from a certain individual, together with the story itself. I was wondering, well, hoping really, that you'd be able to tell me who that individual was?'

'I'm very sorry, Chief Inspector, but as I think I mentioned at the time...'

'You can't reveal your sources,' Tanner said, finishing the sentence for him.

'That's correct, I'm afraid. As I'm sure you're aware, we're protected under the Contempt of Court Act, as are our sources. From memory, I think it's section 10.'

Holding the phone away, Tanner whispered to Vicky, 'Could you look that one up for me?'

Seeing her nod to dive into her handbag, Tanner resumed his telephone conversation. 'If you really think you're unable to, could you at least confirm a name, if I was to give you one?'

'Ah, right, well – you see, if you *were* to give me a name, and it did turn out to be the story's source, I'd still be unable to confirm it, as I'd effectively still be telling you who it was.'

'Would it make any difference if I was to tell you that of the five people on that list of yours, no less than three have turned up dead?'

After a moment's silence, Reynolds voice came back over the line. 'I'm sorry to hear that, really I am, but it doesn't make any difference, I'm afraid.'

'What if your source was one of those already dead, and confirming his identity could help prevent the remaining two from being killed?'

'The relevant law is to help protect us, as much as it is to protect our sources.'

Swearing under his breath, Tanner saw Vicky urgently beckoning his attention.

'Hold on a second, will you?' he asked, holding the phone away once more.

'I've found the relevant law,' she said, in a conspiratorial tone, before beginning to read from her phone. '"No court may require a person to disclose, nor is any person guilty of contempt of court for refusing to disclose, the source of information contained in a publication for which he is responsible."'

'This really isn't very helpful,' muttered Tanner.

'"...unless..."' she continued, glancing up, '"it can be established, to the satisfaction of the court, that disclosure is necessary in the interests of justice, or national security, or for the prevention of disorder, or crime."'

Tanner smiled gratefully at her as he returned to the call. 'Mr Reynolds, we've just looked up the relevant section of the Contempt of Court Act.'

'So you understand where I'm coming from.'

'Insomuch as it says that you have the legal right to withhold the name of your source. However, it also says that the law doesn't apply if the matter relates to the prevention of either public disorder, or in this particular instance, crime.'

'Either way, Chief Inspector, it makes no difference.'

'Er…I'm sorry, Mr Reynolds, but I really think it does.'

'It doesn't make any difference because I couldn't tell you the name, even if I wanted to.'

'And why's that, may I ask?'

'Because, the information was from an anonymous source.'

'You're saying that you don't know who it was?'

'That's correct.'

'But – if that's the case – how were you able to verify the story?'

The line fell silent again.

'Are you honestly telling me,' Tanner continued, in a low, dangerous tone, 'that you published a story without bothering to verify if it was true or not?'

'We had every reason to believe that it was.'

'But you don't know?'

'As I said, we had every reason to believe...'

'Jesus Christ! Do you have any idea what you've done? You've gone and published what could be a complete work of fiction, whilst at the same time providing the names and addresses of five people who some random person could simply have a personal dislike for. And now, three of those people are dead!'

'I'm sorry, but you can't pin that on us. We didn't publish the names.'

'But you did publish the story, before handing the names out to whoever happened to ask for them.'

'The only person I gave them to was you.'

'What about your staff at the newspaper?'

'Only those working on my editorial team.'

'So, the only people who knew the names on that list were me, you, your editorial team, everyone they decided to tell down the nearest pub, and the rest of Norfolk shortly afterwards?'

'I can assure you, Chief Inspector, that those working on my editorial team are the very soul of discretion.'

'You may think they are, Mr Reynolds, but I sincerely doubt if that's actually the case. It's hard enough to keep a room full of police officers quiet, let alone a bunch of journalists who spend half their lives down the pub, and the other half making up the most sensationalist stories imaginable for the delight of their readership.'

'My staff neither spend half their lives down the pub, nor do they just make up what they write, and I take offence at the idea that they do!'

'I don't give a shit what you take offence at!' Tanner replied, almost shouting. 'If I find out that three completely innocent men have been murdered over a story that you failed to take a single step to verify, I'll be recommending that Norfolk Police takes legal action against you, your entire editorial team, and whoever owns that bloody newspaper of yours for criminal negligence. And once you've all been found guilty, I wish you the very best in finding another job, after you've been released from prison, of course, unless it involves handing out someone else's newspaper, probably whilst standing outside a train station at five o'clock in the fucking morning.'

- CHAPTER FORTY TWO -

'DID YOU HEAR that?' baulked Tanner, stabbing at his phone to bring the call to an unceremonious end.

'Didn't everyone?' questioned Vicky, glancing surreptitiously about at the surrounding emergency personnel, all carrying on with their business whilst pretending not to have been listening.

'That Idiot-in-Chief published a story based on nothing more than some random, unsubstantiated source, who probably made the whole thing up just to get back at some moronic old friends of his.'

'Yes, I know. You had the speakerphone on, remember?'

'Which means our entire theory; that the people on the list are working together as part of some child prostitution scheme, and that someone is killing them off, one at a time, who is either one of their old victims, or is someone on the list, looking to silence them, has just been flushed down the proverbial toilet!'

'Unless the story is true,' commented Vicky, 'which would mean we're still on the right track.'

'But we don't know, though, do we!'

'No, we don't,' she agreed, 'but in fairness, we didn't know before, either.'

With his phone still clenched in his hand, Tanner stared down at the pavement to draw in a calming breath.

'One thing that hasn't changed,' Vicky continued, 'is that we still have the bodies of three men, each killed using the same method, and each one on a list given to us by a local newspaper, which means we still have a murderer to find, preferably before he, or maybe she, reaches the end of the list in question.'

'I suppose,' Tanner agreed, somewhat begrudgingly. 'Have you heard anything from Cooper?'

Vicky shook her head. 'I assume they're parked outside the house of the last person on the list, Mr Hanson.'

'They haven't called, to confirm that they are?'

'Well, no, but they haven't called to say they aren't, either.'

Tanner's thumb hovered undecidedly over his phone. 'I better give them a call anyway, just to be sure.'

Dialling Cooper's number, Tanner pressed his phone impatiently against his ear. 'Cooper it's Tanner,' he said, a moment later. 'Just calling to see how you've been getting on?'

'All right, I suppose,' came Cooper's petulant response. 'Any idea how long we have to stay here for? I mean, it's hardly the most exciting job in the world.'

'You're outside Mr Hanson's house, yes?'

'As instructed.'

'And he's OK?'

'Well, we haven't seen him come out, if that's what you mean.'

'But you have seen him, though?'

'Not yet, but as I said, he hasn't come out.'

Tanner bashed his fist against his head. 'You were supposed to drive over there to make sure he was alright!' he seethed.

'We were told to park outside his house to make sure he was OK. Nobody said anything about going inside.'

'How the hell can you make sure he's OK by simply parking outside his fucking house?'

'By not letting anyone go inside, like a serial-killing paedophile, for example.'

'Please God, tell me you're joking?'

'I'm sorry, but why would I be joking?'

Casting his eyes up to the sky, Tanner took a moment to try and calm down. 'Is Townsend with you?' he eventually asked.

'He's sitting next to me.'

'OK, I want the two of you to step out of your car, go up to Mr Hanson's front door, and ring the doorbell. If he doesn't have one, then use the door knocker. Failing that, just bash on the bloody thing with your fists until someone answers.'

'And if nobody does?'

'Then I want you to break the bloody thing down, by whatever means necessary; and call me the minute you have.'

'If you say so.'

'Actually, don't bother calling,' Tanner continued, tugging open his car door. 'We're on our way over there now.'

- CHAPTER FORTY THREE -

FURIOUS WITH COOPER for having been so unbelievably stupid, Tanner gestured for Vicky to climb into his XJS for them to begin speeding their way back to the other side of Norwich, and the address they already had for the final person on the list, Mr Robert Hanson.

Half an hour later, with a sickening feeling at the base of his stomach, Tanner sped them around the bend of another suburban road to see what he'd been dreading since ending the call; a long line of police and emergency vehicles parked on one side, with a row of traffic backed-up behind them.

'It might not be what it looks like,' commented Vicky, quietly beside him.

'I think it's exactly what it looks like,' growled Tanner. 'Even Johnstone is here!' he added, gesturing at the medical examiner's boxy Volvo Estate with his chin.

'At least we're back on familiar ground.'

'Do you have to be quite so positive all the bloody time?' Tanner snapped, wrenching the steering wheel over to bring his car wallowing to an ungainly halt.

'You'd prefer me to be lazy, argumentative, disrespectful, and pessimistic, like Cooper?'

Seeing the prematurely ageing detective inspector she was referring to, leaning against his car about fifty feet up the road, Tanner wrenched on the handbrake.

'Sorry, I take it back. Please remain exactly as you are.'

'I'm delighted to hear it,' she gracefully replied, opening the door to swing herself out.

Doing the same, Tanner followed her up a pavement towards a house near the top of the hill, where numerous uniformed police officers could be seen, most of whom he recognised.

Spying Townsend talking to one of them, looking considerably paler than he remembered him to be, he lifted a hand to garner his attention.

'Sorry about all this, boss,' the young DC said, with an apologetic grimace.

'It's not your fault,' Tanner replied, glaring with disgruntled disdain over at Cooper, doing nothing more productive than staring idly down at his phone.

'I don't think it's Cooper's fault, either,' Townsend continued. 'Doctor Johnstone says the victim's been dead for several hours. Long before we got here.'

'That's not the point, Townsend.'

'No, of course. You're right. We should have taken a look when we first arrived.'

'Yes, well. It would be nice to hear Cooper apologise,' Tanner mumbled. 'Anyway, I don't suppose there's all that much we can do about it now.'

Dragging his eyes off Cooper, who seemed to be blissfully unaware of his presence there, Tanner stared up at the very normal looking semi-detached house. 'I assume it's the same as the others?'

'The victim had been stabbed multiple times in the chest,' Townsend nodded, 'but there was one rather obvious difference.'

'He'd had his genitalia removed to be left inside his mouth?'

Townsend gazed over at him with a mystified expression. 'How did you know?'

'The other guy was left in a similar predicament. Is there anything else I need to be aware of?'

'It would appear that the attacker forced his way inside, the moment the door was opened.'

'Has the body been identified?'

'We're fairly sure it's Hanson. We found his driver's licence inside his wallet in the hall.'

'Time of death?'

'Johnstone thinks it must have been sometime between six and nine this morning.'

'Have you spoken to the neighbours?'

'The ones that are in.'

'Did they see anything?'

Townsend shook his head. 'They didn't hear anything, either.'

'And have you both given statements?'

'We have.'

'OK, then you may as well get back out in search of Joseph Miller.'

'Yes, boss,' he replied, standing to attention before ducking away.

'Before you go,' Tanner called after him, 'could you ask Cooper to arrange a squad car to position itself outside the gates of Sir Charles Fletcher's stately home? Maybe you could remind him that they'll need to make sure he's alive first, before doing so?'

'No problem, boss.'

'Also,' Tanner continued, glancing earnestly around at the dozen or so police personnel, 'can you tell everyone here that if they don't have a specific role, then they need to rejoin you in the hunt for Miller. Our priority remains for us to find him, now more than ever!'

- CHAPTER FORTY FOUR -

'DO YOU WANT me to go with them?' asked Vicky, watching Townsend navigate his way between two stationary vehicles to join Cooper, still staring vacantly down at his phone.

Tanner glanced back to the house to see Johnstone appear beside the front door. 'Stay with me for now,' he replied, making his way towards him. 'I just want to have a very quick word with our medical examiner.'

'Detective Chief Inspector Tanner!' Johnstone called out, in a cheerful tone. 'I haven't seen you for weeks! Two, in fact!'

'I've been treading on people's toes on the other side of Norwich,' Tanner replied, sidling up a path towards him.

'So I've been told. I also hear you've met my counterpart, Mrs Westwood?'

'Only three times,' he replied, gazing nostalgically away, 'or was it four? Sorry, I seem to have lost count.'

'With the amount of work you've been sending her way, she probably has as well! Still, at least it's given me some much needed time off. Speaking of which, how was that honeymoon of yours?'

'Good, whilst it lasted.'

'And congratulations, by the way!'

'Er...congratulations for what?'

'Didn't you come back with a baby?'

'Of course. Sorry. I'm not sure how, but I'd almost

managed to forget,' he laughed.

'All is well, I assume?'

'Apart from the normal torturous lack of sleep, we're all fine, thank you.'

'Newborn babies and sleep deprivation always seem to go hand in hand.'

Being reminded of just how tired he was, Tanner found himself desperately trying to suppress a yawn.

'I suppose you'd like a quick tour?'

'I had enough of those in Spain,' Tanner replied, 'but I suppose one more won't do any harm.'

'OK, well, if you follow me, the victim is in the kitchen,' Johnstone responded, turning to lead Tanner and Vicky into a narrow, dimly lit hallway, to bring them to an eventual halt beside an open wooden door.

Stepping cautiously through, Tanner peered inside to see the body of another half-naked man, this time bent awkwardly backwards over the top of a kitchen island, fragments of shattered cups and plates scattered across a blood-splattered floor.

'I suspect the victim opened the front door for his assailant before they made their way in here. There's no sign of a struggle in the hallway, so I'd have thought it's likely he either knew his visitor, or was comfortable enough to invite them inside. Either way, once here it looks like he was pushed against the island to be stabbed no less than fourteen times in the chest. Thankfully, for the victim at least, his genitalia were removed post-mortem.'

Tanner lifted himself up onto the balls of his feet to see the anatomical items in question, hanging out of the victim's mouth, much like they had been before.

'Do you think it would have been possible for the attacker to have been a woman?' queried Tanner.

'That would probably depend on if the assailant had to fight their way in, but as I said, there's no indication that they did, so I don't see why not.'

Continuing to stare at the body, Tanner folded his arms over his chest to rest a pensive finger against his chin. 'Left or right handed?'

'The stab wounds are from the right hand side.'

'Townsend said you estimate the time of death to be between six and nine this morning,' Tanner continued, his gaze shifting away from the body to take in the scene. 'Is that correct?'

'Something like that.'

'I don't suppose the weapon has been found, by any chance?'

'Not that I've heard.'

'And when do you think you'll have a post-mortem report?'

'Until about an hour ago, I didn't have all that much on. But now you're back,' he frowned. 'How about first thing tomorrow?'

'Tomorrow will be fine, thank you.'

- CHAPTER FORTY FIVE -

LEADING VICKY OUTSIDE, Tanner stopped on the path to watch two squad cars pull out to begin following Cooper's bullet-grey Audi.

Taking a moment to collect his thoughts, he looked down at his watch. 'It's getting late,' he eventually said, glancing around at Vicky. 'I'd better give you a lift back to the station. We can decide where you go from there.'

As they made their way back to his car, Tanner was about to climb inside when he heard the muffled sound of his phone ring from the depths of his sailing jacket.

Digging it out to see it was Forrester, he flinched as he recalled the last time they'd spoken, when his superintendent had bawled him out over his mishandling of the first suspect, the man Tanner had now become so desperate to find.

'It's Forrester,' he whispered to Vicky, over the Jag's low sloping roof. 'I'd better take it. If you can wait in the car, I'll try not to be too long.'

Seeing her nod, he turned away to lift the phone to his ear. 'Tanner speaking!'

'Good evening, Tanner. It's your long forgotten boss, Superintendent Forrester.'

'Yes, sir. Sorry I haven't been in touch. It's just been a particularly busy day.'

'Where are you?'

'With Vicky, outside Robert Hanson's house.'

'He's the fourth victim on that list of names of yours, yet another victim who's been stabbed multiple times in the chest?'

'You know about that, do you?'

'With nobody bothering to update me, I've started listening to the police radio.'

'Oh, right!' Tanner replied, unable to tell if he was being serious.

'I've also been chatting with Haverstock.'

Tanner rolled his eyes. 'I suppose he's been moaning about me traipsing all over his crime scenes.'

'Something like that.'

'Well, sir, as I did try to explain to him, I've simply been chasing leads. If he'd been doing his job properly, I wouldn't have had to.'

'That's hardly fair, Tanner, not when you're the one who's been keeping information from him; the list of names, for example, and its connection to that newspaper's child prostitution story?'

'The list was given to me by the newspaper's Editor-in-Chief. At the time, it didn't appear to have anything to do with his various murder investigations.'

'But I understand it does now?'

'Well, yes, but only because the names on the list would appear to be the same as those who've been murdered. As for the story, I'm not convinced it's even true, given that the entire thing came from a single anonymous source, making it impossible for them to verify before going to print.'

'I wasn't aware that they'd printed the names.'

'Maybe not, but judging by how many people knew about it, they may as well have done. Before handing it to me, he'd already given it to his entire editorial team. God knows how many people they went on to tell, meaning that someone could have easily given it to our first suspect.'

'I take it you're referring to Joseph Miller, the man who you let walk out the door, despite his physical appearance, that he had the knife that killed the first victim, and that he's a diagnosed paranoid schizophrenic, one who was sexually abused as a child?'

'You heard about that as well,' Tanner said, with a capitulating sigh.

'I caught the tail end of your press conference.'

'Look, I'm sorry, sir. Had I known about his past when he came in, I'd have never let him go.'

Preparing to be on the receiving end of another tirade of verbal abuse, Tanner braced himself. But it didn't come. Neither was he told to clear his desk. Instead, Forrester said something totally unexpected.

'Don't worry, Tanner. We all make mistakes.'

As Tanner's head jolted back in surprise, he opened his mouth to reply, only to realise that he didn't know what to say in response.

'As I said before,' he heard Forrester continue, 'I've been speaking to Haverstock. Believe it or not, he's been saying some remarkably good things about you. He even suggested that you should take over as SIO for the murder investigations.'

'He did?' Tanner replied, with open astonishment.

'So anyway, having had a bit of a think, I've come to the conclusion that he's probably right. The cases are obviously linked, and with your seniority, it would seem to make good sense. I assume that would be OK with you?'

'Sure, no problem. Can I start on Monday?'

'Very funny. Now, before you go, there was something else I wanted to talk to you about.'

Raising an eyebrow, Tanner leaned back against his car.

'I don't know if you'd heard, but Westfield Station's DCI has had to take time off for ill-health.'

'I'd heard something about it,' Tanner replied, curious to know where this was going.

'Unfortunately, it looks like he's going to need more time than was first thought. Quite a lot more, as it turns out.'

'I hope that doesn't mean he's....?'

'Not yet!' Forrester laughed. 'He's simply come to the conclusion that the time has come for him to retire. It was earlier than expected, but it has at least allowed us to begin discussing something that we've been thinking about for a while now.'

'Which is...?'

'How to cope with the Government's latest round of budget cuts, whilst still being able to provide Norfolk's residents with an effective police service. A part of that could be to combine Norfolk's Western Division with yours, by closing down one of the offices. We haven't made any decisions yet,' Forrester quickly added, 'but if we did, we were wondering how you'd feel about becoming the DCI for what would effectively be Norfolk's Western Division as well as the Broads?'

'Who, me?' Tanner asked, completely taken by surprise.

'It would come with a pay rise, of course,' Forrester continued. 'Nothing amazing, but something we thought may come in handy, given your family's recent addition.'

Endeavouring to digest what was being offered, Tanner closed his eyes to feel the familiar buzzing sensation sweep from the front of his brain to the back. He was already exhausted. The idea of having to take on more work, with what would no doubt be longer hours, and more travelling, was something he couldn't even contemplate. Whether it came with an increase in salary was neither here nor there. 'Do you have any idea when this would be?' he tentatively asked.

'We don't know, exactly. Certainly not immediately. There would also be a period of transition, during which time you'd be expected to manage both offices, but again, I don't know for how long.'

Tanner took a fortifying breath. 'May I ask what would happen if I were to decline the offer?'

'Don't worry about that. We'd sort something out.'

'But closing down one of the offices would mean redundancies?'

'There would have to be, I'm afraid, but only if we do decide to move forward.'

With Tanner's mind turning to his staff, he asked, 'Do you know which office would be closed?'

'As I said, we haven't decided anything yet.'

'But it could be Wroxham?'

'It *could*,' Forrester replied, before falling silent.

'OK, well,' Tanner eventually replied, his voice sounding tired and deflated, 'if it's alright with you, I'd like some time to think about it.'

'Yes, of course! Take as long as you need. I hope it goes without saying that this is just between you and me, for now at least. I don't want everyone to start running around like a bunch of headless chickens, thinking they're about to be fired.'

'May I discuss it with Christine?'

'By all means. But if it could go no further, I'd appreciate it.'

'OK, thank you, sir, and thank you for considering me.'

'Oh, and I'm sorry about the timing,' Forrester added. 'We'd just like to know your thoughts, before taking the idea any further. I'm sure you can appreciate that good people like you are hard to find, especially in this day and age.'

'Right, sir,' Tanner added, with even more surprise.

'Anyway, have a think about it. If it's something you would be interested in, then maybe we could arrange a meeting at HQ. Sometime next week, perhaps?'

'That soon?'

'Or the week after,' Forrester countered. 'As I said, it really is up to you.'

- CHAPTER FORTY SIX -

ENDING THE CALL, Tanner climbed wearily into his car to slump down into the seat. He knew what Forrester had meant when he'd said not to worry, if he did decide to say no. They'd be forced to find someone else for the job, meaning that they'd have no choice but to let him go. The only question then would be the size of the redundancy package they'd be offering, and if it would be enough for him to join Westfield's DCI in retiring, or at least to give him time to find another less stressful line of work. What that would be, he'd no idea.

'What was all that about?' he heard Vicky ask beside him.

Finding her staring at him with a curious, albeit concerned expression, he forced a grim smile at her. 'Oh, nothing important.'

'He's not firing you, is he?'

'Not yet!' he laughed, with nervous apprehension, as he thought more about what could happen if HQ did go ahead with their plan; that the employees of an entire office would be made redundant, one of whom could easily be the person sitting next to him.

Becoming instantly torn between his loyalty to Forrester and his CID team, he opened his mouth to tell her, only to change his mind. As his superintendent had said, it was still only a proposal. Until he was told something a little more concrete, it would probably be best not to worry her.

'He's made me the SIO for the murder investigations,' he eventually replied.

'That's good, isn't it?'

'I suppose.'

'If you don't mind me saying so, you don't seem very happy about it.'

'It's just...' he began, knowing he'd now managed to put himself into a position where he was going to have to lie, at least about his current emotional state. '...it's just that I – well – I suppose I was kind of enjoying *not* being in charge, for a change.'

'You have a funny way of showing it, being that you'd effectively taken over the investigation.'

'Yes, well, I suppose I couldn't help myself,' Tanner smiled in response.

'What about Haverstock?'

'Apparently, it was his idea!'

'But – I thought he hated you?'

'Me too!' he laughed.

'What did you tell Forrester?'

'I offered to start on Monday.'

'Seriously?'

'Well, yes, I did, but no, I wasn't being serious. Anyway, back to the task at hand. What were we doing again?'

'I think we were about to head back to the office.'

'Then back to the office we shall go!' he stated, in a deliberate up-beat manner, as he started the engine to pull away from the kerb.

- CHAPTER FORTY SEVEN -

AFTER FIGHTING HIS way through rush-hour traffic, Tanner turned into Wroxham Police Station some twenty minutes later to leave his car in the nearest space.

Climbing quickly out, he followed Vicky inside, only to see Elliston's solicitor, pacing up and down reception, her hands clenched firmly behind her back.

'Shit,' he cursed quietly to himself, coming to an abrupt halt in the middle of the doorway. With so much going on, he'd completely forgotten about Elliston being trussed-up inside Interview Room One, waiting for his interview to recommence. He couldn't even remember how long he'd been there, nor when he'd last spoken to him. All he knew was that he had absolutely no desire to talk to his solicitor about it.

'Are you alright?' Vicky queried, turning to look back at him.

'Um...' he replied, wandering if he'd be able to do a U-turn to find another way in. But it was too late. The solicitor must have seen him when Vicky stopped to look around.

'Detective Chief Inspector Tanner!' came her sharp, arresting voice.

Realising he was hunched behind Vicky, in a forlorn effort to hide, he pulled himself up straight to meet the solicitor's double-barrelled gaze with a wavering smile. 'Miss...er...?'

'Ms Heatherington,' she responded, charging over the carpet towards him like a rampaging rhino.

'That's right. Of course!' he grinned, watching Vicky slink quietly away with jealous envy. 'Sorry to have kept you and your client waiting.'

'Kept us waiting?' Heatherington repeated, offering him an incredulous glare. 'We haven't seen you since yesterday!'

'Has it really been that long? Sorry, I'd no idea. So anyway...where were we again?'

'It's been such a long time, I can't remember.'

'No, me neither,' Tanner laughed, nervously. 'Tell you what, let me grab myself a quick coffee, and I'll be with you in a jiffy.'

Seeing her do nothing more than to fold her arms over her ample-sized chest, he offered her a placating smile. 'Maybe I could get you one as well?'

'I've had enough coffee to sink the Titanic all over again, thank you very much!'

'A biscuit, then?' he inquired, only to find her expression remaining obstinately unchanged. 'If you give me five minutes, I'll be straight in.'

'You can have two minutes, Detective Chief Inspector. If the interview hasn't recommenced by then, I'll be escorting my client out the door, and good luck trying to stop me.'

'If we could agree on three-and-a-half minutes, then I'd be able to bring you each a sandwich.'

Seeing the murderous look in her eyes, he wondered for a moment if *she* might be the person they'd been looking for, and was just toying with the idea of asking where she'd been at the time of the various murders, when he remembered; the same place her client had been, at least for the last three.

'OK, two minutes it is,' he wisely capitulated.

Managing to sidle his way past, he hurried through the double doors into a virtually empty main office. As he passed Vicky, hiding in the kitchen, he made a beeline for Sally, the only other member of his CID team there.

'Hi, Sally,' he began, catching his breath. 'How's it going?'

'Oh, good, thank you!'

'I don't suppose anyone's found Miller?'

'Not that anyone's told me.'

'OK, can you do me a favour? Can you check that there's a police squad car parked outside the gates of Sir Charles Fletcher's estate?'

'Right you are, boss,' she replied, reaching for a police radio.

'And can you ask them to confirm that they've actually seen him, and that he's still alive?'

Seeing her nod, he dived into his office to plonk himself down onto his chair. There, he turned on his computer to find the entire first page of his email's inbox crammed full of unopened messages.

Cursing loudly, he scanned through the list, looking for something from either forensics, or Alison Westwood.

Unable to see anything from either, he was about to navigate to the next page when he caught a glimpse of Haverstock's name near the very top. Curious to know what he had to say for himself, he opened it up to see he was simply thanking him for agreeing to take over as SIO, and that if he needed anything, he only had to ask.

Thinking what he really needed was a forensics report from the grave at Swanton Morley, and the lay-by where the body had been found, he realised Haverstock had attached two documents, both appearing to be what he was looking for.

Offering the DI a silent word of gratitude, he opened the first entitled "Swanton Morley – Preliminary Forensics Report" to begin speedreading his way through. The moment he saw the name Joseph Miller, he stopped to read more carefully. The man's prints, and traces of his DNA, had been found on both the victim's body and the surrounding surfaces.

Unable to see anything else of any relevance, he moved onto the second attachment to find it was a fingerprint analysis of the print found on the vehicle recovery van left at the lay-by. Reading the person's name it belonged to, he sat slowly up in his chair.

Taking a moment to think, he reached for his phone to speak to Vicky, when he saw her head appear from behind his door.

'Sorry to have abandoned you like that,' she apologised, offering him a look of sheepish guilt, 'but that solicitor scares the bejesus out of me.'

'You and me both!' Tanner exclaimed.

'So anyway, I made you a coffee,' she added, producing a steaming mug from behind her, 'to try make up for it.'

'Then why didn't you say! Please, come in!'

Waiting for her to close the door, Tanner offered her a seat. 'I've just been reading an email from Haverstock.'

'Anything nice?' she replied, placing the mug on the desk in front of him.

'He thanked me for agreeing to take over as SIO.'

'Oh, right!'

'He was also good enough to send me a couple of their forensics reports. One's from the grave at Swanton Morley, the other is a fingerprint analysis of that print found on the van.'

'Anything of interest?'

Tanner reached forward to take hold of the mug. 'The fingerprint does belong to Elliston after all, which I think has to be the final nail in the coffin for our case against him. Even if it hadn't been his, there's simply no way he could have killed Derek Harvey, Marcus Thornton, *and* Robert Hanson, not when he was either locked in a holding cell, or sitting with his solicitor, waiting for us to continue his interview. So, with that in mind, I think the hour has come for us to let him go.'

'We still have until half-past eleven tonight,' Vicky commented, 'and you do remember what happened last time you did something similar?'

'In an ideal world, I'd keep the entire population of Norfolk under lock and key, but unfortunately, that isn't possible, at least, I don't think it is.'

Another knock at the door was followed by Sally, peering timidly around at the two of them.

'Yes, Sally?' Tanner demanded. 'How can I help?'

'Sorry to bother you, boss. I just thought I'd confirm that there *is* a squad car parked outside the gates of Sir Charles Fletcher's house.'

'And he's alive and well?'

'He's not very happy about them being there, but he is both alive and well,' she confirmed.

'OK, that's something, I suppose.'

Seeing her nod before ducking away, he called after her, 'Actually, before you go, do you think you could do me another quick favour?'

'Of course!' she smiled.

'Could you let Elliston's solicitor know that her client is free to go? You'll probably find her wearing a hole in the reception's carpet.'

Sally glanced hesitantly at Vicky, before returning to look at Tanner. 'Are you sure, boss; after what happened last time with my uncle, and everything?'

'Quite, sure, thank you, Sally. And if you could apologise to her for having taken up so much of her client's time, that might be useful.'

Waiting for the door to close, Vicky said, 'I assume that means we're down to two suspects again, and that the most likely one has to be Sir Charles?'

'Sorry, but why him?'

'Because Elliston's fingerprint was found on the van door, proving someone's been trying to frame him, as he couldn't have left it there himself, and that Sir Charles is the only obvious candidate, being that he's running against Elliston in the forthcoming by-election.'

Tanner gazed out at all the news vans piled up outside. 'To be honest, I still think it's more likely to be the person I was stupid enough to let walk out the door, given his diagnosed condition, and what happened to him as a child. More so if the men who abused him turn out to be the people on that list. It would also explain the ferocity of the attacks, and the fact that two of them had their genitalia removed. Then there's what the forensic report said concerning the murder scene at Swanton Morley.'

'Which was...?'

'That Miller's prints and DNA have been found all over it.'

'But weren't we expecting that, being that he'd already confessed to finding the body?'

'Maybe so, but at least we now have some physical evidence to prove that he was there.'

'I'm sorry, but didn't we have that with the knife?'

'The knife didn't place him at the scene.'

Vicky shifted awkwardly in her seat. 'I hate to say this, boss, but there's something I think you're forgetting. If it was Miller, murdering them all for having abused him as a child, what is Elliston's fingerprint doing on the van?'

Leaning restlessly forward, Tanner planted his elbows onto his desk. 'I must admit, I hadn't thought of that.'

'Which means it has to be Sir Charles, doesn't it?'

'There is just one more alternative,' Tanner mused, tapping a pensive finger against his stubble-covered chin.

'Which is?'

'That Sir Charles didn't place Elliston's fingerprint there to try to incriminate him, but that it was there *before* the van's owner was murdered.'

'I'm sorry, but why would Ellison's fingerprint be on the door of a vehicle recovery van? Unless, of course, he'd...?'

With Vicky's question left both unasked, and unanswered, Tanner pushed himself up from his chair. 'Tell you what, how about we ask him?' he suggested, skirting around his desk to reach for the door. 'With any luck, he's still here, preferably without that bloody solicitor of his.'

- CHAPTER FORTY EIGHT -

LEAVING VICKY TRAILING in his wake, Tanner lurched through the main office, heading for reception. When he reached the double doors, he shoved them open to find the place deserted. 'The suspect, Mr Elliston?' he called to the duty sergeant. 'Has he gone?'

'You – er – just missed him,' came the officer's hesitant reply.

Tanner turned to stare through the glass entrance, only to hear the duty sergeant say, 'He actually went the other way.'

'Huh?' Tanner replied, glancing around.

'The suspect asked if it was alright for him to go out the back.'

Nodding his understanding, Tanner headed for the corridor behind him to see Elliston at its furthest end, stepping out through the door.

'Mr Elliston!' he called, bringing the man to an abrupt halt. 'Before you go, I just had one more question.'

'You must be fucking joking?' the man grimaced. 'I was only released about two seconds ago!'

'Yes, I know. Sorry. If it's any consolation, it's got nothing to do with what you were brought in for, and it will take less than a minute, I promise!'

Rolling his eyes, Elliston turned his head to call, 'Stephanie! The police are trying to interrogate me again!'

Realising his solicitor was still there, Tanner cursed under his breath. The prospect of having to deal with her for the second time in a row made his stomach churn.

He was about to say not to worry, and that he'd call him later, when the woman's head appeared through the still open rear exit.

'Mr Tanner, please don't tell me you're about to arrest my client again?'

'Er...not at all. I just had one very quick question for him.'

'Well, unless you do, I don't realistically see how you expect him to answer it, not when you've had him held under lock and key for nearly thirty-six hours, without barely taking the time to speak to him.'

'I wanted to ask if he's broken down recently?'

'What?' she demanded, glaring at him with a look of egregious befuddlement.

'Maybe sometime within the last couple of weeks?'

'Do you mean physically, as in by the side of a road,' she asked, 'or emotionally, as in crying into one of the many cup-a-soups your staff so kindly provided?'

Pleased to hear that she at least had a sense of humour, he took a breath to continue. 'I meant physically, as in by the side of a road, preferably in a vehicle of some description.'

'I'm sorry, but you're going to have to provide a little more context.'

'His answer will help to determine if someone has indeed been trying to frame him, as your client himself has proposed, or if he's nothing more than an unfortunate victim of circumstance.'

'You do know that his answer can't be used in a court of law, being that he hasn't been cautioned, at least not since his release?'

'Understood!'

She narrowed her eyes at Tanner before finally turning to face her client. 'You may answer the question, but only if you want to.'

'I had a puncture last week,' Elliston shrugged. 'So what?'

'May I ask if you called for roadside assistance,' Tanner continued, 'and if so, which company it was?'

'That makes three questions, Mr Tanner,' the solicitor stated, 'two more than you originally requested.'

'They will help to resolve the same matter, once and for all,' Tanner replied.

The solicitor turned again to Elliston. 'You may continue.'

'Yes, I did,' he nodded, 'but only because I haven't changed a wheel since... well, since never, really.'

'And their name...?'

'Just some local recovery service. I've no idea what they're called, but I can look them up, if you think it might help?'

- CHAPTER FORTY NINE -

WITH THE NAME of the vehicle recovery service Elliston had used being the same as the one owned by the second victim, Mr Derek Harvey, Tanner thanked him for his time and led Vicky back into the still empty reception.

'So it looks like you were right,' he fumed, stopping briefly in the middle, 'which leads us right back to where we started, and the guy who came waltzing in through those doors right there, desperate to make us believe that he didn't kill the first victim, when it was clear as day that he did. I just happened to be gullible enough to go along with it.'

With Tanner continuing through to the main office, Vicky was left struggling to keep up. 'But we still don't know it was him,' she was eventually able to say.

'Probably because we can't find him to ask!'

'Even if we had, we still don't have enough evidence to charge him, and that won't change, not until we hear back from forensics, and the medical examiners from *all* the crime scenes.'

'Meanwhile, he remains as free as a bird, and there's still one person left on that list.'

'Who you've warned. You've also arranged for a squad car to be parked outside the entrance to his estate. I'm not sure what else you can do.'

'I could have kept the suspect in custody, that's

what I could have done.'

'As I recall, you had a good reason for letting him go.'

'I don't suppose you could remind me what that good reason was? For the life of me, I can't remember!'

Reaching his office, Tanner turned to see her gazing at the carpet with a contemplative frown. 'I rest my case,' he muttered, opening the door, 'which is no doubt something HQ's prosecution team will be doing at the end of my rather short criminal negligence trial, and that's *before* we learn that Miller has managed to stab a knight of the bloody realm in the chest about fifty times to leave his genitalia hanging out of his mouth.'

'Forrester has only just made you the SIO for the murder investigations. He's hardly likely to suddenly turn around to recommend that you're kicked off the Force, not without questions being asked about his judgement.'

'That's only because Miller hasn't had the chance to murder Little Lord Fauntleroy yet,' Tanner continued, skirting around his desk.

'May I make a suggestion?' proposed Vicky, stopping in the doorway as Tanner pulled out his chair. 'Go home and get some sleep. Maybe spend some time with that wife and baby of yours?'

'I suppose that depends on which is more of a priority,' he replied, turning on his monitor, 'seeing my family, or being able to sleep through the night?'

'Then perhaps you should buy some earplugs on the way home?'

'Thanks for your concern, Vicky, but I'm fine. Unfortunately, sleep deprivation is all part of being a parent.'

'But you are going to go home, though?'

'At some stage. I just need to make some sort of a dent in my email's inbox before doing so.'

- CHAPTER FIFTY -

AS TANNER'S MIND untangled itself from a quagmire of twisted dreams, he woke up to find his chin resting against the knot of his tie, and his hand slumped over his computer's mouse.

Cursing himself for having fallen asleep at his desk again, he moved his mouse, just enough to wake his computer up.

'For fuck's sake,' he groaned, the moment his eyes were able to see the time in the bottom right hand corner. It had gone half-past nine. He couldn't remember what the time was when he'd sat down, but it was a lot closer to six than it was now.

Seeing the list of unopened emails had only grown in length since he'd dozed-off, he scrolled to the top to make sure nothing important had come in during his comatosed absence.

Confident nothing had, he turned the computer off to begin collecting his various personal effects from off the desk before heading for the door.

The moment he wrenched it open, his head jolted back in surprise when he saw both Vicky and Sally were still at their desks.

'What the hell are you two still doing here?' he demanded, his eyes darting disbelievingly between them.

'I'm waiting for Mark,' came Sally's response, attached to which was a weary smile.

'Who?'

'She means Townsend,' Vicky supplemented.

'Sorry, of course. And where is he?' Tanner continued, directing the question back to Sally.

'With Cooper, out looking for Miller.'

'What, still?'

'You never said they could stop,' she shrugged.

'OK, enough!' he exclaimed, shaking his head. 'Can you please tell them to call it a day?'

With Sally reaching for the phone, Tanner turned to ask Vicky, 'What on Earth have you been doing all this time?'

'I've been trawling through CCTV footage with Sally, trying to find him. Unfortunately, without much luck.'

'Is it safe to assume that Sir Charles Fletcher is still OK?'

'I arranged for the officers on duty to be relieved. Their replacements confirmed that he was alive and well.'

'When was that?'

'Just after eight.'

Tanner rubbed his exhausted eyes to stare down at his watch.

'I told them to stay there until the morning,' he heard Vicky continue. 'I hope that's OK?'

'Yes, of course. Thank you.'

'You know, there could be another reason why Miller hasn't been found, other than because he's trying not to be.'

'You mean, that he could be lying face-down in a ditch somewhere?'

'Or face up, having decided to take his own life.'

'Well, we'll have to see, but I don't think we should stop looking on the off chance.'

'No, of course.'

'One thing I do know is that the search is going to have to wait until tomorrow. With that in mind, the time has most definitely come for us to go home.'

'OK, I'll just...'

'No, Vicky! We've done enough for today. We'll just have to cross our fingers and hope for better luck tomorrow.'

- CHAPTER FIFTY ONE -

NOT ARRIVING HOME until gone ten o'clock, Tanner entered his modest riverside bungalow to dispose of his coat and keys as quietly as possible. Unable to hear a single sound, he continued into the main living area to find baby Samantha, gurgling happily to herself within her secure, prison-like playpen, whilst Christine was snoring on their L-shaped sofa. 'At least someone's getting some sleep,' he whispered to himself, glancing back at Samantha.

Resisting the temptation to pick her up, for fear of reminding her that she was either hungry, tired, completely bored, or in desperate need of a nappy change, he turned instead to the kitchen, only to hear Christine begin to stir.

'You're back,' she mumbled, shifting her head to look over at him.

'You get some rest,' he smiled, 'I'm just going to find myself something to eat.'

'I was only dozing,' she replied, dropping her legs off the sofa's edge to stand slowly up. 'I'm happy to make you something.'

'You don't have to.'

'Honestly, I don't mind,' she continued, stumbling over.

'How's Samantha been?' he enquired, happy enough to prop himself up on one of the breakfast bar stools.

'As if I've been feeding her a diet of amphetamines and LSD.'

'So...normal, then?'

'Pretty much,' Christine replied, opening the fridge to stare unblinkingly inside, as if transfixed by its illuminated bounty. 'Ham and cheese?'

'Ham and cheese...what?'

'I don't know. That was as far as my brain got.'

'Is it alright if I pick Samantha up?' he asked, turning to gaze devotedly at her.

'Better not. She might explode.'

'Fair enough,' he responded, electing to pour himself a drink instead.

Hauling a variety of items out of the fridge, Christine tilted her head to ask, 'How was your day?'

'I wouldn't know where to start!'

'How about with how many bodies you found?'

'Um...' Tanner began, counting with his fingers whilst staring up at the ceiling, '...three or four, I think.'

'Not seriously?'

'It was something like that. The other highlight included falling asleep at my desk, once at the beginning of the day, and again at the end. I've also been made the SIO for the murder at Swanton Morley, together with all the various others. Oh, and Forrester told me that HQ's thinking about closing down either Wroxham or Westfield, and he's asking if I'd like to become the DCI of which ever one they decide to keep open, despite the fact that I made the rather peculiar decision to release a deranged serial-killing psychopath, only for him to start immediately adding to the already impressive body count.'

Downing his rum, Tanner refilled his glass to find Christine staring at him with a kitchen knife in one hand, and a block of cheese in the other. 'If you're trying to decide whether to stab me with the knife, or bludgeon me to death with the cheese,' Tanner mused, 'I'd go with the latter. At least then you'd be able to eat the evidence.'

'Are they really going to close Wroxham Police Station?' she eventually asked.

'Either Wroxham or Westfield. They haven't decided which, at least that's what Forrester said.'

'So...you could lose your job?'

'Only if I said no to taking on what would be a much larger geographical area, no doubt with the same dwindling resources I'm stuck with now. If they do decide to close Wroxham, then I'd be left with a tedious commute, as well.'

'Are they at least offering you a pay rise?'

'Well, Forrester said they would.'

'And what would happen if you said no?'

'Hopefully they'd offer me some sort of redundancy package. What that would be, I've no idea.'

'What about your CID team?'

'I think that would depend on which office they decided to close.'

'But, if it ends up being Wroxham, they could all be out of a job, right?'

'I'm sure it wouldn't come to that.'

'But it might, though.'

Instead of answering, Tanner took another sip from his drink.

'Are you going to warn them?'

'I've thought about it.'

'And...?'

'It's probably best if I don't, at least for now.'

'But, you will at some point?'

'Only if they decide that they're definitely going to

close Wroxham.'

'By which time it would be too late.'

'To be honest, I'm not sure what difference it would make. If I tell them now, then they'd only worry.'

'And for good reason!'

'Not if HQ decide against the idea. At the moment, I need their minds focussed on the job, not if they've got one to focus their minds on. And as I said, HQ haven't decided.'

'OK, well, having been in the Force for as long as you have,' Christine began, beginning to attack the block of cheese with the knife, 'do you think it's more, or less likely that they will?'

Tanner didn't have to think about that for very long. He already knew the answer. The Government had been rolling out widespread spending cuts for years, with the NHS, Schools, and the Police Force consistently bearing the brunt. The closure of small, rural police offices was just one of the results. 'It's probably more likely than not,' he eventually replied.

'Then don't you think you should tell them?'

'I've already promised Forrester that I'd keep quiet.'

'I see. So your loyalty lies with HQ; not your staff?'

'It's not as simple as that.'

'Isn't it?'

Tanner took another sip from his drink.

'Anyway, I assume you're going to accept the offer and stay on, if they do decide to go ahead?'

'As I said, I think that depends on what sort of redundancy package they'd be willing to offer.'

'If it turned out to be a particularly generous one, and you did decide to leave, what would you do then?'

'I was actually toying with the idea of becoming a Broads Ranger.'

Christine snorted with laughter with such force that baby Samantha stopped gurgling to gaze over at them, a wide toothless grin spreading out over her amused, cherub-like face.

'Er...that wasn't a joke,' Tanner responded, unsure if he was talking to his wife or the baby.

'I never said it was,' Christine continued, evidently trying to keep a straight face. 'I'm just surprised you think you'd be interested in spending your days fixing barbed wire fences in the freezing cold, or rebuilding collapsed stone walls, or breaking up fights between fisherman and dog walkers, instead of sitting behind a nice warm desk, whilst being paid good money for doing so.'

'Well, for a start, I don't spend my days sitting behind my desk. I normally have my feet on top of it. The rest of me is fast asleep. Secondly, I thought you spent your days driving up and down the Broads in that little patrol boat of yours, whilst presenting tourists with speeding fines for doing six miles an hour instead of five?'

Delighted with his rebuttal, Tanner turned to wink at Samantha.

'Well, for a start,' Christine retorted, 'there's a lot more manual labour than there is pottering about on the water, I can assure you! And no offence, but when you do have to spend an entire day rebuilding a stone wall, or digging out an overgrown drainage ditch, you wouldn't last five minutes before demanding to take a four hour lunch break.'

Placing a lopsided sandwich on top of a plate that was far too small for the task, Christine turned to find Tanner mouthing the words blah, blah, blah at Samantha, whilst rolling his eyes around his head like some sort of demented clown.

'I hope that's not supposed to be me?' she

questioned, offering him an unamused scowl.

Tanner cleared his throat. 'Er...no, of course not. You're *much* better looking.'

Christine continued to send daggers into his eyes, before eventually saying, 'You should probably know that Samantha can barely see beyond her nose, being that she's less than a week old. I, on the other hand, have got eyes in the back of my head.'

'Really?' Tanner replied, with a quizzical expression. 'I'd no idea! How do they see through all that hair of yours?'

She continued glaring at him for a moment, before laying the plate down on the breakfast bar. 'One freshly made sandwich. Sorry about the plate. The rest are in the dishwasher.'

'What about the sandwich?' he queried, lifting one of its limp, miss-aligned corners, before dropping it back down.

'I'm not apologising for that, not when it's about to be devoured without so much as a second thought.'

'Fair enough,' Tanner replied, picking up one half to jam straight into his mouth, without so much as a first thought, let alone a second.

'Right. I'm going to feed Samantha. Then I suggest we all go to bed. You never know, tonight could be the night that she sleeps all the way through.'

'I doubt it,' mumbled Tanner, turning to look at her. 'From this angle, it looks more likely that she's about to start doing press-ups.'

- CHAPTER FIFTY TWO -

Wednesday, 25th June

AFTER ANOTHER FITFUL night's sleep, and only half an hour late, Tanner found himself stuck in a long line of traffic, just outside Wroxham.

Assuming it was thanks to either a broken down bus, or yet another news media van, reversing into a space opposite the police station that simply didn't exist, he turned off his engine to try to conserve fuel.

With nothing better to do, he pulled out his phone to put a call through to the office.

'Hi Vicky, it's Tanner,' he began, recognising her voice. 'Just to let you know that I'm stuck in traffic outside Wroxham.'

'No problem, boss.'

'Is everyone else in?'

'Just about.'

'Cooper?'

'He's just coming out of the toilet.'

'OK, that was a little too much information, but thanks anyway.'

'Any time.'

'I don't suppose Miller has shown up anywhere?'

'Not that I've heard.'

'That's a shame. I was kind of hoping that you'd arrive to find him sitting in reception, writing out his confession. How about Sir Charles Fletcher?'

'The officers positioned outside his stately home were relieved at eight o'clock this morning. Those who took over made sure that he was still OK before doing so.'

'They actually laid eyes on him?'

'They used the gate's intercom.'

'I suppose that will have to do. Anything more from forensics, or either one of the medical examiners?'

'Nothing that's come through on my email. How about yours?'

'I'll have another quick look, but there wasn't anything when I left home.'

'Dare I ask how you slept?'

'Like a log.'

'Oh, really?'

'Unfortunately, it was more like one being floated over the top of Niagara Falls, than the more traditional stationary one.'

'I'm sorry to hear that.'

'Don't be. I'm getting used to it. When everyone's had a coffee, do you think you could ask them to head back out to recommence the search for Miller?'

'Yes, of course. Do you want me to join them?'

'If you wouldn't mind. I emailed the Westfield office last night, asking if they could help out. I had a reply from Haverstock this morning, which was surprisingly positive.'

'What did he say?'

'That he'd already spoken to the vicar at Swanton Morley. Unfortunately, he hadn't seen him. Actually,' Tanner continued, 'given the fact that the traffic hasn't moved since I called, I think I'm going to double-back to drive over to the Westfield office instead. Could you stay there and hold the fort for me?'

'No problem, boss, but maybe you should call ahead, to let them know you're coming?'

'Or maybe I'll see if I can catch them on their toes, something they're going to have to get used to if I'm going to become...'

Snapping his mouth closed, Tanner kicked himself for having nearly blurted out what Forrester had told him, '...the SIO for all their bloody murder investigations,' he quickly added.

'I thought you already were?' Vicky queried.

'Yes, I suppose I am,' he replied, hating himself for lying to her. 'Anyway, this traffic isn't going anywhere. I'm going to try a three-point turn and head over there. If you could let everyone know to call me on my mobile if they need me, I'd be grateful.'

- CHAPTER FIFTY THREE -

SEEING THE NAME Swanton Morley on a signpost pointing left, underneath one directing him to where he was supposed to be going, a nagging feeling crept into the back of Tanner's mind, as if he'd forgotten something vitally important.

Taking a moment to wonder what that could have been, he refocused his mind back to the road, only to realise that he'd turned left instead of right.

Shaking his head at his own stupidity, he continued along the narrow country lane, looking for somewhere to turn around, when he caught a glimpse of Swanton Morley's imposing church tower on the distant horizon.

Willing to entertain the idea that he'd turned the wrong way for a reason, he decided to carry on, arriving at the picturesque English village about ten minutes later.

With the church carpark on his left, he pulled in to climb slowly out.

Taking a moment to enjoy the peaceful, idyllic surroundings, he cast his eyes up at the church tower.

A flicker of movement near its base brought his attention down to see the vicar, making his way from the back of the church to the front, his head hanging thoughtfully towards the ground.

Remembering Haverstock had already asked him if he'd seen Miller, just the day before, he debated whether he could really be bothered to climb all the way to the top of the hill to ask him again. But why else had he driven there, if it wasn't to see if Miller had since made an appearance?

Taking a fortifying breath, he locked his car to begin trudging up. When he reached its ancient stone entrance to find one of the giant oak doors hanging open, he inched cautiously inside.

With nobody around, he was about to call out, when he remembered where he was, and the silence that such a place seemed to demand.

'Detective Inspector?' came a sudden enquiring voice, from the shadows to his right.

Spinning around to see the familiar grey face of the church's vicar, Father Graham, peering at him from one of the wooden collection boxes, he smiled before stepping over. 'Sorry to bother you,' he replied, in a low, respectful tone. 'I was just passing, so I thought I'd stop by to say hello.'

'It's a funny sort of place to be "just passing"?' he replied, in a gentle, mocking tone.

'You're right, of course. I was actually on my way to Westfield, when I found myself driving here instead, without even realising it!'

'Sounds like divine intervention, to me.'

Tanner took a moment to wonder if he was being serious, when he recalled the man's profession.

'I was very upset to hear the news that so many people have been found brutally killed,' the vicar continued. 'I don't suppose it's possible that the stories are just the result of some journalist's overactive imagination?'

'In this particular instance, unfortunately not.'

A shadow fell over the vicar's pale, grey face. 'Over two thousand years since Jesus's teachings, and we're still going around killing each other.'

As his watery blue eyes came drifting back, he smiled apologetically at Tanner. 'Sorry about that. I should probably stop watching the news. It's all just so upsetting.'

'No need to apologise.'

'Anyway, if I can do anything to help find the person responsible, I do hope you won't hesitate to ask.'

'I actually came to see if you'd heard anything from your groundskeeper, Mr Miller?'

'One of your colleagues was here only yesterday, asking me the exact same thing.'

'Yes, well, I thought it was worth trying again, on the off chance.'

With the vicar saying nothing more in return, Tanner shrugged before thanking him for his time.

Turning to make his way back to his car, he stopped to glance thoughtfully back. 'Actually, there *was* something else that maybe you can help me with. It's more of a moral dilemma, than anything else.'

'OK, well, I'm happy to have a go.'

'It was something my boss told me yesterday, in confidence. Apparently, the powers that be are thinking about closing down one of the local police stations, either the one at Westfield, or where I work, over in Wroxham. He's asking if I'd be willing to stay on as DCI to cover both, no matter which one they decide to close. That's if they do, of course.'

'I assume you're about to ask if you should warn your fellow employees about the potential threat to their livelihoods?'

'That's remarkably insightful of you,' Tanner replied, gazing at him with a look of surprised awe.

'Not really. It's hardly the first time I've been asked such a question.'

'Then you see the problem? I've already told my

boss that I'd keep it to myself, but now I'm left feeling guilty for not giving my staff some sort of advanced warning. So, I was wondering if you'd be able to offer me any advice?'

'I can only tell you what I've told others in a similar predicament, I'm afraid.'

'Which is?'

'To do what you think is best.'

Tanner thought about that for a moment. 'You're right, of course,' he eventually replied.

'I am?' the vicar queried.

'Well, yes, but only because it wasn't very helpful,' Tanner said, offering him a whimsical smile.

'Well, I did warn you!' the vicar laughed.

'Anyway, I'd better be off.'

'Before you go, maybe I could ask *you* a question?'

'By all means!'

'It's another moral dilemma, I'm afraid.'

'Go on,' Tanner replied, already intrigued.

'If a neighbour were to ask for your help with something that could be considered to be illegal, would you do it?'

'I suppose it would have to depend on just how illegal whatever the person in question needed help with? If, for example, it was to rob a bank, then it would obviously be a no.'

'What if it was to simply not answer a question that someone had asked, at least not directly?'

'OK, well, that doesn't sound so bad.'

'When the question was in relation to the person they were looking for?'

Tanner found himself taking a moment to narrow his eyes at him. 'Then that could be considered to be obstruction of justice,' he eventually replied, 'which is a very serious crime indeed.'

'That's what I thought,' the vicar muttered,

wringing his hands. 'When your colleague came around yesterday, asking if I'd seen poor Mr Miller, I replied by saying that I'd heard the police were looking for him. I left it for him to assume that meant I hadn't seen him, in very much the same way I did with you, just a moment ago.'

'You're telling me that you *have* seen him?'

The vicar's head sank slowly to the flagstone floor. 'I've known him since he was just a boy. He could never have done the things the newspapers have been accusing him of. Not in a million years! I know he had an unimaginably difficult childhood, and that he's been burdened with problems ever since, but that doesn't mean he's capable of killing someone.'

'If you have seen him, then you have to tell me.'

The vicar raised his eyes to look directly into Tanner's. 'There's another reason I know he's not responsible, at least not for the most recent deaths.'

'And that is...?'

'Because he's been hiding inside the church crypt, ever since Monday.'

Tanner began to glance instinctively about. 'May I ask how you know that he hasn't been sneaking out?'

'I know, because he asked me to lock him inside. There are no windows down there for him to crawl out of. No tunnels, either. And the door is solid seventeenth century oak. There's simply no way he could have escaped.'

- CHAPTER FIFTY FOUR -

TWENTY MINUTES LATER, Tanner was standing alongside the vicar, watching Miller being led down the hill towards an awaiting police car.

'You will look after him?' the vicar asked, gazing on with an anxious frown.

'Yes, of course!' came Tanner's earnest reply, as his phone rang from inside the depths of his sailing jacket. 'Don't worry,' he continued, fishing it out, 'he hasn't been arrested for anything. We're simply going to ask him a few questions, but not before he's had a chance to meet with a psychologist.'

Excusing himself, he stepped quietly away to take the call.

'Hi, boss, it's Vicky. I heard on the grapevine that you've found Joseph Miller!'

'He was hiding inside the church crypt at Swanton Morley.'

'What on Earth made you think to look there?'

'Divine intervention, apparently, which also led me to having a bit of a heart-to-heart with the vicar, which reminds me. There's something I need to talk to you about.'

'Can it wait?'

'Why, what's up?' Tanner asked, taking a cautionary breath.

'I just thought you'd like to know that we've

managed to unearth pornographic images of pre-pubescent girls on each of the victims' servers. Sir Charles Fletcher's as well!'

'So, the newspaper story was true!'

'What I think's more interesting is that they were all deleted, within hours of the story coming out.'

'Sorry, but – if they were deleted, how do we know they were there?'

'Because host servers keep back-up files for thirty days, just in case someone deletes something by accident.'

'Good to know,' Tanner laughed.

'We've also heard back from forensics concerning the first three murders.'

'And...?'

'They've uncovered numerous DNA samples, most of which are from unknown sources.'

'Was that it?'

'Not quite. One set was found at all three locations. They've even been able to identify who it belongs to.'

'Do I have to guess?'

'He's sitting at the top of our list of favourite people in the whole wide world.'

'Please tell me it's Sir Charles Fletcher?'

'The one and only!'

'Finally!' Tanner exclaimed.

'He'd also been in regular contact with the victims for years, so the idea that he didn't know any of them was utter bollocks!'

'Have you checked in with the squad car, parked outside his estate?'

'I have.'

'And?'

'They're still there, as is our suspect.'

'Excellent! Right, tell them to sit tight. I'll be there in ten minutes.'

'Right you are, boss.'

'Oh, and good work, Vicky!'

'Thanks, boss, although I didn't do much. I just happened to be the one who opened the emails.'

'Well, that's more than I've been able to do recently. Right, I'd better be off.'

'OK, but – didn't you want to tell me something?'

'Don't worry, it can wait. It's nothing urgent.'

Ending the call, Tanner turned to see the vicar approach with a hand raised hesitantly in the air, as if offering to answer an unasked question.

'Sorry, Chief Inspector. I didn't mean to eavesdrop on your conversation, but I couldn't help but overhear the mention of the name Sir Charles Fletcher.'

'Uh-huh,' Tanner nodded, with reticent interest.

'I don't know if it's relevant, but I actually know him.'

'Don't worry. I'm sure a lot of people do. He's running in the forthcoming by-election.'

'Yes, I know. I've seen his election posters, but that's not how I know him.'

'Then may I ask how you do?'

'He's been using the church as a community meeting place for the last several years. At first, he said they were for his photography club, saying they didn't have anywhere else to meet. More recently, they've supposedly been about his election campaign, but to be honest, I've always had my doubts.'

'For any particular reason?'

'Well, firstly, he always seems to hold them in the middle of the night, when I'd have thought most people would have been in bed, but more so because I've never once seen a single woman take part. I'm not saying that such social gatherings are normally dominated by women, but in my experience, there's normally at least one!'

- CHAPTER FIFTY FIVE -

RELIEVED TO FIND the squad car was still parked outside the gates of Sir Charles Fletcher's estate, Tanner pulled up in front of it to climb quickly out.

'He's still inside, I take it?' he asked, stepping over, as the driver wound his window down.

'As far as we know, boss,' came the young man's reply, glancing around at his colleague in the passenger seat.

'You haven't moved since you arrived?'

'We've been here the whole time.'

'And you checked to make sure he was in, when you did?'

'Well, we used the intercom.'

'But you did speak to him?'

'We spoke to his wife. She said he was still in bed. So, without actually going up to look for ourselves, we were forced to assume he was.'

'OK, well, let's just hope he is,' Tanner muttered, turning to gaze up at the resplendent stately home. 'Right, I'm going to see if I can get myself invited in. Once I have, I suggest we drive up together. I'll then proceed inside. My plan at the moment is to place him under arrest, so I suggest the two of you remain in your car, just in case he tries to do a runner. Maybe park directly behind his car, to help dissuade him further.'

'Right you are, boss,' the officer replied, starting the engine with an anxious nod.

'Oh, and he's got an over-sized Bentley Continental, just in case you were wondering which car to park behind, when you get there.'

Turning to march over to the intercom, Tanner heard the young officer call out, 'I assume we've got permission from HQ?'

Tanner stopped where he was to turn slowly back.

'It's just...' the officer continued, 'with him being a lord, and everything.'

'He's not a lord, he's a knight of the realm.'

'Sorry, boss. I didn't know there was a difference.'

Unfortunately, the young man had a point. 'Tell you what,' Tanner began, 'I'll make a quick call, just to be sure, then we'll head up.'

'Right you are,' the officer replied, exchanging a relieved glance with his colleague.

'Forrester, sir,' Tanner began, a few moments later, 'it's Tanner.'

'Who?' came the superintendent's quizzical response.

'Er...DCI Tanner, sir, from Wroxham Police Station?'

'Oh, *that* Tanner! My apologies. I've just never known you to call me before.'

Relieved to hear he was joking, at least in part, Tanner drew in a breath. 'Just to let you know that I'm standing outside the gates of Sir Charles Fletcher's estate.'

'That doesn't sound good.'

'Forensics has found traces of his DNA at not only the scene of the first murder, but also the lay-by where the second body was found, as well as the one

Vicky and I discovered.'

The line fell momentarily silent.

'I thought we were looking for Joseph Miller?' Forrester eventually asked.

'Sorry, sir. We've already found him. About half an hour ago. He'd been hiding inside the church crypt at Swanton Morley. The vicar assures me that that he'd been there since Monday, so there's no way he could have killed any of the victims, apart from the first, perhaps.'

'So, now you're thinking it's this Fletcher character?'

'Well, sir, had his DNA been found at only one of the crime scenes, I'd have been less certain, but not all three!'

'You haven't mentioned anything about a motive.'

'We're not one-hundred percent sure about that, but it has to have something to do with that list of names he was on.'

'What about that other body, the one Cooper and Townsend found?'

'We're still waiting to hear back from forensics.'

'OK, well, perhaps it would be sensible to wait, until you do.'

'To be honest, I'd rather not risk someone getting word out to him that he's become our prime suspect.'

'Is that really very likely?'

'I don't know, but people in his elevated position always seem to have connections. So, anyway, I was calling to ask your permission to bring him in for questioning?'

The line fell silent again, but this time for longer.

'Are you still there, sir?'

'I'm thinking!'

'Oh, right. Sorry.'

More silence followed, before Forrester's voice

eventually came back over the line. 'Very well, Tanner, but for God's sake, when you do bring him in, please make sure to treat him with at least a modicum of respect.'

'How do you mean, sir?'

'I mean, don't punch him in the face if he tries to resist!'

'I wouldn't dream of it!'

'Actually, maybe this isn't such a good idea.'

'Don't worry, sir. I'll be as good as gold. If he does resist, I'll get someone else to punch him in the face.'

'The problem is, Tanner, I never seem to know if you're joking.'

'Right, I'll be heading in then. I'll give you a call when it's done.'

Ending the conversation before Forrester could say anything else, Tanner began making his way over to the gate's intercom.

'Do we have permission, boss?' asked the squad car's driver.

'From Superintendent Forrester himself,' Tanner called back, before glancing away to add, 'just about,' under his breath.

Pressing the intercom's button, he leaned nonchalantly against the gate's post to stare down at his shoes, only to see what looked like either baby vomit, or toothpaste, on one of the unpolished toecaps. Thinking it had to be baby vomit, as he never wore his shoes in the bathroom, he began asking himself how long it had been there for, when a woman's curt, monosyllabic voice came barking out from the intercom.

'Sorry to bother you, ma'am,' Tanner began, clearing his throat. 'It's Detective Chief Inspector Tanner, Norfolk Police. I was just wondering if I'd be able to come in to have a very quick chat with Sir

Charles Fletcher?'

'What's it about?' the woman demanded, in a distinctly clipped British accent.

'I was speaking with him the other day. We were discussing security, amongst other things. I just had a couple more questions for him, if that's OK?'

'Well, you'd be more than welcome to come up, but unfortunately, my husband's still in bed.'

Tanner glanced suspiciously down at his watch. Seeing it was nearly eleven o'clock, he pulled his shoulders back to ask, 'Then perhaps you'd be so kind as to wake him up for me?'

Half expecting her to tell him to sod off, he let out a relieved sigh when he heard her voice come back over the intercom.

'Very well, Chief Inspector whatever your name is, but don't blame me if he's in a foul mood when I do.'

Hearing a metallic clunk, followed by a mechanical whirring sound, Tanner jogged back to his car as the gates began to creep sedately open.

Offering the squad car's driver a perfunctory nod, he clambered inside his own to close the door. With the engine started, he began edging his car through the gate's gradually expanding gap, before speeding his way through to follow the meandering road to the stately home at the top.

- CHAPTER FIFTY SIX -

SEEING AN ELEGANT middle aged woman, waiting for him outside the stately home's resplendent entrance, wearing a pair of sleek black riding boots, skin-tight breeches, and a quintessentially British tweed jacket, he brought his car to a slow, gradual standstill.

'Lady Fletcher?' he enquired, climbing slowly out.

Seeing her nod to drape her arms around her thin, narrow waist, he closed the door to pull out his formal ID. 'Detective Chief Inspector Tanner, Norfolk Police.'

'I thought you were here to ask my husband some questions?'

'That's correct.'

'Then why, may I ask, does your presence here necessitate the police escort?'

Tanner glanced around to see the squad car she was directing his attention to come grinding to a halt behind Sir Charles's Bentley Continental, as he'd instructed. 'They're here for – er – moral support,' he smiled back.

The woman planted her arms down onto her narrow, boyish hips. 'Surprisingly, Chief Inspector, I wasn't born yesterday.'

'OK, well, depending on his answers, we may need to give him a lift down to the station.'

'Oh my,' she responded, returning to Tanner a

particularly bored, unemotional expression. 'My husband, arrested. The scandal. The intrigue. The single newspaper headline. How very exciting.'

'If you say so,' Tanner replied, not particularly surprised by her haughty, uncaring attitude.

'May I ask what he's to be arrested for?'

'*If* we do,' Tanner repeated, 'then, unfortunately, I'm not at liberty to say.'

'It's not about that story in the newspaper, is it?' she eagerly asked, as if desperately hoping it was. 'You know, the one about all that disgusting child prostitution?'

'Is there a reason why you think it could be?' Tanner enquired, curious to know what had made her leap to such an abhorrent conclusion.

'You mean, apart from him spending the vast majority of our marriage sneaking out at all hours of the night to do God knows what, that he's always been more interested in pre-pubescent girls than myself, despite the fact that I used to be one of the highest ranked models in Europe, or that I've caught him on more than one occasion playing with himself whilst staring at images on a computer that had me throwing up in the toilet?'

'Forgive me, Lady Fletcher, but if you suspected your husband of being a paedophile, why on Earth haven't you come forward to tell someone about it?'

'I don't know, Chief Inspector. Why do you think?'

'But – you don't seem to have any objection to telling me now?'

'I was hardly going to hand him over, was I! The man *is* still my husband, which has left me having to endure waiting around for years on end for someone to turn up on our doorstep. And here you are. Finally!'

Tanner shook his head in bemused disbelief. 'I assume you subsequently won't mind if I went inside to ask him about it?'

'Be my guest! I'll even walk you to his bedroom.'

'You don't share the same room?'

'Are you mad? It's bad enough having to be married to some contemptible, malignant paedophile, let alone having to share the same bed as one!'

Watching her spin gracefully around, Tanner gestured over at the two police officers to remain where they were, before turning back to follow her in.

As he stopped to stare open-mouthed at the stately home's lavish foyer, he had to quicken his step to follow her up a wide, sweeping staircase.

'I hope you'll do your best to keep my name out of the papers?' he heard her enquire, as she reached the sprawling floor above. 'But if you do feel the need, may I ask if you could use a half-decent picture of me? Actually, before you go, remind me to give you the name of my publicist.'

'Er...yes, of course,' Tanner responded, rolling his eyes. No matter how many members of the so-called British Aristocracy he met during his career, he still found the despondent manner in which they all seemed to view the world to be both shocking and disturbing.

'Right, he's in here,' she announced, coming to an abrupt halt beside a large white door. 'Do you want me to go in first?'

'If you wouldn't mind.'

'Well, actually, I would, but I can fully understand why you wouldn't.'

With that, she knocked loudly to call, 'Charles, my dear, there's someone here to see you!'

Without waiting for a response, she marched straight in, only to find the voluminous double bed parked in the middle to be devoid of anything but four large pillows and a duvet. 'Oh!' she exclaimed, stopping where she was. 'I could have sworn he was here.'

Shoving unceremoniously past her, Tanner threw back the duvet to reveal nothing but a crumpled bedsheet.

'He must have left unusually early,' he heard her continue.

Leaping over to a wardrobe, Tanner flung the doors open to find it as empty as the bed. 'Shit!' he cursed, glancing fitfully about to notice the drawers of a nearby chest had all been left half-open. 'When did you see him last?'

'Sometime last night. I'm not sure when.'

'Do you have any idea where he could have gone?'

'Not really,' she replied, taking a moment to glance nonchalantly down at her watch.

'You must have a flat, somewhere?'

'Well, we do, but it's more of a chalet than a flat, and it's not in this country, I'm afraid. It's in Switzerland,' she smiled.

'How the hell is he going to get to Switzerland? His bloody car's still parked outside!'

'Well, if he has been good enough to up-sticks and leave, he'd have been far more likely to take his Aston Martin. He only uses his Bentley for parading around town. Not for any serious driving.'

- CHAPTER FIFTY SEVEN -

RUNNING OUT OF the stately home to be welcomed by the smatter of rain, Tanner sprinted over to the awaiting squad car to rap his knuckles against the driver's side window.

'I thought you said nobody had left?' he demanded, the moment the window began sliding down.

'No one *had* left!' the young officer stated.

'Nobody apart from Sir Charles bloody Fletcher, you mean!'

'Swear to God, sir! Nobody came out of the gates. Not since we've been here.'

'What about before?'

'Well...'

'Well, what?'

'The officers we took over from. They said they weren't, but when we arrived, they did appear to be fast asleep.'

'FOR FUCK'S SAKE!' Tanner ranted, slamming his fist down onto the squad car's rain-splattered roof. 'Right, wait there!' he ordered, spinning away, just as the sound of the police radio inside began spluttering into life.

Pelting back to the mansion's pillared alcove, he took shelter from the steadily intensifying rain to put a call through to the office.

'Townsend, it's Tanner,' he began, recognising the

detective constable's voice.

'Hi boss! Long time no see. How are you?'

'Is Vicky there?' he asked, ignoring the normal pleasantries.

'Yes, of course. I'll put you through.'

A rumble of thunder had Tanner glancing up to the sky to find it becoming ominously dark.

'Vicky,' he began, the moment she answered, 'we have a situation. I've arrived at Sir Charles Fletcher's estate only to find he's done a runner.'

'But – I thought there was a car parked outside the gates?'

'He must have driven straight past them. Anyway, I need you to get an all-ports warning out for him. According to his wife, they have a chalet in Switzerland. With their political neutrality, I think there's every chance that he could be trying to make his way there. There's also a possibility that he could be heading there by car, so make sure to let Passport Control at Eurotunnel know. Cross channel ferry operators, as well.'

'Is he in his Bentley?'

'It's more likely to be an Aston Martin, but I'll confirm that shortly, along with its model and registration number.'

Seeing one of the police constable's climb out of the squad car, into what was fast becoming a torrential downpour, Tanner ended the call to make his way towards him.

'Sorry, sir,' the man called out, torrents of rain streaming down his chubby, youthful face. 'More bad news, I'm afraid.'

'Do I want to know?' Tanner enquired, flipping his fluorescent hood over his head.

'The suspect, Joseph Miller. He's managed to escape.'

'What?'

'They forgot to lock the car when they stopped off for petrol.'

'I thought the back doors couldn't be opened from the inside?'

'Apparently, he climbed over the front seats.'

'You must be fucking joking,' Tanner muttered. 'Where was this?'

'Just outside Westfield.'

'Do they have any idea where he went?'

'He was seen entering a local primary school. By the number of screaming children seen running out the other way, they think he's still in there.'

- CHAPTER FIFTY EIGHT -

WITH THE SOUND of rain, rattling off his Jag's roof like a tin drum, Tanner arrived outside Westfield Primary School to find the place surrounded by at least half-a-dozen squad cars.

Parking on the kerb, he wrenched on the handbrake to see a string of uniformed officers on the other side of the road, struggling to keep what must have been at least a hundred petrified-looking children herded behind a line of flickering blue and white tape.

Seeing yet another officer, standing with a fluorescent jacket zipped up to his nose on the other side of the school gates, he climbed quickly out to pelt his way over.

'What the hell's going on here?' he demanded, stopping in front of him to present his ID.

'I'm – er – not one-hundred percent sure, sir,' the young constable replied, staring at Tanner like a frightened rabbit. 'All I know is that it's become a hostage situation.'

'Who's in charge?'

'DI Haverstock, sir.'

'And where is he?'

'In the foyer, just outside the assembly hall. He's waiting for an armed response unit.'

Tanner glared at him with a look of deranged

incredulity. 'Please, God, tell me you're joking?'

'Er...' the young constable began, 'well, sir, apparently, the suspect is armed, and with him being a murder suspect, and everything...'

'Jesus Christ!' Tanner grimaced, turning away in utter dismay.

Leaving the police constable where he was, Tanner charged over the playground, straight into the school's main entrance to immediately see the man who was supposedly in charge, deep in conversation with yet another group of uniformed officers.

The moment he came dripping to a halt in the foyer, Haverstock looked up to glare over at him.

'May I enquire as to what you're doing here, sir?' the detective inspector asked, as Tanner approached.

'I was in the neighbourhood,' he replied, staring through two large open doors to see a man holding something up against the exposed neck of a young woman, at the furthest end of an otherwise empty assembly hall.

'Do I really need to remind you that this isn't your jurisdiction?'

'Not yet it isn't,' Tanner mumbled, under his breath.

'What was that?'

'Do we know who the hostage is?' he continued, ignoring the question.

Haverstock glanced down at his notes. 'Miss Susan Hampton. She teaches Year Three.'

'And the weapon?'

'We think it's a screwdriver.'

Tanner gave him a look of curious incomprehension. 'And that necessitates the need for an armed police unit, does it?'

'I'm sorry, sir, but I'm not risking the life of a school teacher.'

'And you think a bunch of trigger-happy armed police officers are going to help?'

'We have a serial-killing psychopath with the sharp end of a screwdriver jammed up against a young lady's neck. What the hell was I supposed to do?'

'Well, for a start, he's only a serial-killing psychopath in the eyes of the local press.'

'I thought you wanted to speak to him in connection with the murders?'

'That was before I found him locked inside the church at Swanton Morley, where the vicar says he's been since Monday. The person I really want to talk to has somehow managed to do a runner.'

'And who's that?'

'Sir Charles Fletcher?' Tanner questioned. 'The person whose DNA has been found at three of the crime scenes?'

With Haverstock staring at him with a particularly moronic expression, Tanner drew in a reticent breath. 'I take it you didn't bother to read that forensic report you emailed over to me?'

'I'm sorry,' he eventually replied, his face darkening with embarrassment, 'I just sent it straight to you, the moment it arrived.'

'Anyway, it doesn't matter,' Tanner replied, refocussing his attention towards Miller, and the woman being held in front of him. 'He's probably halfway to Switzerland by now. What's your strategy for dealing with the current situation, apart from having our hostage-taker shot in the head, of course?'

'I don't know. I've never had to deal with anything even remotely similar to this.'

'Have you tried talking to him?'

'Of course!'

'And...?'

'He just keeps saying the same thing; that he didn't do it.'

'Probably because he didn't,' Tanner remarked, stepping around to make his way into the assembly hall.

'Where are you going?' came Haverstock's earnest voice.

'To have a chat to him,' came Tanner's straightforward response. 'What did you think?'

- CHAPTER FIFTY NINE -

FIXING HIS ATTENTION on Miller's eyes, hovering behind the panic-stricken face of the female teacher, Tanner lifted his hands in the air to edge his way forward.

'Hello, Joe!' he eventually called. 'It's John? John Tanner? We met at the church, earlier today?'

'I DIDN'T DO IT!' the man suddenly bellowed, his voice left to reverberate around the assembly hall.

As the woman began shaking with fear, Miller shouted again. 'I DIDN'T DO IT! I DIDN'T KILL ANY OF THEM!'

Coming to a gradual halt about twenty feet away, Tanner lowered his hands. 'I know you didn't, Joe. That's why I wanted to talk to you.'

With the only sound coming from the rain, relentlessly lashing the windows outside, and the muffled sobs of the snivelling teacher, the giant assembly hall fell into a cold, sterile silence.

'There's nothing to talk about,' came Miller's eventual response. 'I didn't kill them. I could never have done anything like that.'

'I know, Joe. It's my fault. I should have explained what was happening when I found you at the church.'

With no reply, Tanner resumed inching his way forward. 'I was talking to the vicar. He told me you'd been there since Monday. He also told me that he'd locked you inside. That's how I know you couldn't have killed all those people.'

'I heard Father Graham listening to the radio. It said everyone was out looking for me.'

'The journalists got it wrong, Joe.'

'But – you told them it was me!'

'I know, Joe, and I'm truly sorry. I got it wrong as well.'

As Tanner continued creeping his way over the dusty wooden floor, he was able to see the young woman's face; her strained, tear-soaked eyes, staring at him in silent desperation as the underside of her jaw trembled against the tip of a particularly lethal-looking screwdriver.

'YOU'RE LYING!' Miller suddenly screamed, jamming the makeshift weapon up behind the teacher's jawbone, leaving her eyes growing to the size of discs as she desperately tried to stop her head from being impaled on its grimy steel tip.

'I'm not lying, Joe.'

'THEN PROVE IT!'

Tanner wracked his brain, trying to think of a way to convince him. 'You can tell I'm not because...' he began, his mind racing in circles before finally latching onto something he hoped would work, '...because Father Graham gave me his word that you'd been there the whole time. If I'm lying, then he must have been lying as well, and we both know that he wouldn't do that, don't we, Joe?'

Holding Miller's demented gaze, Tanner watched with relief as he finally began to relax his grip on the screwdriver's handle.

'Another reason I know it wasn't you, Joe,' he continued, 'is because the man who did kill all those people is at this very moment trying to get away, and the longer I'm here, watching you hold that screwdriver up to that poor woman's neck, the less chance I have of catching him.'

As he was talking, Miller's eyes swivelled around to stare at the side of the woman's pale, trembling face.

'Her name's Miss Hampton,' Tanner added, making a point of looking directly at her. 'She's one of the teachers here. You teach Year Three, don't you, Miss Hampton?'

The woman blinked a river of tears from her eyes to respond with a single, hesitant nod.

'Imagine how upset all the children in her class would be if something happened to her?'

Seeing Miller lower the screwdriver a fraction more, Tanner took a chance. 'Did you have a favourite teacher at school, Joe? Someone who was especially kind to you?'

Miller shifted his gaze down to the woman's fragile, exposed neck, and the tip of the screwdriver resting against it. 'I did,' he mumbled. 'Miss Copeland.'

'Imagine if the lady you're holding was Miss Copeland?' Tanner continued, 'and you had a screwdriver held against *her* neck?'

As Miller's head slumped forward, he closed his eyes to let the screwdriver slip through his fingers.

The second it clattered against the hall's parquet floor, the teacher pushed herself away from him to leap into Tanner's awaiting arms, tears of relief streaming down her red, distraught face.

Directing her towards the police officers behind him, Tanner stepped cautiously towards Miller, his knees now held against his chest as he openly sobbed.

'It's alright, Joe. Try not to worry,' Tanner began, picking up the screwdriver before signalling for Haverstock. 'We're going to take good care of you, I promise.'

Climbing cautiously to his feet, he edged his way back before turning to face the approaching DI. 'He really needs psychiatric help,' he whispered, leading him away. 'Maybe you could arrange that for me?'

'Yes, of course.'

'And you may find this useful,' he continued, handing him the makeshift weapon, 'especially if you're going anywhere near Ikea at the weekend.'

Stepping back into the foyer, Tanner was about to head outside when he heard the all-too familiar sound of his phone, ringing from the depths of his threadbare sailing jacket.

'Tanner speaking,' he said, stopping where he was to answer.

'Hi boss, it's Vicky.'

'Yes, Vicky, how can I help?'

'I just thought you'd like to know that we've had some luck regarding Sir Charles Fletcher.'

'Has he been found?'

'We've received a call from Passport Control down at Harwich. They were a little late picking up the all-ports warning, but he's just been seen driving his Aston Martin on board a cross channel ferry.'

'Please tell me it hasn't left yet?' Tanner pleaded, his heart picking up a beat.

'Thanks to the delightful weather we're currently enjoying, it's been delayed. They're asking what they should do?'

'Do you think they can continue its delay until I can get there?'

'Well, I can ask, but it's a two hour drive. I was wondering if it would be better to ask the local police to bring him in?'

'Not when he's a knight of the bloody realm it

wouldn't, and a slippery one at that. Just tell them to hold the boat for as long as possible. I'll be there as soon as I can.'

- CHAPTER SIXTY -

HOPING THE HOWLING wind and near torrential rain would be enough to keep the ferry moored firmly against its dock, at least until he was able to drive down to it, Tanner took the A140 heading for Ipswich, crossing the River Stour, to then speed his way around to the coastal town of Harwich.

Following the signs for the international port, he was soon entering a complex system of white lines and traffic cones, eventually seeing a blue and white ferry, hovering in the distance like an enormous floating hotel.

Using the ferry as a point of reference, he continued to follow the virtually deserted road around, until spying a man dressed head to foot in orange.

Stopping briefly for directions to Passport Control, he continued on, until reaching a barrier opposite a sheltered security booth, with two uniformed policemen standing outside, their black peaked caps pulled firmly down over their eyes.

As he brought his car to a halt underneath the shelter, he wound his window down to present them with his formal ID. 'Detective Chief Inspector Tanner. I hope you're expecting me?'

'PC Hollingsworth,' answered the nearest, 'and PC Manning. We've been asked to meet you here, sir, to provide support, if needed.'

'That would be appreciated, thank you.'

'We have a passport photograph of the man we're supposed to be looking for,' the officer continued. 'Mr Charles Fletcher. Is that correct?'

'It's actually *Sir* Charles Fletcher,' Tanner replied, already grateful for having made the effort to drive down. 'I assume that's the ferry,' he continued, gesturing towards it.

'It is, sir, but we need to be quick. We've been informed that the captain is keen to leave as soon as possible.'

'What about the weather?' Tanner queried, as a particularly violent gust of wind pummelled against the side of his car, leaving the two police officers turning their faces away from the stinging sheet of rain carried with it.

'Apparently, it's more about the state of the sea than the actual weather,' Hollingsworth continued, 'which we've been told has improved, enough at least for them to make the crossing.'

'Then we'd better push on. If you could tell me where I can leave my car, I'll follow you on board.'

- CHAPTER SIXTY ONE -

KNOWING THAT SIR Charles could have been anywhere on board the vast, sprawling ferry, Tanner stepped off the end of its clattering steel boarding platform to come grinding to hesitant halt.

As he stared one way, then the other, the officers behind him exchanged a concerned glance.

'Does anyone know how many decks there are?' Tanner eventually asked.

'Three, I think,' Hollingsworth replied, 'but that doesn't include the two where all the cars are kept.'

'So, five, then?'

'Well, yes, but I'm not sure they allow anyone to stay on the lower decks once the boat departs, which should hopefully leave one each.'

'You're forgetting that the boat hasn't left the dock yet, so he could still be down there.'

'Does he know we're looking for him?'

'He shouldn't, but he might,' Tanner replied, remembering the man's wife, and that she knew they were after him.

'Well, if he doesn't, then he should be on one of the upper decks with everyone else. If we can't find him there, then we can always start checking the cars.'

Tanner looked indecisively about. 'I don't suppose anyone knows how many people are on board?'

The officers exchanged a non-committal glance.

'I take it that means you don't?'

'We can ask the captain, if you like?'

Tanner shook his head, his eyes peering down one of the seemingly endless walkways. 'I'm not sure it would make any difference, even if we did know.'

Turning back, he found the same officer holding out a two-way radio for him.

'I thought this might be useful, sir.'

Accepting it with a grateful nod, he quickly familiarised himself with its controls. 'Right! I suppose we'd better get started. Maybe if I take the upper deck, then perhaps you two could divide the remaining ones between you?'

Watching them leave, Tanner took the stairs to the ferry's uppermost deck to gaze anxiously out at the mouth of the River Stour, and the hazy coastline beyond that marked the boundary between Suffolk and Norfolk. There were literally hundreds of people on board, some milling about the sheltered deck, others queuing up inside the various cafes and bars. There were even some braving the wind and rain on the viewing platform at the very back of the ship. It was when he saw a sign that said, "Cabins 1 – 100", immediately alongside another that said, "Toilets Level 4" did his shoulders drop in despondent despair. If Sir Charles had booked himself into a cabin, or if he was hiding inside what must have been at least two-dozen toilets, then they were going to have little to no chance of ever being able to find him.

Determining that the worst case scenario was that the ship would sail, leaving him working with Holland Police to pick their way through the disembarking passengers, he briefly imagined the call he'd have to make to Christine, telling her that he wouldn't be home that night because he'd decided to take a cross channel ferry to Holland instead.

Laughing to himself, he pulled his shoulders back as he thought how best to begin. 'From bow to stern, or stern to bow?'

Realising that the ship was so big, he didn't even know which end was which, he simply began walking towards what he assumed would be the bow, being that was the end facing towards what he did at least know was the North Sea.

- CHAPTER SIXTY TWO -

HALF-AN-HOUR later, having picked his way through what must have been literally hundreds of people, all of a dizzying variety of ages, shapes, and sizes, Tanner finally reached the windswept viewing platform at the very back of the gigantic vessel.

With the rain still pouring down, he flicked his hood back over his head before venturing out to begin doing his best to stare into the faces of the various brave souls who were there, huddled against the painted white railings with either hoods pulled over their heads, or fighting to keep their umbrellas from blowing away.

As one young couple spun around to run straight past him, giggling excitedly as they did, he took their place to stare out at the complex array of buildings, cranes, and neatly stacked containers that made up Harwich International Port, before turning to lean back against the railing.

Having done his absolute best to study the features of every single adult male he'd passed, he'd only seen one person he thought could have potentially been Sir Charles. That was a man speaking fluent Dutch, enjoying a meal with his attractive blonde wife, and three even blonder children.

Hearing the muffled sound of his borrowed two-way radio, crackling out his name, he dug it out to depress its talk button.

'DCI Tanner receiving, over.'

'It's Constable Hollingsworth, sir. We've had word from the ship's captain. They're all set to sail. He's given us ten minutes to disembark, otherwise, we'll be heading for the Hook of Holland.'

'Shit,' Tanner cursed, quietly to himself. He'd been expecting the news, but knowing that he was about to be stuck on board a ferry, jostled up against hundreds of passengers for what was likely to be a particularly unpleasant crossing, only to have to wait to come all the way back again, was hardly ideal.

'Have you had any luck?' came back Hollingsworth's voice.

Tanner lifted the receiver to his mouth. 'I've done a sweep of the entire top level. Nothing so far. How about you?'

'Not so much as a dickie-bird.'

'And your colleague?'

'Same here, sir,' came the other officer's voice.

'Are we absolutely sure he's on board?' Tanner enquired, somewhat desperately.

'He's been checked in, together with his car, so he should be. He certainly wouldn't have been able to drive off again, that much is certain.'

'No, of course.'

'How about if we ask the captain to make an announcement over the tannoy system, asking for him to make himself known to one of the crew?'

'It would probably only serve to alert him to the fact that we're looking for him, making him even harder to find.'

Silence followed, before Hollingsworth's voice came crackling back. 'What do you think we should do, sir?'

At that stage, Tanner had no choice but to let them

go. It was one thing for him to have to endure a trip to mainland Europe, but it was quite another to expect them to as well. 'Thanks for your help, chaps, but I think you both need to make your way to the nearest exit.'

'And what about you, sir?'

'Looks like I've just got myself a free trip to Holland!'

Thanking them again, he promised to return the radio on his eventual return, before signing off, only to hear the dull, muffled sound of his phone ring.

Shoving the bulky two-way radio into one of his sailing jacket's voluminous pockets, he dug the phone out to see it was Vicky, calling from her mobile.

'Hi Vicky,' he answered, doing his best to keep the phone out of the unrelenting rain. 'What's up?'

'I just thought I'd call to see how you were getting on?'

'I'm on board the ferry that Sir Charles is supposed to be on, but there's no sign of him.'

'Do you need any help?'

'How do you mean?'

'I'm at Passport Control, just waiting to be let through.'

'You've driven all the way down here?'

'Not on my own. Sally, Townsend, Gina, and Henderson are all in the car with me.'

Tanner's face cracked into an emotionally charged grin.

'We thought that if you were going to have to search an entire ferry, that you could probably do with some help.'

'Thanks guys. It's appreciated, really it is. But, unfortunately, I think you're too late. The ship is about to sail.'

'Don't worry, boss. I've already spoken to the

captain. He's going to hold it until we've managed to clamber our way on board.'

- CHAPTER SIXTY THREE -

'THANK YOU ALL for coming down,' said Tanner, meeting the bulk of his CID team at the top of the ferry's galvanised steel gangway. 'It means a lot to me.'

'No problem, boss,' grinned Townsend. 'Besides, it wasn't as if we had anything better to do.'

A loud double-clunk had them glancing behind them to see the platform they'd been standing on just moments before drop suddenly away.

As they each peered over the railings, two-hundred feet down to the dock below, Tanner waited for them to look back before saying, 'I hope you all brought your passports.'

The question left them glancing fitfully about at each other.

'Don't worry,' he laughed, 'I don't have mine either. Besides, we won't need them. We're not exactly on a tour of Northern Europe.'

As the entire ferry began trembling underneath them, Henderson reached for the nearest railing. 'I've never been on a boat before,' he said, his eyes watching the ferry inch slowly away from the dock.

'Then you're in for a treat!'

'But – what if I get seasick?' the detective constable questioned, already looking a little green around the edges.

'Then you'll throw up over the side,' Tanner

replied, in a matter-of-fact tone. 'Anyway, we'd better get started. I suggest we pair up, just in case our suspect kicks up a fuss when we do eventually find him. Sally and Townsend, if you two can go together. Vicky, you can come with me. Gina, if you could go with Henderson?'

'Wouldn't it be better if we all split up?' Gina asked, with an imploring look of pleading desperation. 'We'd be able to cover more ground that way.'

'I'd rather we worked in pairs,' Tanner replied. 'besides, there's no great rush. After all, it is a six-and-a-half our crossing.'

'Six-and-a-half hours?' Henderson repeated, his googly eyes staring back. 'Vicky told me it would only take twenty minutes!'

'Er...I think I said it would take twenty minutes to board,' she replied, a little defensively.

'You said it would be twenty minutes there, and twenty minutes back!'

'I did, didn't I,' she acquiesced. 'Sorry about that. To be honest, I didn't think you'd come if you knew it was going to be a thirteen hour round trip.'

'Tell you what,' intervened Tanner, keen to move the subject along before an argument broke out, 'Gina, why don't you go with Vicky, then Henderson can come with me?'

Hearing the news, Gina did her very best to suppress a grin of victorious relief, whilst Henderson was left looking like he was about to be violently ill.

'Right!' Tanner continued. 'Believe it or not, I've played this game before. Quite recently, in fact. Sally and Townsend, if you take the lower passenger deck. Vicky and Gina, you take the one in the middle, and Henderson, you and I can take the one at the top. There's plenty of fresh air up there, which will help if you do start to feel a little under the weather. You'll also be able to be sick over the side without upsetting too many people, as long as they're not directly underneath you, of course.'

Wondering if he was about to, before they even started, Tanner glanced around at everyone else. 'OK, you all know who we're looking for. I hope you've made sure to make a note of what he looks like. If you do see him, call me immediately. Whatever you do, do not approach him. Remember, he can't go anywhere, and we have plenty of time. If we're unable to find him for whatever reason, then the worst case scenario is that we'll have to wait until he tries to disembark in Holland.'

- CHAPTER SIXTY FOUR -

THE MOMENT TANNER reached the upper deck at the very top of the stairs, he heard Henderson whimper breathlessly behind him, 'Sorry – boss – but – I really don't think I'm feeling very well.'

Turning to see the poor boy's goat-like face had turned from its normal pasty colour to a more ghoulish shade of green, Tanner hurried back to take him gently by the arm. 'OK, try not to worry. You'll feel better when you get outside, I promise.'

'I hope so, boss. At the moment I feel like I'm about to be sick.'

'Here we go!' said Tanner, wrenching the door open for them to be instantly hit by a stinging blast of cold, revitalising wind.

Setting him down on a bench outside, Tanner instructed him to breathe deeply through his nose whilst keeping his eyes fixed on the horizon, before leaving him to continue his search.

Reminding himself that he had plenty of time, he returned to the ferry's bow to begin slowly making his way back, searching every nook, cranny, restaurant, and bar, until again reaching the aft end's viewing platform, but that time having not seen a single person who looked even remotely like the suspect.

Cold, tired, and in desperate need of a coffee, he glared frustratedly around at the half-dozen or so people, leaning over the rails to watch the British mainland slip slowly away.

As the ferry began to rise and fall over vast, mountainous waves, he cast his eyes out over the North Sea's stark, inhospitable landscape.

Smiling at the memory of his time spent sailing around the Mediterranean, he was about to go in search of a coffee when he heard the demanding sound of his phone.

'Yes, Vicky?' he replied, ducking inside the peaceful comfort of a carpeted restaurant. 'How're you getting on?'

'No luck yet, boss. How about you?'

'Same here, I'm afraid. Have you heard from Sally and Townsend?'

'Not yet. They've probably managed to find themselves an empty cabin.'

Tanner rolled his eyes. 'I hadn't thought of that. Hey-ho. Too late now.'

'How's Henderson?'

'I left him on a bench somewhere. I don't think he's going to be much use, I'm afraid.'

'You never know, he may see Sir Charles walk straight past.'

'I'm not sure he's in much of a state to notice *anything* walk past, unless perhaps it was Godzilla, wearing a pair of bright red stilettos.'

'I was actually wondering if it would be worth asking if the crew would be able to help find him,' Vicky continued, 'or to at least ask if they'd seen him?'

'You know, that's actually not a bad idea!' Tanner replied, already scanning the lounge area for someone suitable to ask.

'Anyway, it was just a thought. We're going to keep looking for another twenty minutes or so before taking a break. I hope that's OK?'

'Yes, of course! Maybe we could all meet up somewhere, then I'd be able to treat you.'

'Sounds good. I'll let the others know.'

Ending the call, Tanner caught the eye of a female member of the ship's crew, kneeling on the carpet whilst chatting to the parents of two small children, neither of whom were looking particularly well.

Waiting for her to climb to her feet, he caught her eye to beckon her over. 'Are they going to be OK?' he asked, gesturing back at the family.

'Seasickness,' she replied, glancing around at the half-empty restaurant. 'It's going to be a difficult crossing,' she continued, 'but you seem to be alright.'

'Oh, I'm used to it,' he laughed.

'I see!' she responded, taking him in with more interest. 'You're a sailor?'

'Part-time. Actually, these days more like no-time.'

His response had her nodding with an understanding smile. 'My husband and I have a small yacht which we rarely seem to use, so I know what you mean. Anyway, may I help you at all?'

'I'm actually here in an official capacity,' he replied, discreetly fishing out his formal ID.

Staring down at it, her head baulked back in surprise. 'Sorry,' she said, glancing up, 'it's just that – well – you don't look like a policeman.'

'I'll take that as a compliment,' he replied, replacing it to glance furtively around. 'It's a bit of a longshot, but I was actually wondering if either you, or maybe one of your colleagues, has seen a male passenger on board who we're keen to have a chat with.'

'Can you describe him?'

'Oh, you know, just your average serial-killing psychopath.'

'So, not dangerous, then?'

'Well, perhaps just a little.'

Returning to him an affable smile, she cast her eyes incuriously around. 'If I had to put my money on someone on board being a serial-killing psychopath, using the journey to contemplate my various unholy acts, I'd probably pick that man over there,' she said, her eyes resting on a figure leaning against the railings outside, the hood of a rain coat pulled over his head. 'He's been there since boarding. Either that, or he's feeling a little green around the gills, like just about everyone else.'

- CHAPTER SIXTY FIVE -

THANKING THE WOMAN for her time, Tanner made his way back towards the restaurant's rain-splattered glass door to rest a hand on its cold metal handle. As he felt the ferry begin to fall beneath his feet before lifting slowly up, his eyes remained fixed on the hooded man the crew member had brought his attention to. From where he was standing, it was impossible to tell if he was Sir Charles Fletcher or not. The hood he had on completely hid his face. But there was something about the way he was leaning against the railings, with one gleaming black Wellington boot perched nonchalantly on its lowest rung, that gave the impression that it was at least a possibility.

Trying to think of a reason to go over and talk to him, other than the obvious, he thought he might ask if the man had a light for a cigarette that Tanner didn't have, when he had a better idea.

Heaving open the door, he stepped out into the howling wind to bellow out, 'Sir Charles!'

The second the words flew out of his mouth, the man whipped his head around to present him with a look of curious intrigue.

'Gotcha,' Tanner muttered, under his breath, flicking his fluorescent hood back over his head to jog quickly over.

'I thought that was you,' he eventually continued,

reaching the railings in time to brace himself as the ferry's bow pounded into an oncoming wave.

Even with Tanner staring directly into the man's cold blue eyes, it was obvious he still hadn't recognised him. 'Detective Chief Inspector Tanner?' he prompted, pulling the wired peak of his hood back to allow his face to be seen more clearly. 'Norfolk Police? We met the other day, outside your resplendent stately home.'

As the scales of incomprehension fell from his eyes, Tanner watched him glance surreptitiously around the viewing platform, as if checking to see if anyone else was with him, before eventually opening his mouth. 'Yes, of course! What on Earth are you doing here?'

'Well, it may sound a little strange, but I was actually looking for you.'

'On a ferry, in the middle of the North Sea?' he queried, with a look of spurious incredulity. 'That sounds more than a little strange. How did you even know I was here?'

'We were alerted by Passport Control, shortly after you boarded,' Tanner replied, making sure to study his reaction. 'May I ask where you're going?'

'To be honest, Chief Inspector, I'm not sure what that has to do with you.'

'I'm just curious, really.'

Sir Charles's eyes flickered indecisively between Tanner's. 'If you must know, I've decided to take some time off from the campaign trail to spend a few relaxing days at my Swiss chalet.'

'Wouldn't it have been quicker to fly?'

'No doubt,' he shrugged, 'but I enjoy the drive.'

'What about your wife?'

'Unfortunately, she couldn't come.'

'Did you at least tell her you were going?'

'Of course!'

'Oh, right,' Tanner replied, casting his eyes briefly out to sea with a strange, mystified expression. 'It's just that when I spoke to her this morning, she seemed to be under the impression that you were still in bed.'

Sir Charles shifted his weight from one foot to the other. 'Then she must have forgotten.'

'That you were going to drive all the way to Switzerland?'

'Forgive me, Chief Inspector, but unlike your average person, it's quite normal for me to take a few days out of my busy life to drive my quarter-of-a-million pound Aston Martin DBS down to the Swiss Alps, which is why I'm sure my wife *did* simply forget.'

'It's not because you're trying to run away from anything?'

'What on Earth would I be running away from?'

'Well, for a start, we know about your midnight meetings inside Swanton Morley church.'

'My "midnight meetings"?'

'The vicar said they were supposed to have something to do with either a photography club, or your election campaign.'

'Oh, *those* "midnight meetings"!'

'He just seemed a little confused as to why they always seemed to take place in the middle of the night?'

'Well, firstly, they never take place at midnight. They're normally held between nine and eleven, and that's simply because it's the only time people are able to come.'

'He was also confused as to why he never sees any women.'

'Then he needs to get his eyes tested.'

'So, they do take part, then?'

'Of course women take part!'

Tanner took a moment to deliberately fix the man's eyes. 'May I enquire as to how old they are?'

'What?'

'You just told me that women do take part in your clandestine, just-before midnight meetings, despite a vicar telling me he'd never seen any, so I was just wondering what sort of age they'd be?'

With Sir Charles falling reticently silent, Tanner was left to continue.

'It's just that we found some highly disturbing images of pre-pubescent girls on your cloud-based server. I don't suppose you have any idea how they got there, by any chance?'

'I'd have hoped that would have been obvious. Someone must have hacked into my computer to plant them there, probably in an effort to derail my election campaign.'

'Oh right, yes, I see. Or at least I would have done if someone hadn't tried to delete them just a few days ago. Whoever did, clearly didn't realise that your host keeps them on file for thirty days before permanently doing so, presumably in case they'd deleted them by accident.'

'OK, yes, I admit, that was me. I did try to delete them, but only because I just happened to find them there, not because I was the one who uploaded them.'

'We've also discovered that you've had previous communication with every single one of those men on that list I showed you the other day, the same ones you said you'd never heard of, all of whom have had remarkably similar files found on their cloud-based servers. What's perhaps even more surprising is that, once again, someone tried to delete them, very shortly after that story came out in the Norwich

Reporter.'

'Then whoever planted them on my computer must have done so on theirs as well.'

'For what possible reason?'

'I've no idea, but just because you found a few inappropriate pictures on my computer, doesn't automatically make me some sort of perverted paedophile.'

'But it does at least allow us to suspect you of being one,' Tanner replied, with a presumptuous smile.

'As I'm sure you know, Chief Inspector, given your profession, and everything, in the eyes of the law, I'm innocent until *proven* guilty.'

'And as I'm sure you know, given the position you're hoping to be elected into, in the eyes of the general public, people have a tendency to believe whatever they read in the newspapers.'

With Sir Charles falling silent once again, Tanner took a breath to continue. 'Regrettably, there's something else I need to share with you as well. As of this morning, every single one of the men on that list is now dead, every one apart from you, which does make me wonder what you're *really* doing on a ferry in the middle of the North Sea.'

'Please don't tell me that you're about to accuse me of murdering them all as well?'

'I must admit that, up until very recently, I was more of the opinion that you were in danger of being murdered yourself, possibly by someone you'd previously sexually assaulted. But that was before traces of your DNA were found at no less than three of the murder scenes.'

Sir Charles stared at Tanner with a look of confused incredulity. 'But – that – that can't be!' he eventually exclaimed.

'We've yet to hear back from forensics with regards

to where the fourth body was found, but there's no particular reason for me to believe that they won't find your DNA there as well.'

'Is this some sort of sick joke?'

'So what I'd really like to ask you is not *if* you killed them, but why?'

'But – I didn't!'

'Was it because you'd become concerned that one of them had started to feel guilty for spending year-after-year molesting what must have been dozens-upon-dozens of innocent young children, that he'd leaked the story to the press to try and make amends, but you weren't sure which, so you thought you'd better silence them all, just to be on the safe side?'

'What the hell are you talking about?'

'Or perhaps more likely, that you simply didn't trust any of them to keep their mouths shut when we came knocking on their doors to discuss the disgusting things you'd all been up to?'

'If my DNA *has* been found at some of the murder scenes, then I think it's obvious that someone is trying to frame me, especially when you take into account those images that had been uploaded onto my computer.'

'If that is the case, then someone must *really* have it in for you!'

'I'm sorry, but it's the only explanation I can think of.'

'You mean, apart from the one that you *are* a predatory paedophile, and that you *did* kill all your perverted chums in order to keep their mouths shut?'

'Or that someone's trying extraordinarily hard to make you think I'm responsible, when I had nothing to do with any of it!'

'Perhaps someone like your political rival, George Elliston, for example?' proposed Tanner.

'Yes, him! *He* must be the one who's behind all this! Haven't you found anything to suggest that he was there as well?'

'It's funny you should say that, but we *have* found evidence that he was at some of the crime scenes.'

'Then why the hell are we even having this conversation?'

'Because, up until very recently, he's been held under arrest at Wroxham Police Station, since shortly after the first body was found, which means it would have been physically impossible for him to have murdered the other three victims. But you didn't know that, did you? You couldn't have done, because we made sure that his name was kept out of the press. If you had, then I suspect you wouldn't have set about your plan to murder all your paedophile chums, making the rather clumsy effort to make it appear to have been him, and not you.'

As Tanner's words were whipped from his mouth by a particularly savage gust of wind, both men had to catch themselves as the ferry slammed into another enormous incoming wave.

Making sure to keep a firm hold of the railing, Sir Charles pulled himself up straight. 'I think, Mr Tanner, the time has come for me to seek legal representation.'

'You're more than welcome to, but we need to get you back to Wroxham Police Station first.'

'I'm referring to Swiss legal representation,' he continued, 'not their British counterparts.'

'Unfortunately, I'm afraid that won't be possible. As soon as we're done here, I'll be taking you into custody to await transportation back to the British mainland.'

'You seem to be forgetting that we'll have to stop at Holland first, at which point you'll have to place me into the hands of the local police, as you won't have the necessary jurisdiction to arrest me. You'll then need to apply to the Dutch courts to have me repatriated back to the UK, by which time they would have had to allow me to continue with my journey, as the Dutch Police would have had no legal reason to keep me in custody.'

'That's only if we were to allow you to disembark,' Tanner stated. 'Until then, according to Maritime Law, you remain under the jurisdiction of whichever country's flag is flying at the top of the ship's mask, which, in this particular instance,' Tanner continued, directing Sir Charles's attention to the top of the ferry to see a large predominantly red flag being flogged by the buffeting breeze, 'just happens to be the Red Ensign.'

- CHAPTER SIXTY SIX -

THE MOMENT HE turned back, he saw Sir Charles surge suddenly forward, shoving him hard against the railings to leave him struggling just to stay on his feet.

As the suspect leapt away, Tanner glanced around to see him pelting over the viewing platform, only for him to come cursing to a slow, reluctant halt.

'Are you alright there, boss?' came the welcome sound of Townsend's voice, drifting its way over from somewhere behind him.

Using the railings to claw himself up, he turned to see the young DI, standing in the restaurant's sheltered doorway, with Sally hovering behind.

When he saw both Vicky and Gina emerge from the ship's port-side walkway, and two burly male crew members stepping out from the one on the other side, he pulled himself up straight to begin making his way over.

'Sir Charles Fletcher, I'm arresting you for the murder of William Greenfield, Derek Harvey, Marcus Thornton, and Robert Hanson. Also for being in possession of indecent images of children. If it's discovered that you've been involved in their sexual abuse, or have helped others to do so, more charges will follow. You do not have to say anything, but it may harm your defence if you do not mention when questioned something which you later rely on in court. Anything you do say may be given in evidence.'

Whilst Tanner had been reading him his rights, Sir Charles had been inching his way slowly back. The moment he reached the railings at the ferry's furthest end, he placed his hands on the uppermost rung to glance fitfully over the side, two-hundred feet down to where the ship's massive twin-prop propellors churned mercilessly at the water below.

'I do hope you realise that there's nowhere for you to run?' Tanner queried, watching him with acute curiosity. 'Even if you were to somehow manage to climb down to the next level, there's no way off the boat, not without going into the sea. If that is your intention, then you should know that your chances of survival are somewhere between nought and zero'.

'I don't need to get off the boat,' Sir Charles called back, placing a foot onto the lowest rung to swing his leg over the top, 'neither do I need to go over the side, at least not yet,' he added, bringing his other leg over. 'There are plenty of places to hide on board until we reach our destination,' he continued, leaning out to stare down at the level below. 'Then all I'll need to do is to reach the shore. Once I have, you won't be able to lay a finger on me. I'll swim if I have to. I really don't care.'

'You're not seriously going to try and climb down, are you?' Tanner questioned, leaning his head over the railings in an effort to follow his suspect's gaze.

'Just watch me,' the man grinned defiantly back.

With Tanner looking on in astonished disbelief, Sir Charles lifted a foot off the bottom rail to begin lowering himself down. The moment he removed a hand to grab hold of the steel rung below, the ferry's bow slammed into yet another encroaching wave, the impact wrenching his hand from the top rail to leave him hanging in the air by his other, his legs kicking helplessly at the air underneath.

'Jesus Christ!' Tanner exclaimed, lurching forward to hang himself over the rail his suspect was now suspended by.

As Sir Charles tried desperately to swing his arm up for Tanner to grab, he gritted his teeth to mutter, 'Help me, for fuck's sake!'

'I'm trying!' Tanner grimaced, as the ferry began forging up the wave it had only just crashed into, leaving Sir Charles's entire body hanging further and further out over the boiling mass of water below.

'Then try harder!' the man demanded, glaring up at him in panicked desperation.

Leaning over just as far as he dared, Tanner stretched every tendon of his body to finally be able to grab hold of Sir Charles's outstretched hand.

With the sound of people approaching from behind, he began heaving the suspect up, only to feel the man's cold wet fingers begin slipping through his own.

'I can't hold on,' Tanner grimaced, the muscles in his arm screaming out in pain, as he desperately tried hauling the man up.

When he glanced around to see Townsend appear breathlessly by his side, he felt Sir Charles's hand slip silently out from his.

As the moment seemed to stretch itself out for an eternity, Tanner glared down in incomprehensible horror, as Sir Charles's body seemed to hang suspended in the air. With his petrified blue eyes staring up into his, Tanner screamed, 'NO!' But the single, solitary word could do nothing to stop the law of gravity from dragging his suspect away, the man's arms reaching forever up before vanishing into the unwelcome depths of the churning water below.

- CHAPTER SIXTY SEVEN -

THE MOMENT SIR Charles's body disappeared beneath the waves, the ferry was brought wallowing to a gradual halt. With the coastguard being alerted moments later, Tanner and the bulk of his team did their best to help first the ship's crew, then the arriving RNLI lifeboat, to conduct an exhaustive search of the sea's turbulent surface.

As the wind continued to build, and with the sea state becoming increasingly hostile, the ferry's captain was eventually forced to take the safety of his remaining passengers into account, turning the ferry around to head back to Harwich International Port.

When it eventually docked, Tanner was required to provide a statement to not only the ferry's captain, but also the coastguard and Essex Police, before finally being allowed to head back to the carpark where he'd left his car some five hours earlier.

'How're you holding up,' came Vicky's concerned voice, nudging herself off the side of her car parked alongside Tanner's.

'Tired, but OK, thank you. How about you?'

'Oh, I'm fine, but I wasn't the one hanging over the ferry's railing, trying to prevent a suspect from falling two-hundred feet into the North Sea.'

The image of Sir Charles's horror-stricken face flickered into Tanner's mind. 'Where's everyone else?' he asked, desperate to distract himself from having to relive the moment for what must have been the hundredth time.

'Grabbing some food before we head back.'

'Aren't you eating as well?'

'I've placed an order. I assume you've eaten?'

'I was able to grab something after speaking to the local police.'

'May I ask what you told them?'

'That I was endeavouring to arrest him when he climbed over the railings,' Tanner shrugged, his gaze drifting vacantly away.

'You do know that it wasn't your fault, don't you?' questioned Vicky.

'I suppose.'

'It's not a matter of supposition, John. It *wasn't* your fault, full stop, end of story!'

'But if I'd been able to hold on to him for a few seconds longer, Townsend could have helped pull him up.'

'Pull him up from where he was hanging off the back of a ferry, in the middle of the North Sea, trying to escape being arrested for murdering no less than four people, as well as for molesting God knows how many pre-pubescent young girls.'

Tanner stared at her with a haunting shadow hanging over his eyes. 'But we don't know that he did, though, do we.'

'We had physical evidence, and we had motive. We also had hundreds of sordid pictures and videos, all of which he'd tried to delete the moment the story broke. Then we have proof that he'd been in contact with all four of the murder victims, each in possession of similar files, all of which they'd also tried to delete. I don't think there's a court on planet Earth that wouldn't have found him guilty. I'm sorry, John. I don't often say this, but the guy had it coming.'

'Not if he was innocent.'

'If he was innocent, then why was he so willing to risk his life to avoid prosecution?'

Tanner dropped his head to stare down at the ground.

'Did he say anything to you, before...before he...?' Vicky hesitantly asked.

'Only that he didn't do it.'

'Didn't do what? Murder all those people, or spend half his life molesting pre-pubescent girls?'

'He said someone must have planted the images.'

'You mean, before he tried to delete them all?'

'Yes, I know. It doesn't sound very likely.'

'What about the murders?'

'He said it must have been George Elliston, trying to frame him.'

'Didn't he mean the opposite; that he was the one trying to frame Elliston?'

'I hear what you're saying, Vicky, but a court of law should have been left to decide his fate, not my inability to hold on to him.'

'Sir Charles Fletcher chose his own fate, not you!'

'Maybe so, but, unfortunately, it doesn't make what happened any easier.'

Vicky leant back against her car to stare apologetically at the ground. When she saw Tanner do the same, she looked up to ask, 'Are you going to be alright driving back?'

'I'll be fine.'

'You can take one of my passengers for company, if you like? There's barely enough room for all of us, so you'd be doing me a favour.'

'I think they'd be happier driving back with you. Besides, to be honest, I'd rather be on my own.'

'Yes, of course. Just promise to take a break if you need to.'

'Uh-huh.'

'Was that a yes, Vicky, I promise, or no, Vicky, I'd rather drift off to sleep to drive straight into a truck?'

'Yes, I promise.'

Pushing himself off the car to head wearily around to the driver's side, Tanner pulled out his phone to check for messages, only to see he'd had no less than three missed calls, all from Forrester.

Letting out an exhausted, world-weary sigh, he climbed inside before forcing himself to return his superintendent's various calls.

'Forrester, sir, it's Tanner.'

'Ah, Tanner. Thanks for coming back to me. I was really just phoning to make sure you were OK?'

'I take it you heard what happened?'

'Vicky told me. I assume there's been no further sign of him?'

'Nothing, I'm afraid, and it's hard to believe that there ever will be. We were about ten miles out when it happened, and what with the weather, and everything.'

'Did he say anything, before he went over?'

'If you mean a confession, then I'm afraid not?'

'Wishful thinking, I suppose. Anyway, at least it saves us having to go through a lengthy trial.'

'That's if he did it, sir.'

'Is there any doubt?'

Tanner hesitated for a moment, before mumbling, 'I suppose not.'

'OK, good. Now, I want you to take the rest of the week off.'

'But...'

'That's an order, Tanner!'

'Yes, sir.'

'That will at least give you the chance to get some much deserved rest. I'm also hoping it will give you some time to think about what we were discussing earlier.'

'I don't need any more time. I've already made my decision.'

'Oh, right,' Forrester replied, in a tone of anxious curiosity.

'If you do decide to close one of the offices, then I'd like to stay on as DCI.'

'Are you sure? You don't have to make up your mind yet.'

'One-hundred percent, but there is a condition, and it's non-negotiable, I'm afraid.'

'Go on.'

'If you do decide to go ahead, no matter which office is closed, I want to choose who stays and who goes.'

'Er...I'm sorry, Tanner, but that's not how the redundancy process works. You're welcome to present us with your recommendations, but it's up to HQ to make the ultimate decision.'

'Can you at least allow me to decide who stays within my current team?'

The line fell momentarily silent. 'Well, look, I'm due to sit down with the Chief Superintendent and the Assistant Chief Constable tomorrow. I'll bring it up then, but on the face of it, I don't see it being a problem.'

- EPILOGUE -

Thursday, 10th July

'HONEY, I'M HOME!' sang Tanner, throwing his keys onto the hall's narrow sideboard.

Hearing nothing back in response, he waited a moment, unsure if the silence meant Christine was asleep, when a gurgling shriek rang out from somewhere near the kitchen.

'Someone's up,' he happily muttered to himself, making his way through the house to find Christine, struggling to change Samantha's nappy beside the sofa, whilst her patient kicked harmlessly at her with her chubby little legs.

'You know, this is a lot easier when you're not here,' Christine said, without looking around. 'The moment she hears you come home, the only thing on her mind is to demonstrate how many sit-ups she can do.'

'And how many's that?' Tanner enquired, kneeling beside them to watch Samantha continue trying to wriggle her way out from under her mother's faltering grip.

'Well, none, yet, but it won't be long before she's climbing the walls.'

Taking hold of one of Samantha's tiny hands, he smiled lovingly down at her before pushing himself up.

'How was your day?' he asked, making his way over to the kitchen to put the kettle on.

'Not bad. Samantha's discovered Peppa Pig, which allowed me to catch half an hour's sleep. How about you?'

'I had that meeting with Forrester, over at HQ.'

'Yes, of course. Sorry, I forgot. How'd it go?'

'As well as can be expected. They've decided which office they're going to close.'

With the nappy finally on, Christine picked Samantha up to look at Tanner with an anxious frown. 'Dare I ask which one?'

'Westfield.'

'OK, well that's a relief, I suppose.'

'Yes, I know. The commute would have been a nightmare if they'd chosen Wroxham.'

'What about the staff?'

'Wroxham will be able to absorb some.'

'And the rest?'

With the kettle boiling, Tanner offered her a non-committal shrug to start making himself a coffee.

'And everyone at Wroxham?'

'I've given them a list of those I'd like to keep.'

'Which is...?'

'Everyone, pretty much.'

'Henderson?'

'Uh-huh.'

'How about Cooper?'

Tanner paused before answering. 'I've asked if it would be possible for Haverstock to take his place.'

'What did they say to that?'

'Well, they didn't say no,' Tanner replied, pulling some milk out of the fridge. 'I think it will probably depend on what Haverstock decides to do. All I know is that I'd rather not have to keep putting up with

Cooper's incompetent belligerence all the bloody time.'

The sound of the doorbell had Tanner glancing over at Christine. 'Who the hell's that?'

'Probably something to do with the election. I've had two canvassers around already today.'

'I must admit, I'd forgotten all about it. Did you get a chance to vote?'

'I went with Samantha, after lunch.'

'Then I suppose I should make the effort, as well.'

Hearing the doorbell ring again, Tanner finished making his coffee to take it with him to the front door. When he saw a figure through the frosted glass turn to walk away, he hesitated for a moment, wondering if he should bother, before deciding that he may as well.

The moment he opened it, the visitor spun around to beam a gregarious smile at him. 'Hello, Chief Inspector! I wasn't sure if you'd be in.'

It took a full moment for Tanner to place the man standing before him. 'Mr Elliston!' he eventually exclaimed. 'What are you doing here?'

'The by-election, of course!' he replied, stepping forward to hand Tanner a leaflet. 'Remember?'

'Sorry, yes, of course. My wife and I were only just talking about it.'

'Have you had a chance to vote?'

'Not yet.'

'Well, the polling stations are open till ten, so you've still got time.'

'Right, yes, thank you,' Tanner replied, hoping he wasn't about to ask who he'd be voting for. 'I'll be – er – heading down, just as soon as I've finished my coffee.'

With Elliston just standing there, grinning at him, Tanner found himself having to think of something to say to help fill in the increasingly awkward silence. 'How are you doing in the poles?'

'Leading by a long way, thanks to you!'

'Me?' Tanner queried, with surprised incomprehension.

'Of course! I mean, you were the one instrumental in removing my main political rival from off the ballot.'

'Oh, right!' Tanner replied, as the haunting image of Sir Charles, reaching for his hand, flashed briefly into his mind.

'I wouldn't have stood a chance if I'd had to stand against him.'

'I think you're forgetting that I initially had my sights set firmly on you.'

'Only at first, and only because I wanted you to.'

'I'm sorry?' Tanner responded, his head jolting back in surprise.

As Elliston's eyes gazed into Tanner's with a look of playful indecision, he hesitated for a moment, before eventually saying, 'I never did tell you what happened to my daughter.'

'You told me she took her own life, after initially telling me that she'd been hit by a car.'

'Ah, yes, well, I only told you that she was hit by a car because I didn't want you to start delving too deeply into what really happened.'

'That she took her own life?' Tanner queried, with a questioning frown.

'More the reason why she'd chosen to, something we didn't find out until six months later, when we found her diary, hidden behind her bedside cabinet. The final entry gave a full description of what had taken place. She'd even listed the names of the men who'd raped her, when she was barely thirteen years old. That was the entry we photocopied to send to the

Norwich Reporter. It was also the reason I bought the Bentley Continental, the exact same colour as Sir Charles Fletcher's, and why I decided to stand in today's by-election.'

Listening to the words drift out of the man's mouth, Tanner's mind reeled as he desperately tried to process what he was being told. 'But – it couldn't have been you!' he eventually responded. 'You were locked inside a holding cell at Wroxham Police Station!'

'As I said before, only because I wanted to be.'

'I'm sorry, I don't understand.'

'Lying to you about poor Mr William Greenfield, reversing into my car? The drops of blood I deliberately placed on my walking boots? Making sure you caught me trying to sneak them out of my house?'

'So, it *was* you who killed him?'

'Of course I did!' he spat. 'The guy was one of the men who gang-raped my daughter, leaving her so mentally scarred that she felt she had no other choice but to take her own life. I would have killed him fifty-times over for what he did to her!'

'But...what about the others?'

'Ah, sadly, no, although, believe you me, I would have given my right arm for the chance. That was the only part of the plan I didn't like, but I didn't have any choice, not if we were going to convince you that Sir Charles Fletcher was responsible.'

'We?'

'My wife and I. After all, the whole thing *was* her idea. All I had to do was to act suspiciously enough for you to arrest me. The tricky part was to make you believe that Sir Charles was trying to frame me for the murders, when, instead, we were trying to frame him. That's why I was so insistent that you kept my name out of the papers, making it possible – at least theoretically – for him to think that I *could* have killed them, even though I couldn't. All my wife then had to do was to leave my fingerprints as evidence at each of the scenes, somewhere obvious I may add, whilst at the same time planting just enough of his DNA to make you eventually reach the conclusion that it must have been him after all. Thankfully, everything went according to plan, right up until the moment he drowned in the North Sea. He was supposed to spend the rest of his life in prison, contemplating what he'd done, but I suppose that's where fate stepped in. Our only consolation was that, apparently, drowning is one of the most painful ways to die, which again, I'd like to thank you for.'

With Tanner left staring at the man with a look of mortified incredulity, Elliston's face cracked into a broad, salacious grin. 'Anyway, I was pleased you were in. I've been wanting to tell you that for a while now, I just couldn't think of a good enough excuse to come over to do so.'

As Tanner watched him spin merrily away, he was about to head back inside when he heard Elliston call out in a cheerful tone, 'Don't forget, the polling stations close at ten!'

Retreating into his house, Tanner re-entered the living room to stare blankly down at his now lukewarm mug of coffee.

'Who was that?' he heard Christine ask, as if speaking to him from some distant shore.

'Huh?' he replied, staring vacantly up.

'At the door?'

As her words drifted away, it was only then that the full horror of what Elliston had said began seeping down into his conscious mind. Sir Charles had been telling the truth after all, at least about the murders, which meant his actions, and his actions alone, had allowed an innocent man to plummet to his death. But it meant something else as well; that the man who'd stabbed William Greenfield at the bottom of that open grave, to then assist his wife in brutally executing the other three men who'd gang-raped their thirteen year-old daughter, was on the brink of becoming Norfolk's very next Member of Parliament, and he wasn't sure that there was a damned thing he could do about it.

'Are you alright?' he heard Christine continue.

'Yes, sorry, I'm fine,' he eventually replied, shaking his head in an effort to clear it. 'It was George Elliston, the guy running in the election.'

'He didn't seriously come all the way over here just to ask you to vote for him, did he?'

'Not really.'

'Then what did he want?' she asked, bouncing a drooling Samantha on her knee.

'To thank me for eliminating his competition.'

'You're not being serious?'

'I'm – I'm not sure,' he replied, his eyes drifting down to his coffee again.

'Darling, you look absolutely exhausted. Why don't you come and sit down. Tell you what, if you can keep Samantha entertained for a while, I'll make you something to eat.'

'I think I'm going to have a drink instead.'

'Are you sure? I don't mind.'

'Quite sure, thanks,' he replied, finding his way over to the bottle of rum on the breakfast bar, and the tumblers nestled beside it.

Taking a seat to pour himself a glass, he looked at Christine to ask, 'Do you think it would be possible for us to go away somewhere – maybe for a couple of weeks?'

'What, now?' she replied, glancing down at her watch. 'Well, I'd have to pack Samantha into a bag, but apart from that, I'm game!'

'I'm being serious.'

Christine hoisted Samantha into her playpen to make her way over to him. 'Are you sure you're OK?'

'I'm fine, really I am.'

'It's just that you haven't asked to go on holiday since…well…since never, really.'

'I could just do with a break, that's all,' he replied, realising he was going to have to somehow bury what Elliston had told him into the darkest recesses of his soul, *unless….* he thought to himself, *unless I can find a way to link Elliston and his wife to the murders?*

With that more optimistic idea stirring his imagination, he lifted his head to smile at Christine. 'Anyway, as I said, I'm fine. Now, how about I make *you* something to eat, for a change?'

'I suppose that depends on what you had in mind? Beans, or toast? I would ask you to make beans *on* toast, but you might have a panic attack in the process.

'I probably would,' he laughed, reaching for another glass. 'Tell you what, how about I pour you a drink instead?'

DCI John Tanner will return in Stokesby Grave

- A LETTER FROM DAVID -

Dear Reader,

I just wanted to say a huge thank you for deciding to read *Swanton Morley*. If you enjoyed it, I'd be really grateful if you could leave a review on Amazon, or mention it to your friends and family. Word-of-mouth recommendations are just so important to an author's success, and doing so will help new readers discover my work.

It would be great to hear from you as well, either on Facebook, Twitter, Goodreads or via my website. There are plenty more books to come, so I sincerely hope you'll be able to stick around for what will continue to be an exciting adventure!

All the very best,

David

- ABOUT THE AUTHOR -

David Blake is a No. 1 International Bestselling Author who lives in North London. At time of going to print he has written twenty-four books, along with a collection of short stories. When not writing, David likes to spend his time mucking about in boats, often in the Norfolk Broads, where his crime fiction books are based.

Printed in Great Britain
by Amazon